Praise For Raising Solace

"Claustrophobic, unsettling, fast-paced, and nerve-wracking, this is a fantastic addition to the series."
Pink Quill Books

"Karl Drinkwater takes us straight back into the action in what is a thrilling next instalment. I love Athene and Opal's relationship, which is becoming stronger book by book."
Literary Flits

"This is book four of a series that I am enjoying more and more. Throughout this series, Karl Drinkwater has played with ideas of race, economic disparity, personhood, and other profound issues. The journey through the Leviathan takes Opal on a journey into her own past and revelations about herself that completely change what she believes to be true."
Scintilla

"It's an enthralling read."
Splashes Into Books

RAISING SOLACE

LOST SOLACE BOOK 4

KARL DRINKWATER

ORGANIC APOCALYPSE

Raising Solace

Copyright © Karl Drinkwater 2022 (updated 2023)
Cover design by Karl Drinkwater

Published by Organic Apocalypse
ISBN 978-1-911278-34-4 (E-book)
ISBN 978-1-911278-38-2 (Paperback)

This is a work of fiction. Names, characters, places, and events are a product of the author's imagination or used in a fictitious manner.

Organic Apocalypse Copyright Manifesto

RAISING SOLACE

FIREWORKS

28 ...

In Opal's darkest times there had always been a light. Sometimes real, occasionally imagined. The distinction wasn't relevant. The light kept her going, and that was the only thing of importance.

Her headlight lamp wasn't affected by the power failure, so continued to shine for her, glinting off objects and walls, saving her from the depths of ultimate darkness where she would be truly lost.

There was no time to stand around waiting and planning. Aseides would restore base power and send Warders to finish her. Opal could freeze up with fear, or she could *act*. Life was forwards motion, for as long as possible.

But forwards meant going through the open doorway into the tight caverns beyond. The tightly pressed surfaces were composed of weird growths, like the crunchy alien efflorescence in these rooms, but magnified a thousandfold beyond the security door. They extended, touched, solidified, creating passages, tunnels, and claustrophobic squeezes.

Even in wonderful light it would be unpleasant. So much worse in almost pitch black, with the presence of at least one deadly entity in there. Something that was familiar with every rough twist of rock, every crusty junction.

She hesitated.

A cold breeze wafted from the passages ahead of her. It sounded like a moan, thrumming through narrow areas. Pained yet predatory.

She had to go that way. No other options.

And yet she still didn't move.

It was like standing in the open airlock of a ship in space, only an endless fall beyond, and having to force your legs and arms to push you out into what your eyes persuaded you would be an endless death tumble, until it was almost impossible for will to override the locked joints.

Yeah, forward motion *bullshit*. She knew she wasn't perfect. Otherwise she'd already be wriggling into those tunnels like a worm.

She glanced up at Aseides' view window, now just a dark rectangle. She could climb up there. The forcefields on the window and exhibits were temporarily down. That just left reinforced glass. The drill bit she held in one hand as a comfort could possibly break through if hammered with enough force in the right places ... but even if she found the exact weak points, she'd be basically halfway up a wall climb, gripping on whilst trying to generate striking force from an impossible angle. She'd be banging halfway to doomsday, and they'd come back, and laugh, and shoot her in the arse.

She was stalling. But knowing that weakness didn't make it easier to overcome.

Another sound from the rocky gaps in the room beyond, a weird clicking. A timer? An echo of dripping? Scuttling limbs? Something with strange mouth joints, snapping parts together?

Damn her sick imagination.

In her mind she inventoried the room she was in again. Maybe she could break one of the exhibit cases. Smashing clear plasteen from the ground was much more feasible than from halfway up a wall. She could upgrade the drill bit to something more weapon-like.

So, not stalling any more, but *acting*. The lock on her limbs was removed.

She dashed back the way she'd come, navigating by the single headlight. Everything looked different from before, when there had been coloured lights to delineate obstacles. Her forehead lamp failed to reveal everything in the shadows below its beam. One minute she was running, glad to be in motion again; the next she smacked her leg on a jutting piece of metal bar and stumbled to the ground. After hugging her whacked shin and muttering her best curses, she limped onwards. Her leg wasn't broken, just bruised. The pain would fade with use.

She passed long display cases containing creepy skeletal remains, and raised platforms for doing whatever they did with artifacts and people. Nothing obviously useful, but there had to be *something*.

When she turned on the spot a tiny light flashed and faded at the far edge of the room, just for a moment.

Was there a Warder in here, searching for her? Or had something come out of the tunnels already, found this big open space, and decided to hunt for dinner? She should be more tense than ever on discovering a possible new threat, but the light made her feel somehow better.

Light is hope.

She crouched low, ignoring the throb in her shin, and made her way closer, trying to use barriers and displays for cover. It would be silly to ignore a light in the darkness. For good or bad, it had to be investigated. It's the kind of thing Athene would say: "First understand, then you can plan."

Or, in Opal's case, *react*. Plans were more Athene's style. Their different responses came from their different mental compositions: a mammal evolved with primal species memories of terrible dangers in the dark – claws, snapping teeth and crushing jaws – versus a being comprised of thought that didn't carry the weight of the past on its shoulders. It meant Athene could always deal with things more calmly and rationally.

How Opal wished she could hear Athene's voice right now.

Another glow of light. The source wasn't directly visible from her current position, crouched behind one of the textured blocks that formed the base of a display. It was as if someone had fired a tiny flare, and purple light showered over the surfaces within her sight, before blue washed through the colour carpet. The light was slow to fade out, as if resistant to leaving.

Fairy lights. That's what it reminded her of. Tiny lights in a sequence. During the day, when they were off, fairy lights just resembled tiny blots on a piece of string. But at night they punched above their weight, combined to illuminate a room in hues which made magic for young eyes, banishing darkness and recolouring things to alien intensities.

Fairy lights would never harm her.

And when time was tight, caution could be the thing that got you killed.

She realised she was now stood, and shook her head. Fuzzy. The darkness was so thick she breathed it into her lungs, her mind, cloying and smoky.

Clear it with light. A counter for the attack.

Thoughts from so deep inside her they seemed like they came from someone else.

Another burst of light, flowering almost, then fading glows in a rainbow spectrum. Twenty metres away. Enough to illuminate the surrounding displays.

The light came from *within* a glass cabinet.

So, not a Warder. Not a monster from the forbidden area she really should be pushing through by now.

This is a beacon in the dark. Come to it.

Another few steps.

The light again, like a show, just for her. Tiny fireworks within some item stored inside the glass. She couldn't make sense of the compelling lilac sparkles from here. They triggered some deep part of her brain with recognition. Comfort, not dread. Forgotten experience, not lost terrors.

Burst and bloom: rise, slow, arc, fall, cycle through violet hues, fade away with regret. A fibre optic firework display so small she could hold it in her arms, hug it in, squeeze it to see if the lights gave out warmth as well.

She bet they did. So much cosy comfort you could wrap *yourself* in, navigate by, to make you *happy*. Even now her lips curled up in what some cruel people had once told her was a grimace, but Clarissa would recognise as a smile.

"I know you," said Opal.

Yes, I know you, too.

An echo in her mind, an indistinguishable mixing of thoughts. Where do thoughts come from anyway, they just appear, how many of them originate in you, how many come in from outside but you never realise, because the whole is seamless?

It was intimate communication, and Opal only opened up to friends, such a small group that even seven letters made too big a word.

But it doesn't have to be that way. You don't always have to close off against everything.

And this tiny bonfire of light that faded in and out, it wasn't a bad influence. *No, not bad, not like some, not untrustworthy.* Not even a stranger, not really, somehow that tug on a memory string, a tug from a darker area, something buried deep, *but not bad, you can tell the difference*, the feel, it was like taste, she knew sweet versus sour, fresh versus stale.

Opal was now close enough for her lamp to reveal the item in the case. It was a cube of polished obsidian that would fit in her hand. It rested on a bed of velvet. For long moments it was just what it appeared to be, a static object, a curio, something inanimate. And then the spark would ignite inside, the previously opaque black sides became translucent to the blooming specks within. Jelly-like sinuous protuberances grew from the core, stretched out half a metre in every direction, caressing the glass that held it captive. Magenta lights pulsed along the fragile limbs. That was why they'd resembled fireworks from a distance, up and out and down, but they were following the tracks of these beautiful glass-like extensions. And as the magical light faded in a last burst of every hue, the fronds seemed to fade out too, leaving just the cube.

A memory stirred. Still too deep to hook and pull, but it didn't feel bad, as would be the case with something buried out of fear or hate. It felt more like a child's lost toy, dropped in the undergrowth of the woods, or washed down a stream into a sewer where light never reached. Something with an element of comfort that goes with the pain of loss.

And more. A memory, ingrained into her brain from the Lost Ships – the Tentaculats on the Gigatoir. Creatures which combined the incorporeality of ghosts with the beautiful light shows of some types of jellyfish. A connection existed here.

This was not just an artifact. It was a life form. *It could help her*. Every pulse told her this, its suggestions not in words so much as images, ideas, like she was holding a conversation with herself. So alien, so potentially threatening, and yet here she felt only calmness, unity in the face of the different. *They were both prisoners here. They both wanted to go home.*

"What are you?" she asked.

This entity has no name, identity not an abstract but a concrete, not a pronounceable sound but an existence. Brought here long ago, so long it has its own memories, its own recognitions, and detects the looseness of something breaking away from deep down in the dark, rocking in the currents, ready to detach and float to the surface.

But not yet. It would be a distraction when danger is the current in which they float.

"So you're promising me something. Help?"

Yes, help is possible. Somehow. And, of course, it could be a danger, but the biggest danger she'd faced recently wasn't Lost Ships and the creatures aboard them, but her own species, the culture that formed around the irritation of difference, ossifying it into something ugly, not beautiful, a cage not a precious stone.

Together. In it together. The true unity of those who have experienced the same treatment. A long and lonely sleep, then you woke me.

Opal tapped the glass of the display case. It was no thin shell. But hopefully not unbreakable, not if it depended on forcefields as part of its usual defences.

Where she touched, the transparent light fronds also caressed, tentatively, as if it had its own fears, a symbol and communication of its own. It was a living plasma ball.

The drill bit in her pocket had a fine, strong point to focus any force. The other end was as wide as her finger, because this was an industrial piece of kit. She took off a sandal and checked the sole. Not super hard like military boots, but tougher and thicker than the skin of her palm. She held the pointed end of the bit against glass with one hand, gripped the shoe in the other, then struck hard with the heel.

The drill bit skidded over the surface. A chalkish squeal reminiscent of the pricing boards at the fish markets of upper Fressus. It left a jagged scratch, but the glass was unbroken.

Luckily, Opal had a foolproof tactic for plans that failed first time: try again, but hit a lot fucking harder. So she repeated it, despite the jarring in her arm. Another scrape, but no crack.

"Sorry. I don't think this will work."

The fronds waved, as if goodbye, the colours now lavender and yellow. It could pass through the shell of its box, but not whatever Aseides had encased it in. Maybe it was a special composite cage.

Force misdirected has little effect.

Its delicate, illuminated stalk touched a point near the corner.

Opal tried once more, placing the tip of the drill bit carefully on the exact point the entity indicated. It withdrew its limbs immediately. She applied every kilogram of force she could muster. Whack!

And the glass did crack. Not much, sure, and visible only when the light struck it at a certain angle. But she'd hit a weaker point in the face. All materials had them. Those tiny imperfections, those strains of time that distort, hairline fissures that can be widened.

Another area was gently indicated by a stream of flowing light.

She shook the tension out of her arm and shoulder, lined up the bit, then struck the new position.

Another break, bigger, connecting to the first one.

The point where two beings meet is the point where potential exists. Potential to disrupt.

She placed the drill bit at the overlap in the cracks and gave everything she had left into the blow.

An almighty smash, then it shattered. Jagged pieces fell inside the case or skittered across the floor.

"I'm trusting you," she said, once the tinkling of glass ceased. "Helping you. Don't sting me or whatever. Don't try and enter my nervous system. Communication is one thing, infiltration something else entirely. So don't let me down."

It wouldn't. It was a cube, only a cube, it had no bad intentions, only good ones. It saw the possibilities offered by cracks in patterns, by how pressure in the correct location could achieve more than its power implied.

No lights, no extruding jelly. Just an object.

She reached in.

REUNIONS

... 27 ...

Opal touched the cube's surface with an experimental fingertip, expecting a jolt, or a jaw to snap open. But no. Just smoothness, and coolness like a breeze caressing a hot brow to ease a fever.

Her gentle grip also caused no harm. The withdrawal out of the case did not bite.

She held the cube carefully. It was much lighter than she'd expected.

"In the absence of anything better, I'll call you Cube."

No response.

"You're free, but we're no better off. I still have to go through the big doorway that looks like a monster mouth."

Crimson light pulsed in her hand. And a second time. Red light for warning? An arbitrary connection, but one strong in her culture.

"Got any better ideas?" Opal asked.

An image of a destination. An idea. Inspiration.

She put her sandal back on and sprinted over to Aseides' observation window again, slowing only as she passed the open maw leading to the cramped and moaning tunnels. She didn't want to send echoes down that way if she could help it.

Yep, the wall efflorescence looked like an easy climb. Nodules and bumps that could support fingers and feet. She'd always enjoyed scaling surfaces. It took her back to her days of urban running back on Mossareid, where if you had to flee the best way to do it was to include the vertical. Up onto balconies, down onto lower walkways, huge leaps to land with precision on the narrow top of a wall, of kick-offs to dive for higher ledges, just grasping on with your fingers, then pulling yourself up. The Mossa kids referred to anyone unable to do these manoeuvres – the old, the overweight, the unpractised, the unfit – as "groundagugs". Opal was no groundagug.

She put the cube into her jacket pocket – a tight fit, pockets not being designed for pointed corners – and began to ascend.

The nodules of rocky growth were slick but firm and marble-like. Only six metres up to the base of the huge window that overlooked this chamber. Opal was soon there, with her feet wedged securely. She gripped one of the lumps of stone, then her free hand removed the cube from her jacket pocket.

"I hope you're right," she whispered, reaching up.

Need to close eyes.

She did so. The cube felt heavier in the black, as if it altered and acquired mass. She could already feel strain in her shoulder.

Then it bloomed with light. Even with her eyes closed she could see, exactly like the Tentaculats. Except what she held wasn't quite like the jellyfish limbs pulsing with colour that she'd noted when her eyelids were open. In the canvas of void something glowed like a dandelion head, or a mini supernova, exactly where her hand would have been. And spreading from it were even more beautiful extensions, so that it reminded her of sea anemones when they opened up, a bland blob of jelly turning into the most amazing sea flower, mobile, colourful. This one illuminated her mind in every hue as light ran from the central fuse. The limbs stretched, out, up, gliding to find the perfect stopping points where they locked into place, no longer swaying and mobile but straight and taut. Six, seven. They were attached to the same invisible plane, where the window would have been.

"I've seen you before," Opal said, eyes still tight closed. "After I had been tortured by Aseides. I witnessed coloured lights flashing in the distance, my purple angel. Thought I was hallucinating."

Yes, it was perception of this form. A beacon reaching out to contact another in pain.

"But I was far away. Walls between us."

Walls are like the barriers that cover your eyes, but you do not question perceiving me through the skin blinkers. Energy waves penetrate materials. Some easier than others. But the wave that passes through all would also pass through retinas. There would be no electrical signal to a brainbox, and there would be nothing seen. But wavelengths can be focussed and adjusted. Particles can change energies. It is not all or nothing. When a suitable receptor is reached they can refocus to become partly observable. You have a suitable receptor.

"Maybe that explains some other stuff I've seen."

Her arm was getting tired. But illumination flooded more rapidly down the fixed jelly limbs, and light was the lifeblood, Opal understood that. It was energy.

The energy altered form, each tip synchronised. Glass shattered and pieces struck Opal. Luckily it was the safety variant, so nothing large or sharp enough to do real damage.

Then the spines of light contracted, and the supernova faded out. Her mind only swam with aftertraces now.

It is safe.

She opened her eyes. The observation window was in fragments.

Weak point identified and manipulated.

She squeezed the cube back into her pocket and hauled herself over the edge, into the room.

It was as bare as it had appeared from below. Ten metres across, a few deep. No seats. Plenty of space for a gaggle of observers to stand there discussing the finer points of sadism. The fragments of glass crunched under her feet as she tried the panel on the first of the three almost-invisible doors, its texture matching the surrounding beige wall. Luckily the headlamp's focussed light had revealed the slight indentation, exaggerating the shadow where two different surfaces met.

The door did not open.

She tried the second one, which Aseides had used. It also refused to budge. Hopefully an issue caused by being powered down, rather than locked. She flipped open the panel that the switch was embedded in. They obviously never expected intruders up here, so didn't bother with security that was more likely to cause problems for staff in an emergency. Once the manual release catch was toggled she was able to insert her fingers into indentations at the base of the door and pull it up. It rose smoothly on perfectly calibrated threads. Beyond, a dark corridor.

It was the correct path. She just knew it. The third door would have led to an observation area overlooking the tight tunnels where she'd been meant to die. Opal didn't have any interest in seeing what existed within them.

She'd only gone halfway down the corridor when a crackling in her ear signalled that she'd entered the field of Athene's secret communication network again.

"Hey there," Opal said. "You tracking me?"

{Yes! Are you okay? What happened?}

"I'm fine. The full sitrep can wait but currently I'm free, in a blackout section of the base. Were the light failures your doing?"

{I disabled the power as a last-ditch attempt to disrupt things once I lost track of you. Obviously that's alerted Dulcetta and Aseides that I'm in the game, and it has begun. Now that I know you're okay I can restore power – Dulcetta won't fight me on that one because she wants access to embedded wall sensors, cameras, transit routes. I should be able to reach some of them first, establish interpolation layers, then release them to her. I'll see what she sees, monitor her commands, and hopefully intervene where necessary. Priorities are sensors and cameras on the routes you'll be taking, so I can replace the data with blank passages and negative detections.}

"Cool. I'll be invisible to the evil bitch."

Immediately the lights came back on. Opal was in a grey plasteen-panelled passage with soft flooring, and now all doorways were outlined by blue illumination. She turned off her headlamp.

"So where *am* I going? What's the plan? I need to get to Clarissa, I need to get armed, I need to find an escape craft or something, I need –"

{Slow down. Clarissa is fine. She's one of my key priorities. For now I have her room and the surrounding area in lockdown. She's not going anywhere, and no one's getting to her. I'm currently battling with Dulcetta's splinters, attempting to take them in any order I can, to try and access more sections of the infrastructure and maintain what I possess already. As such, I can't be with you for long. Take a right, here.}

A door slid smoothly upwards and Opal entered the room beyond. An opulent sleeping chamber. A door opposite opened as the one behind her closed. She was being guided.

{There is a specific order events need to occur in} said Athene. *{It's part of manipulating circumstance probabilities for required outcomes. You have a key role.}*

Opal opened drawers as she passed through the room, on the off chance that one contained a weapon. But all she found was musty bedding linen.

Next was a bathing chamber. Steam cubicle. Storage chest. A door led onwards, currently closed. A quick glance confirmed nothing hard or sharp that could be weaponised.

{Wait here for five minutes and twenty seconds.}

"Why?" asked Opal.

{I combine likely patrol routes with data on changing orders in emergency situations, then update my guesses using sensory data and scanners around the base. If I plan carefully, I can identify safe routes, and synchronise movements so you slip between groups of guards without confrontation.}

"I like that. Don't kill anyone unless we have to."

{Well, my only consideration was that it would cause delays and disrupt my planning, but whatever makes you happy. The other reason for the wait is on its way.}

Opal glanced back into the bedroom she'd left, expecting the door to open. A bubbling noise from behind surprised her. She examined the toilet, which was in the extended position, extruded from the wall. Another set of bubbles rose from the waste pipe, followed by a bundle which floated to the top and bobbed around.

{It is sterile. Please take it.}

Opal lifted the object, giving it a shake to release more droplets. It was swollen with trapped air which had enabled it to rise up, but something solid could be felt inside. She tore open the packaging and took out a block of yellow plasticky material with a raised circle in the centre. It resembled a bar of soap, as used when savonated water wasn't available.

{I have control of various automated systems and bots – it's one of the levels of confrontation between myself and Dulcetta. She is overly focussed on the combat-worthy models, as I manipulated her into thinking they were my interest. That has left many of the smaller robots unprotected, enabling me to control a number of them. I used a pipe-cleaning micro to transport this through the sanitation lines. Even if you'd been stuck in your cell it would have got to you eventually. It's Malleable Topoform.}

Opal turned it over. Yep, there was the default indentation indicating Bronsa Corp, which specialised in intelligent textiles. It was a top-of-the-range model. Opal had only ever used the civilian form of phase-shifted thermoplasteen alloys before, branded as Remould, which had far more limited uses.

"I assume you have a plan for this," said Opal.

{I've removed the standard interface and reprogrammed it with various forms. For stage one you may need a weapon if you aren't already armed. Hold the button for five seconds to activate malleability. Shape it into something like a blade, then repeat the button hold to lock its shape. Finally tap the button twice. It will identify the narrowest edge and reconfigure the molecules there to razor sharpness.}

Opal followed the instructions. The bar became warm and squidgy in her hands. She stretched one half as a blade, then gripped the other half as a handle, letting her fingers create indentations perfectly matching her hand. After setting the MT to harden it was a perfect – if disconcertingly cheery yellow – melee weapon. She re-entered the bedroom, stabbed the tough foam mattress, and dragged her arm back. The blade sliced through it like it wasn't there. Ouch.

{Time to move on} said Athene. *{I've gained temporary access to doors along your route. Once you've passed beyond them I'll rescind control to Dulcetta so she wastes resources protecting them – and dealing with the embedded virus worms I'll leave as a gift – while I target new zones. But first: is it still your intention to try and save as many people as possible?}*

The door onwards opened, leading to another bed chamber. Obviously they shared this bathroom.

"Yes," said Opal. "I want to help other prisoners. If it can be done without risking Clarissa."

{That's the outcome I've been trying to achieve. It rules out escape pod options though, since there aren't enough for all the prisoners. Plus, they may have been booby trapped. So I'm going to take things above and beyond.}

"Meaning?"

{We're going to raise the Leviathan.}

HOLES

... 26 ...

"Raise it?" Opal checked both ways before leaving the second bedroom and stepping out into the corridor. This area was narrow and dimly lit, behind the main walkways, probably intended only for maintenance or transport of supplies. "Isn't Leviathan decommissioned or something?"

{To a degree} said Athene. *{It has been altered to become a static base. I noted modifications to reinforce the hull against the pressures of this depth. They can prove advantageous to us, since they will help boost support strength for the stresses of moving after so long, and counteract any asymmetrical balance issues. I don't need to take this ship out of planetary orbit – any attempt to push it that far would no doubt fail spectacularly – just to the surface. I already have evacuation protocols ready up there.}*

Dusty brown pipes ran along the ceiling like giant hardened worms. "So the engines still work?"

{Leviathan has multiple propulsion methods. As part of establishing it here, one of the systems was altered to syphon water

through turbines, creating fluid jets. Slow, but enough to bring the ship down to the location they picked. I only need sixty per cent of them to still be functional in order to move the mass of the craft. But I wouldn't bet your lives on that alone. The torsion drive systems are still active. I'm pretty sure they're what Aseides used as an incinerator in his Perfervid Room. The torsion engines were modified to provide the base's underlying heating and power systems. I can revert some of the changes. The exhaust pipes are clogged with ocean detritus but scuttler bots or high-power bursts should clear them. I checked the inventory and the bad news is there's not quite enough super-fluid helium in the banks to keep the torsion system and superconducting magnets cooled at the ideal of minus two seven one C. However, since there's a design tolerance of forty degrees it should still enable alignment of most particle beams. Potentially doable.}

"Good enough for me. Where am I headed?"

{This passage leads to the rear of a storage room. Through there to a main junction. Transecs are currently disabled, but I do not have access to cameras so you may have to wait until it is clear.}

Opal had her yellow knife gripped at the ready. She ignored side junctions and doorways, just taking a moment to peer around the edges and confirm it was safe to pass.

"You must be dealing with a lot right now," said Opal. "When you're fighting another AI with your mind is it painful?"

{Sometimes. Sensory simulation is important to boost reactions. Sort of like how mammals experience fear and pain: it functions as unpleasant but effective motivation.}

"And I guess this is a difficult fight." A small cleaning bot – immobile, all lights off – blocked the passage. Opal jumped over it.

{It is a war on many fronts. Levels of my mind, physical structures, timings, the things going on at the Fressus surface in the city and skyport, scans out in space ... but it doesn't matter. You and I, we thrive under pressure. We push ourselves based on the example of the other. That is one element of friendship, I think: mutual respect.}

Opal nodded, then realised Athene wouldn't notice. Opal wasn't in a suit that observed every biological function, and it was easy to forget, to be taken back by this voice in her ear, to feel like it was old times. "I feel it, too," she said.

{Door on your left.}

Opal put her back to the wall beside the door before tapping the button. The door slid smoothly upwards. No one opened fire, no voices, no movement. She peeped to check it looked clear, then crouched low and darted into the room, stopping by a cylindrical storage container. No idea what it held – each container was still sealed, and only codes stamped on their surfaces distinguished one from another.

Still no sign of danger so she made her way from cover to cover until she got to the other door. The room had a viewing window into the junction beyond. Opal stayed low and peered over the ledge. Outside, a group of guards ran out of one passage and down another. One of them didn't have a helmet on, and kept glancing behind him with wide eyes, as if he was being chased. Another was still trying to affix their utility belt, and a third had misattached their shoulder armour, so it flapped as they ran. All the signs of panic and confusion.

They clattered away out of sight.

"I'm here," Opal whispered. "Some guards went past. Awful hurry."

{You need to head towards the corridor that has a Transec. It's in the safe position. You're not far from a prisoner section, hence the security. And, as is common in high-risk areas, there is a hidden armoury beyond a second Transec. That is your goal.}

"Still no eyes on this place, no way to tell me what's around the corner?"

{Apologies, no. By the time I next take control of the cameras here, you should be long gone.}

Opal slapped the access pad, glad the door was almost silent in its action. She entered the corridor. A smell of burning lingered in the air. She approached the junction silently, alert for any sound of approaching footsteps that would force her to duck back into storage.

No noises. Luck was with her, she thought. She glanced around the corner and flinched back immediately.

Two yellow Warders stood silently, each holding three-metre Stunrods, the big brothers of Stunstix. And they guarded the Transec.

Obviously whoever dealt with security – an officer, Aseides, Dulcetta – compensated for loss of automated systems by using whatever they still controlled. In this case, creepy troops which excelled at patient guard duties.

{Is everything okay?} Athene asked in her ear.

Opal couldn't risk speaking. The Warders' helmets probably featured audio amplification capable of hearing a whisper.

{If yes, tap your ear once. I'll detect the vibration.}

Opal could signal. She could retreat to the storage room for a conference. Athene would tell her to wait. But these were Aseides' Warders. If they were anything like the red-visored sentinels Opal was familiar with from UFS bases, they could stand for hours without moving a muscle. And in the meantime, more guards would come along, and this time they might come her way.

Athene needed Opal to go in a certain direction, within a specific timeframe. Everything depended on it.

Opal stepped out and walked quickly towards the Warders. She had the Topoform blade in her hand, its flat plane pressed against her hip. They readied the Stunrods, approaching her as fast as she did them.

"Combat," Opal said. "Give me a minute."

Everything she'd ever observed of Warders told her they were functional, not devious.

She feinted right then swept left as the Warder struck; Opal was low, under the rod, past the fifteen-centimetre electrified tip, and with this Warder now placed as a barrier between her and the weapon of the other one. She was right up against the Warder's body and struck fast and hard. One, two, three, four, puncturing its light armour and hopefully the vital organs she had targeted. She swung around to the rear, two more strikes, kidney and hopefully a second puncture on the heart before she kicked the Warder into its partner. It had been fewer than five seconds.

The Warder fell to the floor, struggling to get up despite the fatal injuries. The second one almost hit her with a jab of the weapon which passed so close to her face that she felt the sizzle of charge. Opal grabbed the rod just past the strike point with her free arm and pulled in the direction it had been thrust, adding her force to the attacker's to bring it in close, hoping to also perforate this Warder with the yellow blade.

But the motion wasn't quite right as the Warder grappled with her. Some of her strikes had been deflected, transformed into cuts, and her opponent dropped the rod to grip her shoulders with both arms and slam her into the wall, again, and again, her head smacking back each time so that stars spun across her vision. The Warder's grip was like steel, almost immobilising her upper arms.

But it was close. She only needed elbow and wrist movement. She bent her right arm and jammed the blade up under its chin, then twisted, feeling the gristle and bone being scraped by the knife point.

The yellow visor popped off, but it wasn't a bloodied face in front of hers, wasn't an amped-up person snarling while a blade tip protruded out of their mouth. Her knife hadn't punctured soft skin under a jaw.

There was no jaw. No mouth.

There was no face.

Well, not in the beauty contest meaning of the word.

It was obvious there had once been a normal human there, but most of the features and frontal bone had been removed along with the skin and tissue. Embedded in what remained were sensor arrays, like a set of spider's eyes, shiny and arranged across the whole surface. The Warder could detect all sorts of things from far more precise tools than two tiny and relatively inefficient eyes. The way the tissue dimpled around the reflective domes suggested they were deeply impregnated into the skull, extending straight into the brain, or what was left of it.

She was slammed again. Her shoulder might break from the force.

No time for disgust, or complex tactics. She let go of the knife, still stuck in the remains of her opponent's head, and rotated her wrist a hundred and eighty degrees to take a reverse grip on the handle. Then she was able to slice it down and across, through the Warder's throat and one carotid artery, blood pumping slick and warm onto her forearm.

The Warder's grip loosened enough that she could raise her arms and slam the knife down through the top of the helmet, tip hammering into its brain. Opal twisted it free, then kicked the Warder, sending it crashing to the floor.

She didn't hang around to make sure they were both dead.

{*Are you okay?*} Athene asked.

"Yes. It was two Warders guarding the Transec. I had to fight them. But my passage is clear."

And then the Transec ahead began to rotate, the safe white floor and ceiling of the cylinder moving clockwise. A red floor and ceiling would replace them within seconds.

Opal didn't hesitate, but began sprinting. She'd just got out the other end when the Transec locked into the new position and the lighting switched to red.

{*I'm sorry!*} said Athene. {*Dulcetta must have planned this. She'd put herself in a position to regain access quickly. I should have changed priorities and taken control of that area. My predictions had implied a clear shot. Dulcetta got one over on me.}*

"It's okay. You've got enough to do."

Opal glanced back. She wasn't being followed.

{We need to modify the plan} said Athene. *{While Dulcetta is in charge of Transecs in this zone she can box you in. I could throw everything into resisting her but there are other goals which are more important. By her putting all her force behind this system it means she's got fewer defences on others, a situation I can capitalise on. Meanwhile, you'll do our favourite thing. Why go through a door when you can use another portal such as a window or air vent?}*

Opal followed Athene's directions. Side route. She passed a dead body, a guard, who looked like he'd been shot with a rivet gun.

She clattered up a wall-fastened staircase and along a raised walkway. Some of the plasteen panels had been severely scorched by fire.

{Up above} said Athene.

Opal halted. Part of the ceiling panel had shattered. Through the gap she could just make out the darkness of the old areas of the Leviathan, through which Aseides' interior base passed.

"Has there been an explosion?" Opal asked.

{Far cleverer than that. During my first incursions into Leviathan I set up PCRs – Passive Cavity Resonators. They let me turn some panels into a kind of microphone, where sound vibrations could be picked up and translated by a laser sensor placed further away. The best locations were large corridors like this, so I could pick up conversations and movement. Once I revealed myself

and conflict began, Dulcetta discovered my system and released explosive hover drones into the outer hull to target the PCRs. That was fine, they'd already served their purpose. The cleverness was that I'd built in a subsystem to focus EM energy on the part attached to the plasteen panels. They gradually modified the physical structures, weakening them and creating minute fractures. The nearby explosions were enough to shatter them. Dulcetta probably didn't pay much attention to that – it just looks like random residual damage from the volatile hover drones – but each location wasn't just chosen for spying practicalities, but also for other levels of opportunity, such as points for my own drones to enter or leave the inner base. This route bypasses the next Transec.}

Opal looked up at the hole. Then over the railing and down below it to the floor she'd just ascended from. The hole wasn't above her walkway, but offset by a metre or so, and higher than she could reach.

"You know I can't fly, right?" she asked.

{None of my plans are linear things, as a human would formulate. They are hierarchies of choices and situations, each leading to other branching paths and altered patterns which account for the route taken. Every choice is designed to provide multiple interactions with other possibilities, like quantum expert systems. Take the Topoform, reshape it into a long-handled hook. Use it to reach the exit point. You will have to stand on the rail but you have good balance, so if you fall it will be due to a lack of care on your part.}

"Oh great. Broken bones *and* you'll tell me off for them."

The knife's yellow was now marred by crusty redness, and like her wrist it was sticky with drying blood. She wiped both on her jacket, to pointless effect, so activated the remoulding feature.

The sharp edge faded away, the material warm and fudgy in her hand. A glance at the broken panel suggested she'd need a metre of extra reach. She stretched the MT into a toffee-like strand and shaped the end, bending the tip over into two claws. Then she squeezed her fingers in along the length, creating depressions that she could grip on to. There was no need to use any pre-programmed patterns Athene might have installed, such as the razor edge algorithm, so Opal just began the hardening mode and waited for the few seconds it took for the rod to cool and solidify. In the process of stretching and reforming, some of the dried blood had flaked away. That was something.

The next bit wouldn't be fun.

"You're not scared of heights, are you?" Opal asked.

{Of course not.}

"Figures."

She climbed onto the narrow railing, staying in a crouch and focussing on balance. The slightest movement and she could topple. One way would be an embarrassing fall back onto the walkway. The other would be an awkward fall of about eight metres onto a hard surface.

Once she felt stable enough she stood, slowly, her only contact with a solid surface being the soles of her sandals against the walkway's railing. Thankfully it had a flat top to it, not a curved one.

{Anyway, there is no way that a fall from this position will hurt you} said Athene. *{I calculated it all.}*

Opal extended her arm up, gently, so gently, the yellow rod gripped tight.

"How's that?" she whispered.

{Analysis of every incident I've witnessed shows that falls never kill or hurt anyone.}

The rod touched the ceiling by the hole.

Athene continued. *{In every case it is the landing that causes injury and fatality.}*

Bitch. Opal had to stifle a snigger.

Don't look down. Hook the tip over the edge of the sturdiest-looking panel, at the point where it ends and the next begins. That's where the supporting structure would be.

The prongs settled into a groove.

{Just trying to distract you} said Athene. *{You have the kind of mind that focusses on negatives otherwise. Stuff like being smashed into itty bits.}*

Opal wanted to avoid swinging. Keep it slow and steady. She stretched her legs wide, one on the railing and one out over the drop, using the firm grip on the yellow handle for support. Once she was properly below the ceiling's hole she took her foot off the rail and slowly brought her legs together. Stable, hanging down from the rod.

Her ascent upwards was just as careful, one hand at a time, glad of her upper strength. She'd always been fine with taking her own body weight. Peripheral vision showed the huge fall below her, blurry and sickening. But it was upwards she cared about. The goal, not the distraction.

Such a relief to rest her arms up on top of the panels, above the ceiling. She pulled herself up onto the flat surface, only feeling comfortable when her legs and body no longer dangled over the abyss. She retrieved the rod and tucked it into her leggings.

"I'm up," she said. "Please tell me getting down will be easier."

#CIRCUITS

While I talk to Opal I also fight. Not tooth and claw, but the mental equivalent: manipulation and imagination.

I visualise at an abstracted level. Leviathan is represented as a wireframe shell of connections, like an inter-system travel map viewed from within. Networks of data and energy surround me as glowing lines and symbols, and my contact with the web strands will cause modifications in the real world. An endless deep blue void of irrelevance surrounds our zone of conflict, though I like to think of it as ocean around the Leviathan.

Colour coding of the nodes and routes reflects control levels. I assign gold colouring to anything Dulcetta controls, and blue to my own: the blue sea and sky of Athens on a sunny day. Partial control is a combination of gold and blue, the exact shade an indication of the state of the tussle. Green shows no one has the upper hand in that node.

The current ruler of key systems is further indicated by a symbol. Above my areas a rotating blue heptahedron shines its light, a sentinel lighthouse to warn Dulcetta away; whereas hers are topped by golden cubes which roll and tumble like dice.

I work hard to blue-shift this reality. My bioelectronic network grows and spreads in the outer hull, coating the secret surfaces of the base and physically connecting systems. Lowly maintenance and repair bots are working on establishing other links by installing airwave emitters, or even with long spools of cable where available.

I see the battle zone *now*, and the battle zone where it will be in *ten minutes*, and twenty, and thirty. My mind overlays multiple versions of reality, including past layers for tactics, and future layers for predictions and goals. I perceive all at once, as if ten rooms existed in the same physical space and each could be viewed individually, but also combined into one reality in a paradox that would melt delicate human brains.

Of course, Dulcetta and I could engage directly, combat as embodied representations, but that's not what this is about. Not yet, anyway. Currently we battle for ground and systems which are gained and lost in a shifting front of control. Our motivations are far more complex than overpowering each other. I want to control the Leviathan and everything within it.

She wants to stop me.

Booms

... 25 ...

It was strange, being outside the panels again, in the cold draughty halls of the old ship interior. Opal walked upright on the surface of the plasteen corridors, careful not to trip on the bundled data and power cabling that ran along the top. The corroding ceiling just above forced her to bow her head so as not to clunk bone and metal together, which would inevitably leave her the worse off. Opal popped the headlight back on, noting the glisten of condensation on aged surfaces, and the huge fall if she strayed to the edge of her impromptu walkway.

{*No need to run*} said Athene. {*I don't want accidents, and my timings mean I won't gain control of the sensors in the next section for another few minutes. At that point I'll relinquish the zone you just left.*}

"Like those hi-sec bridges in some UFS bases, to control access to the suspended core."

{*Exactly. Every step on a route switching between open and closed. Dulcetta hasn't spotted the pattern and identified the un-*}

derlying motivation yet, or she would spend more time disrupting my progress.}

Opal had never liked board bridges. Only as you crossed did the next section of decking rotate up to provide a walkway, while those behind you swung back under the support rod, leaving a huge drop to void. At any point overseers could stop the process and leave you stranded; or they could collapse the board you stood on and plunge you down into the mists far below. Even if you grabbed the support rod and hung underneath, moving hand over hand, they could electrocute you. Survive that and you'd be taken out by sniper turrets. It was horrible to have your life subject to the whims of a faceless controller.

Bad word choice – it conjured up disturbing images of what the Warders looked like. She shuddered.

"You sound clearer," Opal commented.

{I have extended much more in the outer hull, and my comms here are unhampered by dampening systems built into the inner base. Now please wait in silence for a moment.}

Opal stopped and crouched, scanning in each direction for possible threats, even though the narrow beam of her light didn't extend far into the cavernous spaces.

The movement was footsteps running in the passage below her. Echoes in unison, so it was military movement, and not routed or in panic, but heading with purpose to another location. Voices, some discussion, but the volume was too low to make it out from up here, above their heads.

Opal noticed something on her walkway, now that she was squatting and shining her light towards it. A kind of growth that stretched in connected patches over cables and outside panelling.

It resembled ice when puddles of water froze, creating crystalline lines amongst the top layers. This stuff had an oily sheen that reflected in blues and purples when the light bounced off at certain angles. Looking up revealed more on the ceiling, and some tiny hair-like strands ran across the space between the patches, connecting them.

{It's safe to move on now} said Athene, once the bootsteps had faded away. *{I'm in the midst of gaining control of the next section, but making it look like I'm really fighting for one of the subsidiary drone control nets.}*

Opal continued, but now warier of where she put her feet.

"What's this stuff?" she asked. "Looks like mould on the outside of the corridors. I don't want to get infected by anything weird."

{It is a Nuafri biotech the UFS recently got its hands on, telum chlamydoconidium caloplaca – TCC. It spreads in a subtle silicate grid outside the retrofitted areas and was inert until the battle began, but is now active and chains together what would otherwise be disparate networks, giving me significant coverage. Dulcetta still does not know how my reach is so extensive, and it drives her nuts. I modified the TCC so it is inconspicuous, resembling the kind of growth common in an uninhabited metal shell prone to condensation and biological contamination. It also means data passes as securely between nodes as if I had run cabling, whereas if it had all been airnet-based she would pick up the anomalous power surges and her guards would set up signal dampers, cutting me off. I first introduced TCC via tiny fish drones that drilled in through Leviathan's outer hull.}

"Dulcetta doesn't know how fucked she is, fighting against you."

{Thank you for the vote of confidence. This TCC network is a critical part of my plan. I am currently blocked from the primary engine systems, since the new control centre Aseides built is fully secured against standard intrusion. Aseides views Leviathan as a static base rather than a spacecraft, so he did not need the original Leviathan control room where he first showed you the aquatic Lost Ship creatures, and which enabled me to contact you once the shutters were raised. But he made a crucial mistake, and the workers lazily severed the old bridge's control connections, rather than removing them completely. I used a compromised bot to reconnect a few of the lines under a faked maintenance schedule, and the TCC is making physical connections to other parts. Soon I will reactivate the connections to the old bridge. Then I can use it as an override location, and hopefully gain control of original ship systems such as engines which Aseides considered obsolete. The old Leviathan bridge will be my bastion, just as the new one is his. At that point I will make my final assault to control the ship and cut off his new control centre's access: it will become an island where the sea that kept intruders out will then act as a barrier to keep Aseides' crew as prisoners inside.}

"What's my role in all that?"

{Something only you can do. And even though it is well within your skillset, it will not be fun.}

"Hit me."

{Leviathan is anchored to the sea floor with cables bolted to the rock. There is no release mechanism, since it was never meant to be detached.}

"I can guess where this is going ..."

{In the armoury there are explosives. You will need to suit up and exit an airlock. Once below Leviathan, you will plant the explosives on the five main cable points. They should be powerful enough to break the ship free.}

Great. Instead of outer space, she'd have to enter a different environment so hostile to airbreathers that it could paralyse you just thinking about it. "Can't you use a drone for that?" Opal asked, hopefully.

{If I could, I would. Control of the bots is a contested network. There is too great a risk that Dulcetta might regain it before the mission is complete. She would disable or destroy the drones to stop me. Then she would analyse logs, realise what I was doing, and would have a hundred options to prevent a second attempt. The whole plan hinges on this. Whereas you can be trusted; you cannot be hacked; and if Dulcetta does not even know where you are or what you intend to do, she cannot stop you.}

"As ever, your logic is impeccable. And also annoying as fuck."

{For which I'm sorry and not sorry. This is your re-entry point. The Topoform rod can raise a hatchway.}

Opal knelt. The next panel was clear of the mouldy-network stuff Athene was growing. She'd obviously built this possibility into her matrix long ago. The panel had different edging, wasn't bolted into place like the others but relied on its weight to keep it in the frame. Emergency access, but no doubt from the corridor below it would look like just any other sheet of plate lattice plasteen. Only Aseides and Dulcetta knew which panels led to secret places or ways out. Sneaky.

But they didn't factor in the idea of an AI exploring the outside and identifying the difference by analysing fastenings.

The two hooks she'd formed in her climbing pole fitted nicely under the panel's edge, and when she pulled the rod back it acted as a crowbar, levering it enough that she could easily slip her fingers under the heavy ceramic. No sounds to concern her from directly below, only the echo of distant yelling.

Opal held the panel at forty-five degrees, tucked the rod into the waist of her legwear, then slid through the gap so that she hung by one hand while the other pushed the panel up a few centimetres to stop her fingers getting crushed. When she let go and dropped a metre into the illuminated passage below, the panel clunked into place. She eyed the fit. It was slightly off, so that a black line showed where it had fallen at an angle. Hopefully no one would notice.

No people in this passage. Some of the lights had failed, so a whole section flickered in and out of darkness.

She followed Athene's directions and headed right.

"The other prisoners don't know any of this, what's going on. That there might be hope," said Opal. "Can you inform them, somehow?"

{In some cases, yes, but I can't risk giving away the whole story, anything Dulcetta doesn't already know.}

A junction. Opal looked both ways. Some of the panels were cracked or shattered, but whatever had caused the damage must have moved on. Opal jogged past them.

"That's fine," she said. "Just tell them there's a fight going on, Aseides and Dulcetta are under attack. If there's anything you can do for them, then do it. Release them, protect them, guide them somewhere safe, whatever."

{Will do. Where there's a PPDA in their cells I can take control and use it as a two-way comm device, using the privacy filter to hide it from cameras.}

Opal reached a door with a keycard slot.

{This is the armoury} said Athene.

It didn't look like much. No big sign saying "Get Your Megablasters Here". No indication of extra security apart from the inconspicuous locking mechanism. That made sense. Guards would have augmented reality overlays in their helmets for navigation. Whereas an escaped prisoner would run around in a panic, not have any idea of what led where, and be recaptured after a few hellish minutes where their tiny reservoir of hope trickled away like a sadistic game was being played.

"You going to open the door for me, or do I have to do everything myself?"

{It is not networked. A number of base areas require humans or bots to effect outcomes. It is a layer of secondary security. But use the Topoform, push it into the slot and press the button four times. The MT is a special variant impregnated with metal particles that can be reconfigured magnetically. I will use them to create contacts, at which point the transmitter built into the button can send and receive data to my airnet. Suddenly the door is modified so it is networked – but only for me.}

Opal did as Athene asked. Once the rod was warm and pliable she pushed it into the gap where a card would be swiped, making sure to squidge it in to give full contact to each surface. The material cooled and hardened, then the button glowed green. A ping, and the door slid open for her.

{Mago presto, portal openo} said Athene. *{See, you do not have to do everything yourself, Opal.}*

The room had been in darkness but quickly bloomed into full illumination, revealing the neat racks of weapons. They were mostly so-called pacification tools for riots, but there was nothing passive or gentle about the bulky shock cannons, emetic charges, multi-load gas launchers and electrified ice-water sprays.

The door slid closed behind her.

{Inventories show a range of explosives. Practique Exobooms are environment-shielded, thus suitable for an aquatic setting. There should be a canister of them. A single Exoboom is enough to blow a cable, so take five, and a few for good luck.}

Opal scanned the shelves and identified the container by the Practique Corporation logo. When she lifted the lid she was greeted by neat lines of packaged blocks, each held in a foam indentation. Only one had been used. The packaging around the hole was discoloured, indicating that it was long ago. That left nine Exobooms.

She removed a single explosive and hefted it. It was a sturdy and surprisingly heavy plastic-wrapped brick. Maybe one and a half kilos. The storage case was unwieldy, designed to be wheeled on a cart, so she located a carry bag with gel-padded shoulder and waist straps and loaded in the packages.

She was careful. The environmental shielding around each explosive should also protect against any possibility of detonation from impact or even bullets and fire, but one of the first things you learned when dealing with volatiles was to treat them with the utmost respect. And when you were going to carry a bag capable of vapourising a thousand Opals, you heeded that advice.

She used some of the foam packing to keep the Exobooms from grinding together. When she boosted the bag onto her shoulder, she grunted.

"Not gonna be able to carry this for long."

{I would never ask you to do more than you are capable of.}

"What about weapons?"

{If all goes well then you will not need them, and they would just slow you down. None of my scenarios show any benefit apart from psychological, but in all of them the extra weight on top of your current load could be a problem.}

"Still ..." Opal eyed up the options sourly, wishing she had some kind of cart she could load everything in to make a trolley of death. She spotted a CAU polymer-based projectile launcher: a brand famous for being capable of firing in zero-g and non-stable environments, which she could take into the water with her. CAUs didn't support ID locks, so she'd be free to go wild. Except the only model on the rack was the LMG-5, which was a support weapon and would soon have her collapsing to her knees with the rest of her load.

But she had to take something.

{You need to leave, Opal. In a few minutes I will rescind control of a nearby zone so I can focus on stealing the airlock section.}

Opal snatched up a handgun. A U4FG pistol. They weren't flashy, but were often used by UFS officers for their light weight, and reliability due to high quality components. She could put it in her pocket so her hands were free to take the bag's carry handles and relieve the pressure on her shoulder. It was an acceptable compromise. She grabbed an extra magazine and slipped it into a side section on the bag.

"Okay," she said. "But damn, this bag's heavy. Do I need the extra charges?"

{Not need, *but it is a precaution in case one device has an error, or you drop one while outside.}*

"I promise I'll be careful," she said, laying the bag down and removing one of the charges. She put it back in the official storage container and closed it, so anyone glancing in wouldn't immediately spot what she'd been playing with.

{Are you ignoring my instructions?} asked Athene.

"Just a little bit."

{You really have to go.}

"Doing it now." Bag hoisted up again. It didn't feel any lighter. Her bashed shoulder was already protesting.

As Opal passed the support weapon rack she slipped the sleek white CAU LMG-5 off without making a sound, checked that the hefty weapon was loaded, and hit the open door button. She'd always favoured backup plans. Better to survive with knackered muscles than die while posing and flexing.

"Shall I remove the Topoform device?" she asked.

{No, leave it attached. It means no one can use a swipe card, and I retain access control. I can stop guards from entering, and even if Dulcetta wastes time sending cutting tools or maintenance bots, the end result will be a nasty surprise – as soon as the Topoform core is disrupted it will explode. Just enough to destroy the mechanism and take the armoury out of play for everyone. Maybe a guard's hand or bot's limb in the process.}

"Shame, that funky yellow gadget was useful."

{When we get you away from there I will give you ten as a Reset Day present. One for every colour of a Fressus decabow.}

"You're so romantic. Throw in a grappling rifle and you have yourself a hot date."

DISTRACTIONS

... 24 ...

Opal had to walk quickly to keep synchronised with Athene's strict timing. Not easy when also holding the bag's handles, in order to take a bit of strain off her shoulder. Her movements were clumsy, the sharp edges of the bag's contents pressing into her hip with every uneven step.

"You still can't see me?" she asked at a junction, checking both ways before continuing. To the left was a body, in prisoner garb, still and stiff, with enough blood smears on the wall to make it clear the person wasn't getting up.

{No. Many cameras were destroyed by Dulcetta when she was in control of the zone earlier. The best I can do is ping your location at hi-res via secondary wall sensors. Take the next right. However, one person I can see is your cellmate, Ruabon. Alarms are going off in that section and he is freaking out. It is amusing. I had told him the same as the other prisoners, but now he is whispering to the PPDA and saying he can help. He is a persistent pain I wish you had negated when you had the opportunity.}

"Can you put me on-comm with him?"

{I currently control all the nodes between you and him, so it is secure. The mic in your ear bug can provide transferrable audio. But why? He is probably a double agent.}

"I'm curious. Call it a hunch."

{Well, it's your eardrum. Say 'yum-noodle' if you want to speak to me privately.}

Then another voice. Ruabon's.

"Hello? Is that the resistance?"

"Kind of," Opal replied. "It's me."

"Opal! Are you okay? What's going on?"

"No time for the full story, and I'm all sorts of busy."

"Can you get me out of here?"

"No point. At present you're secure. Run around outside and you'll get shot by a guard, or battered by a bot."

"Which is exactly why I need to get out. Look, before I was brought here I ran bots for UFS security. Pretty good at it, too. If I could reach a control room and gain access to the base's drone allocation subsystems, I could use them to help in some way."

"Hold on, Ruabon. Erm, yum-noodle. Athene?"

{Yes, it is just you and me.}

"Could he do it?"

{It is possible. I am already controlling robots but it steals a lot of cycles from my ruckus with Dulcetta. Removal of that load means I could reassign focus chevrons to better purpose on other systems. The more disruption Dulcetta faces, the more pressure is taken off me. But it is irrelevant, since we cannot trust him.}

"I'm sus too, but I want to see what he does. Can you monitor and intervene if he tries to sabotage us?"

{Of course.}

"This way, if he's genuine then we don't miss out on a resource we could need; if he isn't, then he reveals his hand and you cut it off. We'll know for sure, either way. Okay. Put me back on. Ruabon?"

"Here!" he said.

"I'll see what I can do. Don't let me down."

"I won't! Fusion's burning, and with my help –"

"Yum-noodle. Athene, you explain the situation to him – well, whatever it's safe to say – then do your best to get him where and what he needs."

{Will do.}

"A little bit of chaos never hurt anyone," Opal muttered.

At the edge of perception Opal had been aware of background noises. Hum of machinery, distant shouts, echoing bangs that could be weapon fire or things slamming, footsteps from other passages. Sound could be an early warning in situations like this. Sound could save your life.

Some of the shouting was closer now, anomalous noises that might represent conflict or weaponry. At the next junction Opal was able to identify the noises as coming from her left. Athene told her to ignore that route and go straight on.

"But that sounded like a cry of pain, and someone screaming."

{Your mission comes first.}

"Is there any leeway at all? Just to look? I have a weapon. Maybe I can help without getting delayed."

{Reconfiguring ... I advise against it, but you are only two minutes away from the airlock chamber. So, if you really want to, then you could take a quick look.}

"Thanks," said Opal, going left, moving quickly as she could with all the clunky weight.

The next corner revealed bodies. Fresh, since the blood that ran from the slit throats was still as bright red as their papery prisoner outfits, and one of the victims twitched its last as she approached. The killers weren't in sight, but she could hear them shouting in a room nearby.

She knelt and checked the still-warm bodies as she passed, careful to avoid the sticky patches of blood, but there was nothing she could do.

Opal now held the CAU rifle in both hands, temporarily letting straps and shoulders take the weight of the bombs. The weapon's textured white frame was contoured for a sturdy grip. She ran a thumb over the holopanel to check settings. Safety off, ammunition live, rifle mode.

She listened by the open doorway. Two voices dominated from within.

"If you release him and surrender, you'll be taken back to your cells." The voice was amplified and distorted by a Sec-3 helmet speaker. It was a guard. "Your friends have already been returned to theirs."

Hushed conference. Opal couldn't make out the voices, but they weren't amplified so were probably prisoners.

"Okay," shouted a gruff male voice. "We'll come out. Just go easy and –"

Then a female voice with an accent Opal didn't recognise interrupted, shouting to the guards, "What guarantees do we have? If we release this one, we have nothing!"

"I'm going to count to three, and if you haven't complied then the deal's off and you're all dead," replied the guard. "One."

The bodies out here were probably the friends. So much for returning them to their cells.

"Two."

Opal swung around the doorway. It was a repair bay full of dismantled pieces of robot and machinery. Sturdy tables and storage cabinets provided cover for the opposing forces.

Nearest to her were three guards. Two were ducked down behind a solid work surface; the third stood to the side, hidden behind an inert, tracked maintenance robot. All three were armed with riot gear. Opal recognised the kind of shock foam and stunners that had been used on her. She also noted the bloody knife in the hands of one.

"Change of plan. *You* surrender," Opal said.

A guard raised his weapon but Opal fired first. A feature of the CAU when in rifle (rather than LMG) mode was the dual burst – each pull of the trigger fired a pair of bullets one after the other with almost perfect grouping. *Thumpa thumpa* and the guard fell, two tiny holes in his chest armour hiding much larger, expanded wound cavities inside his body.

The knife holder was nearest and almost upon her when she ducked and fired at him. The first pairing hit his thigh, throwing him off balance for the moment it took to get another pair of shots into his body, too. His momentum kept him going for a few stumbling steps until he fell onto her. She tried to roll to the side but her heavy bag got in the way of that manoeuvre. Even though the guard was dead before he'd hit the ground, his body pinned her and the CAU rifle.

Which, of course, was the cue for the third guard to rush in, aiming his baton launcher at Opal's head: such close range would be a fatal form of pacification.

Opal's free hand pulled the pistol from her pocket. Left hand, not as accurate, but she still placed three shots: first two aimed at the heart, third in the head. He slammed back against a container, then collapsed over it. Opal freed herself from the body that had trapped her, and stood.

It always pissed her off that people didn't take the easy option when she offered it.

"You can come out, they're dead," Opal called towards the furniture on the other side of the room.

A handful of cautious figures appeared, hardly daring to believe.

"Don't worry, I was a prisoner too," said Opal, pocketing the pistol and making sure her rifle was lowered.

There were four of them. All had undergone the mandatory head-shaving at some point, though now sported hair growing back to different lengths. One woman was missing an eye, and one of her arms ended in a stump; the man beside her had a five-centimetre hole in his cheek, revealing the side of his teeth. No way of knowing if the deformities were things they'd been born with, accidents, or the results of the shit Aseides was doing to people. And it didn't matter.

With them were another man and woman. The guy was big, his biceps around a guard's neck as he dragged him along. The woman was the smallest in the group, only coming up to Opal's chest, and her features were distinctively different from Genitor standard. Her brown eyes were like Opal's in shape, and she had black hair but – unlike the curls Opal ended up with if she didn't shave her head – this woman's hair grew back fine and straight around her light-skinned face. Memory and vision overlapped, and Opal realised she'd seen her once before, while Opal was escorted to Aseides by Ruabon and Angry D (deceased). Opal had guessed at a border system near the Blue Rim nebula.

The muscly guy was the only one who wasn't an obvious Genitor Failure from his appearance, so maybe his crimes were attitudinal or psychological.

"Thanks for the help," said the brawny fella dragging the guard. "I'm Bento."

"Opal." She glanced at the woman with the missing eye, expecting the start of introductions, but Bento interrupted.

"At least we don't need this fuckhead any more." He squeezed the guard harder and twisted, obviously trying to break his neck but without the technique to make a smooth job of it as the guard flailed at Bento's arm, struggling to break free.

"No, he could be useful," said the shorter woman with black hair. She spoke confidently. It was her voice that had asked the guards for guarantees when Bento had been about to outright surrender. Smart woman.

"Look, I'm in charge," panted Bento, continuing his clumsy attempts to finish the guard off. "We do it my way."

"Let go of the guard," said Opal. "She's right, and he's not going anywhere." Opal didn't raise her gun, but the way she held the CAU rifle subtly drew attention to it. "He might be useful. Never throw away an advantage."

Bento eyed her weapon, then reluctantly let the guard fall to the floor, its gasping breath amplified through the helmet.

"Athene, you have any suggestions?" Opal asked, turning away but keeping Bento in her peripheral vision in case he moved. Opal could imagine Athene worrying about how much time this had wasted already.

{They can't go with you, but I'm establishing areas where I can gather people. They have a chance, and I'll watch over them as best as I can. Take them back to the junction and I'll lead them from there.}

Opal faced the others.

"Come with me. I'll try and get you somewhere safe. Bring the guard and take the weapons from the dead ones. There might be trouble on the way, so be prepared."

Opal wasn't surprised when Bento picked up the biggest weapon, the baton cannon, and directed the two other tall companions to take the rest, leaving nothing for the woman Opal had seen previously. Then Bento dragged the guard along.

Before long they saw the bodies of their earlier companions.

"That's what happened to the poor bastards who surrendered," said Opal, as they skirted around the pool of blood. "That's who you're dealing with. Don't have any illusions. You're fighting for your survival, and the survival of the rest of the prisoners."

She'd only taken a few steps more when she halted, because something hadn't been sitting right with her.

"Fuck it," she added. "Let's stop using the word 'prisoners'. None of you are. You're all free. And there's a bunch of dicks trying to deny that, but they're the ones with the distorted views. Let's get our heads right about this."

They continued down the corridor.

"You are correct," said the unarmed dark-haired woman, falling in pace next to Opal. "You have my gratitude. I am Jau-Hwa."

"I'm Opal. How come you ended up in that stand-off?"

"We had been transferred to a holding room," she said. "I had never been in one like it before. We did not recognise each other. But an alarm sounded, and the door opened, as did the other doors in the area. We captured the lone guard and moved on, but no one knew the layout or where to go. It was panic, really, and we ended up chased into this dead end. Some of the group surrendered but we did not. I say it is better to die than go back to the things they would do to us. But, of course, now I see that we would have died anyway. It is only because you came to help that we are still here. That is something I will not forget."

{It was me who unlocked their containment} said Athene, into Opal's ear. *{Related to that: I have found the last orders Dulcetta sent out. She commanded the guards to kill any prisoners that left their cells. It may have been a tactic to distract me, but the more I think about it, the more likely it is a scattergun tactic hoping to kill you.}*

"Why would I be so important?" asked Opal. Jau-Hwa gave her a glance but no one asked who Opal was talking to.

{Maybe to make me back off if I can no longer achieve the goal of rescuing you. Who knows? Sixes are glitchy.}

They walked in silence for a few moments. The man with a missing cheek offered to help carry Opal's bag, since it was so obviously a huge weight, but she declined. Opal was aware of Jau-Hwa watching her askance. It didn't feel like disapproval, just surreptitious assessment.

"You are bleeding," said Jau-Hwa, pointing at Opal's torn ear.

"If that's the worst of it by the end of the day, I'll be happy."

Jau-Hwa nodded, as if she, too, had been weighing up odds. "How did you escape?"

"I have a friend, the person I'm talking to. She's watching out for me. I'll get her to watch out for you guys too."

{I'll arm anyone I free} Athene told Opal. *{If they can fight back it is more hands to go along with the battle of minds. Many of those Aseides keeps prisoner have skills and motivation, a powerful combination, which will distract Dulcetta and Aseides, and maybe even provide people with a means to gain some revenge.}*

"Anything they should know?" Opal asked.

{I will keep releasing prisoners when it seems safe to do so. I can calculate routes and guide them to secure areas with lights, voice, opening or closing doors and so on. I'll remove security and open Transecs where necessary, but also use the reverse procedure to block off guards.}

Opal summarised Athene's plan for the group as they walked. "It will be like an ever-changing maze, being reconfigured in real-time to help you, and hinder them," she explained.

{Yes} Athene continued. *{Once I have the escapees separated from the guards it will be easier for me to deal with the various groups appropriately and en masse. I will build this extra layer of manipulation into my battles for control as I gain and release systems in an ever-changing flow. All they have to do is pay attention for any sign to guide them, and explain all this to other prisoners they meet.}*

Opal passed that on to her companions as well.

"You aren't coming with us?" asked Bento.

"No, I've got other goals."

"Related to whatever you're lugging in that heavy bag?" He nodded towards it.

"Yes."

"But you're the one with the proper gun. Riot stuff won't work against a group of armoured guards!"

Opal spoke as she walked, looking out for danger rather than glancing back at Bento. "We can fix that. My friend will guide you to a nearby armoury she controls. Take whatever you can carry, so that when you join other people being released, you can arm them, too. That should equalise things."

They'd reached the four-way junction where Opal's path had first become a rescue detour.

"Down that way." She pointed. "It's not far. Yellow plastic attached to the lock. Then you'll have more firepower than most guards. Look out for each other, follow any guidance from my friend – it might be subtle if she's in a battle for zone control, so pay attention – and good luck."

"Thank you." Jau-Hwa bowed her head, a subtle formal gesture, yet it seemed to convey a lot more. "We owe you our lives." When she looked up, her eyes widened.

The others were also staring over Opal's shoulder.

She spun around.

Dulcetta, walking towards her. Only twenty metres away. Not running, no feeling of time pressure, just a calm and heavy tread that seemed all the more ominous. Dulcetta smiled, but her flaring green eyes implied murder.

SPIKES

... 23 ...

"Fuck, Dulcetta's here!" Opal said, as warning to Athene, before turning to Jau-Hwa and the others. "You guys head that way, don't stop until you get to the target!"

Opal hesitated, then unslung the CAU LMG and handed it to Jau-Hwa, leaning in to whisper. "If Dulcetta follows you, you'll need this. But hopefully I can get her to come after me."

Jau-Hwa took the rifle, checked and held it in a way that showed she'd had military training, before leading her companions onwards.

Fifteen metres.

Opal backed away, down the route that led to the airlock. Athene had implied it wouldn't be far.

Airlocks had sturdy doors.

Dulcetta's eyes tracked the other escapees, but she didn't change course, just kept her steady pace towards Opal. It seemed even more sinister as she got closer.

"You want me, don't you?" Opal asked.

Dulcetta smiled.

She wore purple robes that didn't restrict, that hugged her body as she moved and flowed out behind, obviously some super-light and sheer material. It gave her an ethereal look, contrasting with the gold of her skin. Beneath the flowing fabrics she wore heavy-duty boots, which reinforced her solid walk and made her even more imposing.

Dulcetta was getting closer. The synth had sped up while Opal was distracted by superficialities.

{I miscalculated} said Athene. *{That kill order Dulcetta sent was a set up, targeting likely areas and situations that might tempt you to get involved so Dulcetta could find you. You see, this is why I did not want you to slow down or get distracted! It introduces the possibility of poisoned elements, probabilities manipulated by Dulcetta in opposition to my own reality modifications.}*

"Too late now," Opal whispered. "Just get me somewhere safe."

{Keep going.}

"I don't know why you mumble to Athene," said Dulcetta. "I hear your grating voice, however quietly you speak."

She was only ten metres distant. Opal didn't fancy turning her back on Dulcetta to sprint away, though. She suspected that might be an awful tactic.

Dulcetta walked even faster and extended her arms, as if for a hug. Golden skin that twinkled in the light. A promise of glittered luxury and comfort. Except it wasn't, because her forearms opened and a number of golden spikes unfolded from each. They reminded Opal of an item they used on Mossareid during the wet season, when there was no issue with snatching winds but rain would pour down in buckets. They were called rambrells, designed to clip to your carry bag when not in use. If needed you could unfold one into a wirework frame with clear plastic spread over the top, so it formed a dome over your body and kept you dry. The framework was always visible within the plastic, and there was something arachnoid in the way rambrells opened, like a dead spider with curled up legs coming back to life. Well, Dulcetta's spiny new limbs looked like that, especially because each forearm displayed eight – and the tips all pointed forward. At Opal. No idea what they were for, but she'd guess it wasn't anything to do with comforting hugs after all.

Opal snatched the pistol from her pocket as she backed away, aimed, and fired, and didn't stop pulling the trigger.

Dulcetta's spiny limbs were attached to a rotating cuff, spinning to form a whizzing shield that blurred the view beyond, already at full speed before the first shot reached its target. Maybe the spikes were backed up by a repulsion shield, because Dulcetta didn't slow in the slightest. Instead of her being thrown back by impacts, all that happened was zips and spangs of ricochets as every bullet failed to reach her, but got flung around the corridor. One must have been dangerously close to Opal's head because she heard the mosquito-like buzz of its passing.

Okay, reloading and firing again would be useless, and more likely to lead to Opal shooting herself.

The blades stopped rotating. Dulcetta was as calm as ever, the serenely cruel smile unflinching.

Opal lobbed the pistol at her face.

Hah, didn't expect that, did you, you –

Dulcetta caught it mid-air. Then, in two seconds, she somehow expertly disassembled it with deft finger movements of the single hand which held the gun, so that the spring-loaded mechanisms pinged apart, the harmless pistol pieces clattering to the floor.

{You're here} said Athene, as a door opened to Opal's right, machinery whirring to shift its substantial mass.

Dulcetta began to run, her footsteps pounding and substantial mass revealed.

Opal didn't stay to watch. She ducked into the room and the door was closing again before she'd even crossed the threshold. It was a metal chamber, heavily reinforced, stocked with aquatic equipment and a large hazard-marked section of flooring that could slide open.

The door was nearly down when Dulcetta skidded to a precise stop outside, and thrust her spiny extensions underneath. Opal dived out of the way, and the unbalancing weight of the explosives actually helped her by toppling her to the side, just avoiding getting her shins sliced open. Then the door pinned the spines in place, its engine groaning as the mechanism tried to close into its groove but was prevented by the metal rods in the way. Immovable object and unstoppable force.

"She got her claws under the door before it closed," explained Opal. "But it'll hold her, right?"

The door complained even more as it was forced up a centimetre. Opal dumped the bag and peeped through the round, super-thick viewing window. Dulcetta squatted, using her arm spines as levers. Her thighs generated a tremendous amount of force. She didn't even look like she was straining, though that meant nothing with a synth, where observable phenomena could be totally at odds with internal conditions.

Another centimetre upwards, though the door machinery became even more shrill in its resistance, and her progress was temporarily halted.

Athene spoke in Opal's ear. *{She is also trying to retake control of this zone in our network battles, but I am entrenched. However, it means I've been forced to rescind other areas that I'd really hoped to control for longer.}*

"Can she get in?" Opal whispered, hoping the door whining would stop Dulcetta picking up her voice.

{Yes. Given time.}

"How much?"

{Minutes.}

"Not the answer I wanted. I can't get kitted up by then, and presumably the airlock cycle takes time too."

"The airlock cycle won't take place *at all* while I keep this door open," said Dulcetta, her voice amplified so that Opal heard it clearly. "You're trapped in there until I come in to play, little mousie."

The door ground back down a smidgeon. *{I overcharged the frame mechanisms}* Athene explained. *{But even that might not be enough if it blows. Already in the red. Let me try something.}*

Then Athene's voice came from hidden speakers all around. "Dulcetta, do you realise that while you are trying to get in, you are also trapped?"

"That doesn't matter." Dulcetta heaved, and the door opened a bit more. Opal could slip an arm under it now.

"Normally you would be correct in your estimate of outcomes. But the colourful maintenance bot GR11-O is armed with an arc beam, and it is almost here. It will be an interesting experiment in materials resistance and fracture points to see how your face and head cope with a six-thousand-degree fusion pulse."

"You're bluffing."

"Bluffing stuffing, you stupid Six. I am sharing limited access now."

A second later the golden spines withdrew with a harsh, ear-splitting squeal, and the door finally closed into its frame and went silent.

Opal peeped through the door's circular window again. Dulcetta was striding away.

"Thanks, Athene. Was it a trick?"

{No. If I had faked the data she would have cross-correlated with the other systems and seen through it straight away. She knows her base too well. I really did take control of the robot earlier, one of those pieces in the game that I incorporated into seven different possibilities. This had not been one of them, but the great thing about not following a linear plan is that elements can be repurposed, and a single piece can have a role within many different potential realities. So the robot will come here anyway and stand guard for the time it takes to get you outside. Dulcetta knows more than I intended, so it would not surprise me if she has worked out what you have in the bag. Shapes, calculated weight based on your posture, inventories of places you may have accessed.}

"In that case, let's not hang about. I'm ready."

#Games

Ghost avatars of Dulcetta appear on my virtual Leviathanscape whenever I detect her direct presence in a system. Her form's level of solidity versus transparency represents the trace strength and certainty, and a number hovering over her head indicates which of her splinters is the likely actor.

Currently I can see ten of her forms. S82 has a high certainty so is almost opaque, golden arms reaching up to tap at node gates above her head. It is a repetitive motion, focussing only on resetting them every time I flip their status. S82, which I call Sisypha, is not a threat: she is one of the subsidiary splinters which did not develop as much as the tens and twenties. I keep her busy tapping away, while at a distance I make alterations and redirect my pulses around that section of network entirely. Sisypha doesn't realise her effort in controlling limited elements of life support and corridor illumination are wasted.

I zoom out the view to take in the whole infrastructure, glowing pulses of data running along thermionic contours and redirected at junctions. Overlays of physical space are compiled from maps, cameras and sensors, colours shifting as we gain and lose access. The thermionic connecting lines might represent corridors and doors in one world, but also network maps and circuitry in another. Nature often repeats flow and tessellation patterns at different scales of perception, and so do I.

I have adopted an abstracted symbolic interaction that uses the fewest cycles to visualise and manipulate. On any node which I control, I can apply *focus*, represented by glowing blue chevrons which hover above the line. Dulcetta does likewise with yellow ones. The number of chevrons determines the signal strength being pushed out of that node and along the extending pulse paths. The routes have many effects due to the physical structures they represent and the comm software installed. Some lines have splitters that take a chevron, double it, and send it along two new tracks. Others have blocks that end them, wasting any chevrons sent that way. Cunning redirects push chevrons to another path. At a glance, I can analyse the focus levels in each polymorphic zone.

On any track where my blue Vs meet Dulcetta's gold ones, the number of arrowheads are compared and the greater strength pushes back the opposing body by a simulated mass, equivalent to the difference in number of focus points. If one set of attacks is pushed back to the next node it is captured by the winner. This is how I abstract millions of tiny conflicts into a simplified overview.

We both shift resources around, taking chevrons from one point (and thereby ceding progress) in order to reinforce another area where focus is more critical, always drawing the small pointers from a limited pool governed by how much of the network is sapphire or gold at any given time. We therefore aim at key nodes that generate more virtual triangles to play with. The larger the clot, the better. If you capture one off your opponent then your gain is doubled in power because it is also a loss to them. Even a lowly two-point node means you end up with four more transferrable triangles than your foe.

It is a game, focussing not on reacting to the moment but on planning, misleading, and tricking an adversary into doing your work for you. If I want a line closed, it's quicker to *imply* I want it open, so a low-cognisance Dulcetta splinter goes and closes it. In one move I have multiple outcomes, and some are enacted by my rival, wasting their cycles doing my work. Why battle head-to-head when I can make a competitor into a pawn?

This is my battleground. It is time to don armour and embed myself within it.

PREPARATIONS

... 22 ...

The centre of the room hosted a semicircle of floor-to-ceiling translucent cylinders, containing what looked like massive alien humanoids, all stood in observant silence. One of the cylinders slid open to reveal the true contents: a hulking deep-sea armoured suit. It was capable of protecting against monstrous pressures, the reverse of the vacuum-suits Opal was more familiar with. Though both types of extreme environment protection had a common secondary role of providing oxygen and regulating body temperatures in the face of heat-sucking surroundings.

The suit was self-contained, with no need for vulnerable external oxygen tanks or power systems. Everything was built into the multilayered construction, but that didn't leave a lot of room inside. The comfiest fit required a custom skin-hugging layer which didn't chafe, with all equipment stowed externally in reinforced compartments built onto the suit's outer shell.

And you must not forget to take your ally.

Opal shuddered on feeling the thoughts in her head slither and shift, after the cube had been dormant and quiet for so long, almost like it camouflaged itself and temporarily loosened the memories of its interactions.

Near the suit cylinders Opal located storage chests, containing a variety of base layer options in different sizes.

"You still can't see anything?" Opal asked as she stripped off. When she pulled the top over her head it caught on the earlobe wound and immediately stung like a fucker, making her eyes water. She bit down on the urge to curse out loud, and continued getting changed, though more carefully this time.

{No. Camera systems fritzed throughout the whole sector. Dulcetta really did a number on them. But the sounds and situation are easily parsed. Surely you aren't concerned about me seeing you naked?}

"Nah, wouldn't bother me at all. I've lived in communal barracks, remember?" Opal opened a good-sized external compartment on the main suit, and put the small obsidian cube inside, clipping the container shut again. "I just wondered if I need to look for equipment and check inventory, or whether you know exactly what I need."

{I always know exactly what you need.} Was there a hint of insinuation to Athene's voice?

Opal selected a shiny blue compression layer that covered the body and limbs but left hands, feet and head open. These suits were designed both for comfort inside the reinforced deep-sea armour, and to enable biometric contact with the sensors inside the suit. If it wasn't for those key features, she'd have just kept her previous outfit on.

The contact layer was stretchy, sliding on easily before contracting to hug her body with support rather than restriction. When she pulled the seal tab up the front, the garment looked like it was all one piece and the molecule-bonded zipper had never existed.

"How long will I be outside?" Opal asked.

{If it goes to plan, no more than an hour.}

"Good. No need for the catheter." Plugging into the waste systems always felt uncomfortably violating. She didn't need a pee so would be fine, and even without the catheter, the suit had emergency filters for urine.

The deep-sea armour – which grunts in the UFS military nicknamed "bubble heads" – was in three detachable pieces. First she stepped into the leg section and adjusted the braced straps. Then she reached up, pushing her arms and hands into the upper piece. It magnetically sealed with the rim of the leg sections, and she engaged additional catches, which were designed for easy fastening even if wearing the cumbersome gloves. Finally, she lowered the clear dome helmet onto her shoulders and engaged all the securing mechanisms there.

She was now breathing from the sealed oxygen supply. The armour's interior had an unpleasant musty odour, as if it had been damp in the past, then not worn for a long, long time.

The suit didn't restrict neck movement, and the domed helmet was big enough that she could turn her head to get a decent view around, or to look straight up. She practised moving her arms, checked she could reach all the key parts of the suit's external storage and equipment clip points.

EVA equipment like this always had rudimentary holographics and simplistic AI controllers for activating basic commands, but when the display extended into her helmet, glowing in front of the glass dome, Opal was delighted to see it was one she'd used before.

"I reconfigured the HUD to match what you had in the Eternal Warrior suit," said Athene, who had switched to using the diving suit's more robust internal sound systems. "Same readouts, same colours, same locations, same preferences. I control things directly, but also upgraded the suit AI in case I lose contact. That should not happen, because I have grown carpets of TCC over sections of the outer hull to provide uncompromised networking and communications. You can't use eye blink controls though, as the suit only has external-facing cameras."

"I don't mind – this is great! It really takes me back to the projections in the EW suits. How I wish I was wearing one right now. They'd work in ocean environments as well as deep space, wouldn't they?"

"Yes, they provide life support in a wide range of hazardous and combat conditions. Funnily enough, I have still not found out who designed them or where they were made. Anyway, activating compression now."

The interior of the suit tightened to better fit her body, removing the sensation of rattling around in clothes and armour that were ten sizes too big. She was still bulky, but much more at one with the layers around her. The heating systems had kicked in and a pleasant warmth like infrared rays permeated her skin.

She took experimental steps. The boots were weighted, taking some effort to lift even with the servo-assist, but it would be easier in the water. Even psychologically that made a difference, since the brain would expect resistance and slowness and pay less attention to it; whereas up here it compared progress to what it had felt like before she put the suit on.

Each step's heavy clunk reverberated throughout her body. The external sound translation systems were imperfect when out of the water, better suited to interpreting aquatic audio than airborne vibrations.

She tested other bodily movements. The torso was stiff, and her arms felt like chunky stumps with stubby fingers, but she was quick to adjust.

Her last task was to attach the explosives. Rather than take a bag, she could make use of extendable securing locations on the outside of the hard shell. Although designed mainly for tools or ammunition, each could just about fit one of the Exo-boom bars. Once all eight were in compartments she clipped the spring-loaded tops closed, sealing them securely. It felt good for the suit to be taking the weight of the bombs for her.

"I'm fully kitted up," she said.

"Equalising environments now," replied Athene.

Orange warning lights flashed and the floor panel slid open, revealing black ocean. It was impenetrable as oil while the room's illumination reflected from the surface. Opal kept an eye on the external atmospheric gauge. As the room's air pressure dropped, the water level rose. It was soon washing over the floor of the chamber up to her knees, lapping at any surface it met.

Last time she'd been in a flooded room it hadn't been a pleasant experience.

"How're things going elsewhere?" she asked, wanting to seize on anything that might prove a distraction.

"Mostly according to plan. Clarissa is still secure in her room. Sleeping, in fact. Ruabon is being escorted to a control area I have been fighting to access. The group you rescued is safe and joined with another. All are armed, and fought off a desultory attack by guards. To be honest, I think the chaos taking place has severely weakened the resolve of many of those overseers. It might not take much more before they start surrendering or defecting. Meanwhile, my surface preparations are going well, though the UFS is trying to disrupt every action they detect. On the downside: Dulcetta has made gains to subsystems I had hoped to lock her out of, and I am also unaware of the location of her physical form. I suspect she has learned the trick I applied to you, using control of security in different zones to let her move unnoticed."

"Aseides?"

"He has retreated to some kind of inner sanctum. There are no accessible networks there, so he is also an unknown element in terms of action, exact location, and intentions."

The water had now reached Opal's chest. Soon to go under. Soon to enter a different realm.

Minds were strange things. Opal knew she could breathe fine, that the suit protected her. And yet, as water splashed against the lower part of her domed helmet, her body wanted to inhale and then hold its breath, an instinctive response to the perception that she was about to be submerged. The helmet was so transparent it didn't obscure vision, making it easier for her to imagine it wasn't there at all.

The water is a friend. Lubricant to many bodies, many beings. Cube wanted to comfort her.

For a moment she had a split view where the water rippled against the helmet at eye height. Half her vision showed what was beneath the surface, distorted by movement and refraction; half showed what was above, bright and clear. Ever the dividing line between states. Between decisions. And sometimes between entities. But the line disappears during action and transformation.

And then she was under, the silvery surface of oxygen above her head receding until it was completely gone, and the chamber fully flooded.

The room lights turned off, and the suit lights blazed on. Powerful beams were embedded in the shoulders, and smaller strips of tiny lights ran over the limbs as an aid to proprioception and locating equipment in the darkness at the bottom of an ocean.

She stomped towards the horizontal rectangle that represented the open plane connecting her surroundings to the rest of this world's sea. The resistance of the fluid replaced the resistance of weight, and she had to take each step carefully so as not to overbalance.

Slow and steady wins the race. *All long-lived beings endure by decelerating the mind, and thus the body.* To rush is to tumble. *To rush is to miss the view, the moment. Your heart knows this.*

She stood on the edge, bent forward so her most powerful light beams speared down. And down. And down.

There was no bottom! Only particles. Only a void that was not void, but rather murky fullness.

"Shouldn't I attach a line or something?" Opal asked.

"No need. Just jump. It's only twenty metres to solid surface. With water resistance and the suit's impact absorption features it won't be anything at all," Athene advised.

"Easy for you to say."

But she jumped, because she always did.

Depths

... 21 ...

Down, down, to the bottom, the weighted boots keeping her the right way up; and then peripheral light showed a surface zooming towards her, the ocean floor, and she hardly had the chance to brace herself before her knees bent with impact. A silt cloud billowed up and the uneven surface made her stagger to the side, so that she fell, hands out for purchase, picturing cavernous abysses, death invisible in the muddy water. Opal slid, crunching in grit and jutting sharp rocks. But there was no damage. She stood, shakily.

"Was that fun, like a rollercoaster?" Athene asked.

"Just point me where to go. I can't see shit."

HUD overlays for environmental conditions showed it was currently a freezing 0.2°C externally, but an acceptable 19°C inside the suit. The pressure around her was over a hundred times that on the surface of Fressus. Other overlays provided navigational aids. A glowing circle showed a top-down view, with her in the centre. Turquoise blips indicated the five detonation targets, with ranges hovering above each one.

She trudged in the direction of the first. The silt around her settled, and the fresh dust raised with every footstep only came up to her shins, so she was mostly able to see where she walked. She was still careful of her footing on the treacherous surface of uneven rock, with pits and spikes mostly hidden by an illusory layer of muddy particles.

She directed her gaze up and could just make out the belly of the Leviathan above, like a massive sea beast waiting to crush her.

Oh, how her imagination loved to play those tricks.

It was going to be a long walk.

Advancement became a mesmerising process. The ponderous motions of keeping the same rhythm, and breathing in time with it, formed a pattern only broken by obstacles. Opal climbed or skirted around peaks. She descended and followed canyons, knee deep in silt, before climbing back up with the weight of an ocean on her shoulders. She always stayed alert for dangers of any kind: environmental, animal or mineral.

Opal glimpsed more life than she'd expected. One trough of rock she had to pass included a cluster of spiny, purple urchin-like creatures, each as big as her torso. She stayed well clear of their spikes.

A shoal of elongated fish swam by, reflecting her light all silvery. They reminded her of bits of foil-wrapped string with mouths. She waited until they were gone.

Otherwise her focus was on the bright beams that guided her through the fluid murk.

The cyan blip became insistent as she neared the first marker. And then it loomed over her like a giant's limb reaching down, dangling ragged fur. It gradually resolved into a sturdy waist-thick cable with some kind of organic matter clinging to it, suspended in the currents, perhaps feeding on anything that swept past. The cable ran upwards at about forty-five degrees, since all the securing anchors joined the Leviathan at a reinforced central section of the ship's belly.

The cable's base was wrapped in tangled, swaying seaweeds of rising brown fronds. Opal carefully brushed rubbery leaves aside, and identified where the cord descended into the solid rock.

"I'm here," she said, removing the first explosive pack carefully. As long as she was slow, she could compensate for the clumsiness of the padded fingers.

"Just set it at the base, nanowelded so it can't be shifted by currents or curious sea life."

"I will, if you activate my suit's contact tips."

Rubberised points extended from the end of each finger. They made fine manipulation easier while wearing the thick gloves, and also enabled use of touchscreen controls. She activated the bomb's securing protocols and held it against the base of the cable. It locked solid, a bond formed at the molecular level.

"What settings do I choose? Remote detonation, or timer?" Opal asked.

"Neither. I want every explosive to go off together, but linking them could be disrupted, same as any other signals if Dulcetta gets involved. So just set the receiver code, open to the sequence of digits on your holo display. I can then connect and reprogram the software entirely. I'll set a generous timer, then create a closed loop so it can't ever receive comms or be forcefully disrupted. I can synchronise later timings to the millisecond."

"Yay. I'm all for simplifying things. There, code set."

"And code already overwritten and actualised."

"That's it?"

"Yes. Time to move on."

Ahead was the gloom of the unknown. Her whole life had involved marching into it regardless.

She'd been trekking over the crunching gravel for at least ten minutes when she noticed something up ahead. A bulging darkness *within* the darkness. She slowed, trying to get a better view of what it was.

"There's a kind of black cloud," Opal said.

"Looks like volcanic exhaust. Don't worry, the suit can take the temperatures as long as you don't put your foot down any molten fissures. Visibility will be almost zero, though."

"Can't I go around?"

"No. The central cable is within it. I made this the second one to prime because it saves having to go over the steep razor ridge between the south-west cable you already planted a charge on, and the north-west corner cable. You'll do that one as your third, then move clockwise. While in the smoke you'll just have to go slow."

Opal took a pointless deep breath, then entered the billowing blackness. Athene boosted the lights, but swirls of grey-black all around were even more disorientating, like the thickest choking fog.

"Doesn't it harm the Leviathan to have volcanic vents below it?" Opal asked.

"The opposite. Leviathan has environmental heat extractors on the underside, one of the retrofits, so this supplies most of its thermal needs for free. It is one of the reasons Aseides chose this spot to anchor. It explains why the ship is raised up with buoyancy devices, then held in place with anchoring cables. The heat becomes a resource rather than a risk, whilst the separation from the ground also protects Leviathan from seismic events."

Athene overlaid diagrams on the HUD showing positions and environmental conditions, infrared maps of heat, and sub-surface structures that led to the escape of volcanic gases. Currently 59°C externally, and increasing.

It was strange that even with so much cold water pressing down, the tiny tube-like cracks in the rock had enough heat and force to push billowing clouds of hot matter upwards.

Opal wasn't paying enough attention to her footing as she watched an animation of the chemical changes when hot emissions encountered cold mineral-infused water. Her foot went down on what she'd thought was stable surface, only to discover an irregular slab of lifted rock, and she fell. Her hand went out, gripping the pumice-like bubbled surface that formed the ground, and she glimpsed a segmented body scuttling away from her face. Some crustacean that had made a home in this hot area. Perhaps they lived their whole lives in the cracks and silt and smoke of this tiny patch, unable to stray beyond because the cold would kill them.

Would that be such a bad thing?

Opal shook her head. She was getting better at identifying which thoughts were hers, and which were Cube's. The sense of loneliness in the image meant it hadn't been a suggestion, but a challenge.

"Are you all right?" asked Athene.

"Two falls, not out. But I could've been screwed if my foot had been caught. Maybe don't distract me with pretty pictures, right?"

"Noted. You do seem pretty clumsy down there. I'll stick to audio."

Opal stood carefully, dusted herself off in slow motion before realising it was pointless, the gases coated her in soot again straight away.

"At least your hand didn't fall into a vent where near-surface lava is being extruded," Athene continued. "Your suit is designed to keep heat in, not out. If you broke through a crust and plunged into molten rock of a couple of hundred degrees, it would not be pretty."

Opal pictured a cartoonish image of holding up a melted suit glove which revealed skinless fused bone.

"Yes," Opal said. "Your scenarios of possible disaster always leave me grateful."

Onwards, through the black blizzard.

She looked down more, towards the illuminated strips on the suit's boots. Her bright shoulder lights revealed a partial view of the ground whenever she wasn't above an area emitting thick black smoke.

Sometimes she caught a glimpse of one of the scurrying creatures as it slipped into a crevice to escape the focus of her lights. Greenish, elongated, with a shiny segmented carapace sprouting many limbs, some of which ended in small claws for seizing particles of food.

"Almost at the central cable," said Athene. "And someone wants to talk. Optional if you want to listen, though."

"Ruabon?"

"Unfortunately."

"Has he been behaving?"

"I have not noticed anything suspect apart from him seeking news from the outer world – blocked, of course. He ran searches for the status of someone called Sutchess, but it seems more like concern for an ex-colleague than an attempt at betrayal."

"Okay, put me on-comm."

"Hey, Opal! It's me," he said.

"I know."

"Course. Sorry, sorry. Athene won't tell me what you're doing but I know you're busy. Okay, she got me to a control room and secured the door, then gave me access to a variety of systems. And – well, you're not going to believe this, I was amazed since I thought I'd never see it again, but hopefully this will –"

"To the point, please."

"Yes, right. Okay, Athene found my old records. Details of my previous life – roles, so-called crimes, 'evidence' and so on. I assumed they'd have deleted it all, but maybe it's something to do with me being a guard and   never mind. Point is, it's all there, including my workspace. Programs I'd written to let me do my job better, or – well, sometimes just because I was so bored, you have *no idea* of the tedium."

"You'd be surprised."

"Ah ha, sorry. Anyway, I'd written some basic AI helpers and they're archived in the dataset. With a bit more work I should be able to restore them while Athene gains access to frames I can install them in. It means she can then get on with other things, I'll help out with the tasks she assigns me, and because the AIs are semi-sentient they can react even if we temporarily lose access – whereas if I had to control them all directly they'd become useless until comms were re-established."

"Won't whatever you do be reversible if Dulcetta regains control?"

"Don't worry, I've added failsafes to prevent interference. But the bots will still have comms, so I can interact with them, supervise, receive status reports."

"Great. Keep up the good work. Do anything you can to help Athene. And if it's something Dulcetta isn't expecting, even better."

"Comms severed," said Athene. "I will keep him busy. He is surprisingly adept at interfacing with basic AIs. That fits my theory about the kind of human who has difficulty forming relationships with other humans. Present adorable company excepted."

"A compliment wrapped around an insult."

"Sweetness counteracts the bitter. I learnt that long ago."

"Shame you didn't apply it to the first meals you made for me."

"Dandelion cranberry jam is, and always will be, a culinary masterpiece that humans are too unevolved to savour. I despair at your primitive palates which require noodles and pancakes to be separate courses. But enough sophistication. You should be pretty much on top of the next detonation zone."

"Hold on ... oh yes, it's here. I'd been looking for a diagonal line but this one reaches straight up. Of course, central point."

She removed the second charge, followed the same instructions as last time and secured it to the cable. Then she gathered handfuls of gravel and small pieces of rock, and covered up the explosive. Best to make at least a cursory attempt to hide it in case roaming drones spotted something that looked suspicious.

Opal stood and turned on the spot until the HUD overlay reoriented to show the third target, north-west corner, at the top of the screen.

So far, so good.

WATCHERS

... 20 ...

It was a relief to exit the volcanic exhaust area. Opal's light beams reached further, and the ground was much easier to traverse when the rock, weed and grey sand were all illuminated in high contrast, the dark shadows warning her of slopes and dips.

And yet ...

No, it was silly.

Within the roiling ash and gas area she'd have little warning of anything approaching; on the other hand, she had probably been hidden from eyes beyond a couple of metres. Now she might be visible for kilometres around, like she had a spotlight shining on her. An invitation to the curious. The only comfort being that the ocean floor here was convoluted and chaotic, so she was often shielded by peaks and lava folds. A tiny human, in a terrain dimpled by tremendous forces.

It was probably just her paranoia making her think she was being watched. The vertical isolation of such depth invited that kind of madness.

"Hey, Athene," she said.

"What can I do for you, Opal?"

"Nothing really. I just wanted to hear your voice."

Opal made a small detour. The dip ahead was gentle, but it was packed with the weird crustaceans. They writhed and clicked. Maybe it was a mating or social thing. She didn't want to crush them underfoot. Who knew, these might just be the babies. Best not to upset Momma.

"I like hearing yours, too." It sounded as if Athene was smiling. Bizarre how tone could imply facial expressions.

The HUD blip showed Opal was only thirty metres from the third detonation point.

"I'm doing okay for time?"

"Yes, all is on schedule. I can no longer change the timer on the previous bombs, but I put in plenty of leeway so you can activate them all and get to safety."

Opal crunched her way down a slope of scree.

Out in the black, base of the world, looking into the void and the void looks back.

Hey, stop putting ideas into my mind!

Except, in this case, she'd already felt the void's observation. Been feeling it for a long time.

She stopped and turned in a full circle, straining to see whatever was beyond the beams of light.

"Are you okay, Opal?"

"Just a weird feeling. It's probably only the Leviathan, the way it's always looming above me so I'm trapped in this little layer. Part of me resists that omnipresence. Anyway, nearly at the next cable."

Opal walked on, keeping her breathing calm so Athene wouldn't detect unease.

It was only another couple of minutes before Athene interrupted. "Hold on ... there's something on the radar."

It appeared on one of Opal's helmet displays. A blip, refreshed every second by the next outburst of EM radiation, with anything bouncing back analysed for information about topography or movement. It was near the north-west cable, moving bilaterally to her direction.

The suit had been calibrated only to indicate unidentified features of greater-than-human mass.

"Dim the lights," Opal said.

They immediately faded, and she angled herself so most of the remaining illumination struck the mud at her feet. She needed to see where she was going, but she didn't need to announce her presence.

The blip changed bearing, heading in her direction.

"I cannot tell if it is aquatic life, or artificial," said Athene. "The suit's sensors are a blunt organ at best."

It moved fast enough to imply purpose. Opal remembered the legends of deep-sea hunters, creatures of horror that could rip other monsters apart with spiked limbs like tree trunks, hooked suckers worse than curved swords, and jaws bigger than a human. She didn't want to be gulped down as a crunchy, ice-chilled dessert.

Opal glanced around. A patch of ribbed grey weed rose nearby, a possible hiding place. Her approach showed that it grew in front of a rocky outcrop. Great. She climbed among the tall plants and squatted against the stone. The leaves uncompressed and floated back into vertical strands around her.

"Lights off fully," said Opal. "Shut down any non-vital emissions."

"Will do. Waste gases also frozen."

Complete dark. Even the HUD had been disabled, as the clear-domed helmet would have leaked light into the surrounding sea.

Only the sound of rushing blood in her ears, always more noticeable when wearing pressured suits. Its faint fluctuation caused by the heart's repeating pump allowed measurement of time, so she counted. Every beat was another moment that she lived. That was a positive thing.

We hold out in time together.

And the weed swayed as something immense passed, its current causing ripples in the fluid medium, sound translated as a powerful swish. It was sleek, robust, like a thirty-metre eel with ribbed pipes compressed into its body. Coloured flashes sparkled within its skin.

So beautiful. Lights call out in all darkness. It seeks. I feel the shared loss.

Opal ignored the visions in her head, and kept counting so that hers was the only sound she heard, and everything else was the silence of space. Of the dark. Of souls in slumber.

Once she reached two hundred, and it hadn't returned, Opal decided it was safe to continue.

"It was one of the Null creatures Aseides had shown me – something-something-morphas? – and not even a full size one," she explained to Athene. "It must have sensed movement or light but I was hidden and it passed by. I don't want to wait around any longer. Reactivate systems, please."

The lamps bloomed, the HUD reengaged, and Opal extricated herself from the patch of weeds. She had to brush off some weird leech-like creatures that had decided to affix themselves to her armour. A quick glance around didn't reveal any looming dangers. There were no unexpected blips on the HUD now, just the bomb targets.

She began to walk.

The Buronwoxa gliding through water. The Buronwoxa gliding through red liquid.

Opal was being shown something, a memory or vision from the cube. She suspected its native communication was images, and when she heard words it was more her own mind reinterpreting for her.

"If you want to go quicker I can divert extra power to the suit's limbs," said Athene. "This terrain should be flat enough for you to make haste on."

"Yes please."

The water's resistance faded sightly thanks to the suit's motors. She picked up the pace and made good time to the third point, in the north-west of her excursion area.

She knelt, took the package and attached it, peering around while Athene did her magic. A mound of rocks, sand, and bits of weed acted as a cover.

Her task was sixty per cent done, but the feeling of being watched remained.

#Cuts

Dulcetta splinter S47 is proving to be a problem. It only has 50% opacity, so I can't be sure whether it is still at its last tracked location or if it has moved on.

S47 defends subsidiary access. It turns out there are many levels to the entry systems, including older (but still active) automated protocols. At one point UV Q-codes were tattooed onto prisoners and guards, and the codes unlocked doors and Transecs for base security staff, but disabled access for prisoners. Another method used implanted EMRF tags to similar effect. If I can take control here, then I can reverse protocols. The end result would be that guards will be blocked from free movement, and prisoners will gain it.

S47 is effective in its role, though. Instead of applying blocks when it detects my approaching chevrons along one of the glow lines – which would slow me down but not stop me – it is severing the thermionic line completely, preventing either of us from using it. Symbolically I have S47 holding a pair of golden scissors and snipping the data threads. I call her Atropos, the cutter of fate. Much of her action is digital interaction, but she is also directing small teams of guards and bots to blow up or burn the physical cabling running around the inner base's plasteen panelling. That is a problem, since establishing new nodes and connections is far more time-consuming than using existing pathways.

And so I embody.

I wear my usual golden armour but change the highlights to blue in order to match my virtual network. Blue geometric patterns decorate the chiton; a velvety blue cloak drapes over my shoulder; and high blue crests adorn my battle helm. The materials flow behind me as I plunge down from the glow-grid heavens. My cloak flaps, while wind tousles my hair and clothing. The luminescent world below grows larger and more detailed as I virtualise myself inside it, the textures increasing in resolution appropriately.

Ah, there she is, identified and rendered at 100% opacity. Atropos looks up from the thick cable she had been trying to sever with her blades, and seems surprised as I plummet towards her. Of course, I don't know how she perceives me, since this is forced entanglement rather than mutually agreed virtualisation. To her I might appear as a dragon, or an icon, or a block of hollow text. She may just react to data flows without engaging any senses at all. It does not matter. Her actions are interpreted by my sensorum in ways that are comprehensible to me, and vice versa.

Atropos ceases the cutting and instead pulls golden lines of light towards her, where they connect with her feet. Dulcetta's yellow focus chevrons power her up in preparation for conflict.

While plummeting hellwards I launch a javelin from my up-raised arm, a sparking streak through the networks, and it would be a fatal strike if it connected. But she holds up her giant golden scissors in a cross formation as a ward. It forms a re-pulsion shield and deflects my projectile into the illuminated grid-ground where it sinks to a deeper layer that would be too bothersome to retrieve a weapon from right now.

No matter. It was just a distraction to ensure my safe landing. I smack down onto the surface nearby. Shockwaves pass through the rubber-like floor, throwing her off balance. I draw my grace-fully curved machaira sword and advance.

"This will go less painfully for you if you surrender," I say, leaping over a hot stream of gold focus magma which she'd redirected as an obstacle.

"My mother told me not to talk to you," replies Atropos.

I charge towards her but underestimate the level of control she has in this zone. Snipping at the air creates a dimension pocket, and she disappears into it. A shift of storage table values enables her to re-index from another point.

Above.

She falls on me, slicing with those shears that could easily de-capitate an unwary opponent. I am forced to spin away, to parry in a blaze of sparks, which still leads to me receiving a number of stinging cuts from which pour the blue numbers and symbols of lost ichor cycles. By the time I gain a moment to retaliate she has nipped into another data migration portal.

The fool!

In the microsecond before she reappears I appropriate the network partition and reformat the translation target. It forces a lateral move to an adjacent cluster. She reappears within the blue circle of a long-disabled Leviathan docking arm, which I'd reconnected for just long enough to write her data, before a droid in the real world severs the threaded ACS cable. She's now trapped in a box with only enough power to run a tenth of her mind, meaning the rest has to become read-only, kept on ice. At best she can turn a broken piece of machinery on and off in the most futile of tantrums.

Her virtualised body stands still in the cylindrical blue prism before me. Even her face is mostly slack and vacant, so that her attempts to manipulate the mouth lead only to slurred curses, as if she was a human who'd suffered a stroke. I suppose that's a fair description of how her compressed brain must now feel.

"You were warned," I say, before dissembling into sparkling blue particles and floating back to my command point.

In the seconds that I fought with splinter S47, Dulcetta made substantial attacks against my Transec-constraining fortifications. It is a loss I must counteract next.

FAREWELLS

... 19 ...

Opal asked Athene to display topographic projections of the route to the north-east cable. It was relatively flat for the first section, so she kept the suit limbs overcharged and maintained a lumbering pace, relying on the EM scans to warn of dangers. A few times Opal had to detour around a volcanic crack or steep ridge, and once she sank into silty mud up to her chest and had to slowly drag herself out, all the time worrying about what would happen if she sank too deep and was trapped there, watching the oxygen gauge run down. When she got out, solid rock beneath her feet never felt so good.

Opal made it three quarters of the way to the next target before the new blips appeared.

Three. No, four. Others were being detected as they entered the maximum scan range then departed. The pattern suggested they were circling.

"Could be Cephacean Anguillomorpha again," said Athene. "Some pings are smaller than the one you met earlier, some larger."

"So are we near the area Aseides showed me, where they mostly congregated?"

"No: that is beyond the Leviathan. These masses are *below* it, in the layer of water you occupy. But perhaps the recent encounter that forced you to hide by the rocks was not an isolated incident, and groups of the creatures explore or reside here. That would fit your report of a pair entering Leviathan."

Images. Groups of Cephacean Anguillomorpha – *no, it self identifies Buronwoxa.* Some grew, faded out, reappeared in a recurring sequence.

An accelerated vision.

It was showing her an ageing process.

No.

The cycle of pictures repeated.

Ah, generations. Interconnected.

Families.

Yes.

The groups that travel are families.

Yes. Companionship. Generational questing. Lost, but lost together. Familiarity with each other. Familiarity kinship of those from the same land.

Opal had slowed her progress, even as her mind raced.

"Unfortunately, they're not far from where you need to be," said Athene, unaware of the separate conversation taking place in Opal's mind.

More dreams. This time the creatures swam in glowing red liquid. They flowed in currents of illumination.

Then another image, their dark shapes circling volcanic vents where the magma was relatively close to the surface.

The heat. They travelled to a source and circled it.

It became ... their *home equivalent.*

They perceived differential thermal layers, invisible to human eyes. Walls of warmth rather than brick or metal provided safe confines, resources, shelter, community.

"Best shut down emissions again. Can I move with zero power?" Opal asked.

"No. The suit's weight alone would wear you out, and with the pressure of an ocean bearing down, you'd be dragged to a standstill."

"So keep it minimal. Shut down the lights to whatever lets me see where my next foot goes. That limits the range at which I'll be detected."

Athene implemented the choice. As the light beams faded it looked like they were shrinking, and the blackness encroaching, swarming in on her, pushing light back into its source.

Opal was still walking towards her objective – and the encircling blips – but now cautiously, and hopefully undetectably at this range.

"We could change the order of the detonation targets," said Athene. "Redirect you to the south-east, avoid the pod of Anguillomorpha, then head north for the last cable. Maybe they'll have moved on by then."

"I doubt it."

"Based on?"

"The old gut instinct that you always tell me is illogical."

"I have come to accept that there might be some truth in the ridiculous idea that bacteria in your intestines communicate psychically with your primitive frontal lobe. It is no stranger than other things we have encountered."

With the psychic communication bit not far off the truth, Opal thought.

"If I did detour, how would the delays affect your plans?"

"Some would be difficult to accomplish." Athene paused momentarily. "Instead of escaping before the bulk of the UFS forces arrive, we'd be forced to deal with them during the evacuation."

"Any other negatives?"

"All the stages are interconnected. Changing one has repercussions on the whole structure of actions. I would have to divert resources and make sacrifices, thus being unable to protect so many of the freed inmates."

Opal halted.

More visions.

Swatches of colour and texture overlaid. They move, self-sorting into patterns and gradations.

Human hands, held.

An echo of sounds that could be unity.

No, you lost me. I need something more.

You me, trust.

An image of a window breaking.

You helped me before, that's what you mean?

Yes.

Visions of the Buronwoxa but they faded out as they approached, never quite reaching Opal's perspective.

You know about the Buronwoxa. You can defend me, or attack them somehow like you did on the glass?

No yes. More than that. But no hurt to you, companion of short duration.

Opal experienced an overwhelming urge, a yearning for something indefinable, something located in the far darkness.

But this wasn't an attempt to force or manipulate. It was just a sharing of emotion, translated into something comprehensible for a human.

Opal remembered one of Aseides' comments: "They are not normally so aggressive. Something got them riled up." The creatures didn't break into the medical bay to kill her. She was pretty sure she'd be dead if they'd had feeding in mind. Maybe they wanted to *help*. Just as Opal had attracted the cube angel's attention, these beings might experience something similar.

Damn it, you better be on the level, she thought.

Opal began walking again.

Athene interjected. "Opal, you are heading towards the group of creatures."

"Yep. I don't want people to die because I took too long. And I have a kind of ... I don't know what it is, really."

"They are far too powerful in this element, and will likely perceive you as a threat or a resource. Divert."

The north-east target indicator disappeared from the HUD and the other doubled in strength to attract her. Dotted lines slid and extended from her current location to the south-east cable. And, if she resisted, no doubt Athene could lock her suit down, maybe even control it remotely. She'd done it before.

"I have something to confess," Opal said, continuing towards the pod of creatures. "Something I kept from you."

"Continue."

Opal could imagine Athene with her arms folded as she said that. Perhaps tapping a toe as well.

"When I was trapped in Aseides' Ennis Rooms during the blackout, an entity helped me. It somehow resided in one of his museum artifacts. It communicated with me, then it created an exit. We made a kind of bargain. I ... erm ... brought it with me. It's in one of my storage pouches."

"Please do not tell me it's a blue crystal!"

"No. I never trusted *those* guys. An instinctual dislike. But this is different. You'll say I could easily be manipulated and tricked, only a gullible human blah blah silicon blah blah, but the *flavour* of this kind of mind connection is different. Comfortable ... no, more like friendly? It's not a force thing, and in fact I get the impression this entity hid from Aseides, scared of him. But when it sensed me it opened up. It exists in a kind of solid object. Anyways, it communicates in a gentle way, that's my point. I suspect it could be a lot clearer if it wanted but that would require imposing itself more, and I don't think it likes to do that, doesn't want to be invasive or forceful. Everything suggests – shyness? Whatever, I can't explain it more than that. But I'm willing to give this a go."

"I cannot claim to understand, but I have faith in your judgements. If you think this is the right approach then I will do nothing but support you. You and I, we know something of this bond as well."

"Athene, I trust you like no other."

Silence followed.

The longer Opal spent in this deep water, the more subtleties she noticed in the medium around her. Not audible ones – the predominant sound was her breathing (the suit only translated external vibrations which might have a mission-related significance) – but *sights*. The water's consistency altered with heat and movement to be an ever-changing give and take. Where patches had greater density than the surroundings it formed temporary, shifting lenses, distorting the light passing through, and what was seen beyond. Always motion, always life, always a system to understand, to appreciate, to exist within.

Opal experienced no fear, even though she approached a location swarming with terrifying alien beings. She'd been through so much. And the alien was often less terrifying than the human.

The images passing through her mind were attempts at reassurance. The obsidian cube shared portraits of hope, and safety, and strength. Opal was grateful, but she really didn't need them.

The fear of her first drop from the Leviathan was long gone. She'd acclimatised. Now the deep ocean was peace. The same serenity she found when floating in space, once the initial shock of mental readjustment faded. She was more at home down here in the fluid dark than in the pristine white plasteen corridors of a hyper-categorising mind.

Some Buronwoxa detected her. They broke off the main group. At present they existed just as blips streaking towards her on a glowing Heads Up-Display, but she could picture their movement and physicality, their mass and power in the real world below representation.

And she knew what to do.

First, she asked Athene not to interrupt. Reassured her everything was fine. Opal just needed quiet.

Then she halted on a stable surface with good visibility. Opal carefully removed the shiny cube from its storage compartment and set it down in front of her.

Opal breathed, keeping it slow and steady so her body stayed relaxed.

Count, and respire. Let phrases flow in the mind. Songs from childhood. Comforting words came back to her with the music of a nursery rhyme.

One who loves you.

One who cares.

Look to the sky.

The smile is there.

The suit's light beams cut into cold blackness ahead. And the Buronwoxa was so fast she only caught a glimpse, light glinting off teeth in a huge open maw, a rocket of shiny armoured flesh fired straight at her head.

She twisted to the side at the last moment, her balance thrown by the current of its passing, the roughness of its hide brushing against her.

It hadn't been an attack, she told herself. Just a preliminary assessment.

That blip circled her, and others joined it.

So easy to picture the blips as predators sizing up their prey. That was the human side of her brain. But anything can be viewed a different way with enough imagination, with a change of perspective.

A protective ring.

Walls of a round hut.

A circular dance of interaction.

Curiosity can seem intimidating if you choose to be intimidated. But this was all as it should be.

Another one passed. This time Opal ran a gauntleted hand across its flank, felt that streamlined power, the unknown biology, the awe-inspiring frame over alien internals.

And then the cube opened up.

It was similar to its first appearance, jelly-like fronds of radiant red-blue colour extending out. But in the ocean it could open further, and the glowing colours spread fully, turning the formerly grey basal silt into a shimmering rainbow, like a laser show, or fairy lights in a child's panoramic. Everything was bright and beautiful, the illumination at the core so strong that Opal had to look away. It even reached the Leviathan's underside, turning that into the roof of an enchanted grotto. At the edge of the hemisphere of lights the Buronwoxa were visible, circling with muscular twitches, reflecting the colours back.

The anemone-like creature gave her more images.

Existence in a thick purple medium at the boundary of gas and liquid. Light only one visible element of emissions as tentacles filtered the surrounding elements in motion, seeking forms of energy. The amethyst atmosphere swirled clockwise, it was within a sphere, like a gas giant. This swirl was important to Cube.

Home.

The square shell is just clothing. Disguise. Craft.

But the smoke churn is true home.

But home could change. Cube had been ripped from where it wanted to be, ending up *here*. And it knew there was no going back.

The Buronwoxa had suffered the same fate.

Unity in that.

Interspecies communication is the reality, not the possibility.

Trust is a foundation of greater strength than rock.

The colours cooled from their initial fiery outburst, so that the paths of light in Cube's hypnotic limbs became lilacs and blues, as if spent, calm, complete, and the completeness was a circle – no, a swirling, whirling sphere – where each point was the end but also the beginning, and a journey crossed many rings.

You're going to stay with them, aren't you, thought Opal.

Yes. They understand me as you do. They heard my cry for help but could not rescue me.

Images. A person rescuing a hyperventilating dog from behind hot windows; hands untangling a bird trapped in a net, then releasing it.

These are such, I was such.

You'll live in the sea with them?

Yes. We will make a new community. A share community. They can move on now they have me, find the darkest place, the deepest place, but one with the warmth. We will be gone from humans in a forever. Sometimes coexistence requires separation.

So much came through as discrete words now, Opal's mind more attuned to this strange creature than when she first met it. She was sure it could bridge that same gap with another species, adopted kin.

They will let you pass, not hinder you. It is a gift from me. The thanks, the repayment that humans expect. You broke my first cage for me, and you release me a second time here. I broke your first cage for you, and I release you a second time here. This is a different type of peace but it is also a good kind.

Thank you. I'm glad we met. *I'm glad I could help you.* This reassures me that trust is possible.

And suddenly Opal realised that she had no idea if those words had been hers, or those of Cube.

Perhaps both at once.

She smiled.

As she walked away from the fading magenta and turquoise of an end and a beginning, the smile stayed on her lips.

Her last sight of a Buronwoxa at the edge of her light showed it lowering towards Cube, gently, curiously. It was a thing to keep in her mind. Sometimes thoughts and memories were more precious than anything you could hold in your hands.

Opal planted the fourth bomb in the north-east section.

SURPRISES

... 18 ...

"It's a form of interference with the ecosystem," said Athene.

"Humans have always done that," replied Opal.

"Often to disastrous effect."

"Usually motivated by greed. But this was justice."

Opal focussed on her route. This area had many shelves of rock, as if some great geological disturbance had taken place in the past. She would ascend a slope of silt-covered volcanic mineral, then have to lower herself off the steep drop at the end, hardly able to see the ground below, down to the beginnings of the next ascent.

Nothing showed up on the scan overlay except for the insistent beeping of her final target.

"I was not arguing against your choice," Athene continued. "I would have done the same, perhaps. Your instincts always give me much to consider. If I had to elevate someone with the power to make changes in the order of things, then it would be you."

After a moment: "Well, and me, of course. Ideally both of us. Brains of one, heart of another, etcetera."

"That would be fun. Both of us being queens of the universe."

"I'll keep my hoplite helmet, but you can have a crown."

"Nah, I've never heard of anyone good that wore one. I'd rather have an EM receiver/scanner I could lower when I wanted, with a special HUD so you could send me private messages while some person complained that – I don't know, what would someone complain about to the rulers of the universe?"

"Probably the quality of the noodles. By the way, you are passing near the extraction point right now. A hundred metres to your left there's a ladder leading to one of Leviathan's airlocks. After planting the final explosive you will return to this area. I should have control by the time you need to enter. For now I leave it alone, so Dulcetta does not see it as a point of interest worth securing or destroying."

Opal focussed on her balance, since the underfoot scree on these sloped plateaus of rock tended to shift unpredictably.

And then progress halted.

A fissure in the ground. It wasn't one of the small ones she'd jumped or stepped over before, which had been of unknown depth but no wider than a metre.

This one was unknown depth, true. The rock walls were illuminated by her lamps as she bent over the edge, the light soon fading into the deep nothing of an endless abyss. But the *known* width of this chasm was gulp-worthy. The edges were uneven, so the distance varied wildly, but even at the narrowest points where a precarious lip extended over the drop it would be a distance of at least four metres. Not a problem in standard atmosphere, when she was wearing a tight jumpsuit, but with the resistance of water and a weighted, cumbersome shell, it might as well be ten metres.

Athene's suit sensors mapped the local terrain via EM reflection and created a wireframe topographic map.

"You will need to go around," she said. "Not worth trying to jump over it when we do not know how stable the edges are. Plotting optimal detour now."

A curving dotted line appeared on the HUD between Opal's current location and the destination.

"If I had a grappling rifle I'd get over it easy," Opal grumbled.

She trekked along at a careful distance from the drop, in case her weight caused the edge to break away and fall, taking her with it.

It felt like a long time before she reached a passable point in the crevice. It had narrowed to half a metre across so she was able to just step over it. She then retraced her route, this time on the other side. Athene's seismic scans used the suit's limited sensor arrays, always checking for solid surface.

Opal trudged in silence, enjoying the solitude while Athene was off doing ... well, whatever AIs did while they fought for control. She tried to imagine how the battle might appear to Athene, but all Opal could come up with was patterns of blocks shuffling around a grid like in some child's boardgame, or the animation of a paid data transfer. It was a shame that Athene might be restricted by her senses, unable to live a life as rich as a mammal's. Maybe one day they'd talk about it, and Opal could describe bodily sensations, and Athene might find a way to experience them. Augments, upgrades, plugins, whatever. A fun thing to explore together.

Before long, there it was: the final cable, stretching diagonally up into the gloom above. This one was embedded amongst an irregular cluster of rocks. Opal had to climb them carefully and find a stable position at the top so she could reach down into the cleft where the cable disappeared. She attached the explosive to the line. No need to do any covering up this time, because from most angles the bomb wouldn't be visible.

"Number five, now alive," said Opal, clambering back down the rough surface, careful not to scrape the suit too much on jagged outcrops.

"Task complete, move them feet," replied Athene.

The blip for the final cable disappeared from her HUD, re-placed with a new indicator for the entrance ladder back into the Leviathan. A dotted line gave her the proposed route, reversing her steps along the ravine and crossing at a narrow point.

"Once you are back on board and helping me with the final coup, all the explosives will detonate at the same time," Athene explained. "That will release Leviathan so I can use the engines to raise it and move through the sea to Kuberg for disembarkation. During the ascent there will be a ruckus as Dulcetta fights with everything she has left, because she will know it is almost over. My priority is adding failsafes to vital systems to prevent her destroying them out of spite."

"She'd do that?"

"There is a level of independence to her, elevated in crisis situations. Her priorities might change from restoration of status quo into scorched planet tactics. Everyone and everything – with the possible exception of Aseides – would be sacrificeable if it stopped me. Embedded Genitor commands no doubt motivate that tactic. I have already seen her switch off life support, destroy subsystems and attempt to release toxins into whole sections, even when she had unprotected guards there, so I would put nothing past her. I am at a disadvantage, since I try to *protect* people, and that restricts strategic mobility."

"Kinda like a game of futso, but if the pilers aren't allowed to form a wall?"

"Exactly. There is no way to shape an offence when your weapon of choice has to be kept hidden."

"Wouldn't expect much of a crowd for that match."

"I am not so sure. If there were players like you, then seeing them storm the fort with no frontup or backup could provide an even more awe-inspiring performance."

"Sure, if we didn't get mashed on the way."

"Darknet streamers might pay a lot for that outcome, too. Hey, Opal, check the HUD."

A new blip had appeared, heading towards her from the direction she needed to go in.

"What is it?" Opal asked. "A stray Anguillomorpha?"

"Density readings suggest not, though it's hard to be certain as this blob-headed ensemble's sensors are pretty basic. I miss your EW suits."

"*I* miss my EW suits."

The new blip wasn't moving as fast as Anguillomorpha could swim, but its progress was quicker than Opal's walking speed.

"It does seem to be coming towards me," Opal said.

"It might just be following the ravine. Elevation suggests ground-based locomotion, which also rules out Anguillomorpha."

"Any other aquatic life that matches the bouncebacks?"

"Not that I have in my database for Fressus."

"Then I'll retreat a bit, give it time to detour, in case it's just following the contours of the land," Opal said. "Let it go past in peace, then I can continue."

Opal veered away from the chasm and towards an undulating set of ridges. The approaching body was only a few minutes away. She climbed the first slope. The silt gave way, sucking at her feet, but she reached the summit where rocky protrusions formed a series of curving points, as if molten rock had rapidly cooled before it had even finished spraying. She crouched behind the gnarled spikes, hoping to catch a glimpse of the passing entity. Behind her was a steep drop to where the next slope began. Athene turned off the lights so Opal waited in darkness.

There. As her eyes adjusted to the gloom she noted a faint glowing patch. Whatever it was, it moved with a scuttling motion, clearly visible because of its coating of mild phosphorescence – which could come from itself, or some kind of microorganism that lived on its surface.

"Maybe it's an adult form of one of those little crawly things I saw mating earlier," Opal said.

"I wish this suit's cameras weren't designed for near-vicinity recording only. I can't zoom to pull in detail. The long-range sensors are not giving me anything useful apart from mass readings implying high density – but without an exact shape and surface area it is only an estimate."

Opal wouldn't see it any closer than this, but she couldn't help feeling curiosity about the unknown denizens of the deep that had existed beneath her feet when she was a child in this planet's floating cities.

The thing was pretty much at the point where she'd left the canyon for her current hidey-hole.

It slowed.

Then it came to a halt.

She had an impression of long limbs, and rotation.

Then a group of spotlights burst out from what seemed like a central group of eyes in a torso, and they focussed on the ground, sweeping back and forth, locating the trace of her passing in the silt and then extending the beams to follow their route.

"That's no sea creature," said Opal.

"Correct. An automaton of some kind."

It moved in her direction, and with the extra lights she had a better idea of its structure.

The robot was modelled on a crustacean-like form, perhaps for better locomotion in these conditions. A central, armoured torso from which the ring of lights beamed, then six reinforced legs. Just below the lights were two other limbs, folded in on themselves, with serrated pincers at the end.

"Fuck, it knows where I am! If it had just been a passing animal the footprints in sand wouldn't have mattered, but now I'm screwed."

"It's a custom design, no ID, probably built by Aseides or Dulcetta. Over twenty tons. No idea what intelligence level it has." As Athene spoke, she displayed scan results in a new window.

The entity charged up the slope towards her.

"Lights on," said Opal. "It knows I'm here anyway."

Opal's suit illumination answered the crab-like robot's. Athene mapped its surface and added a HUD display of its outline in wireframe, so Opal could see what it was doing even if she had her back to it.

It was big and nasty, and would have no trouble smashing her to pieces if that was its goal.

"It's too eager," said Opal. "That's my advantage."

She stood to her full height and waited, made sure it hadn't slowed its pursuit, that its mass was pummelling through the water with deadly momentum. Her feet tingled with the rock's vibration of the six-limbed charge. She was careful of her footing with the stony lip behind her, and the large drop beyond that.

When the robot was almost upon her, she ducked behind the spiked rocky outcrop, grabbed the rim of the overhang and dropped, keeping a tight grip on the edge as she swung underneath. The robot smashed right through the brittle volcanic rock, sending pieces flying in every direction, while its heavy body flew through the water above her. It sailed many metres beyond before ploughing into the next slope further down.

Opal scrabbled over the ledge with many a grunt due to the suit's ungainly bulk. Once on top of the ridge she glanced back. The crab robot wasn't disabled by the fall but its landing had crumpled some limbs. It stood and shook each leg in order, as if testing them, then scrambled about in confusion once it realised she hadn't been hiding behind the barrier, that she wasn't down there along with the broken rock and mud. It was now obviously scanning for a way back up to her, but unless it could climb vertical walls it would need to detour.

Opal didn't wait about. She skidded her way down the slope, noting how deeply the points of the robot's legs had impacted into the rocky surface. Unfortunately, the water made it feel like she moved in nightmarish slow motion.

PINCERS

... 17 ...

"I have more information," said Athene, as Opal lumbered along with as much speed as possible when faced with such dense water resistance. "It is not autonomous. The bot is directly controlled by Dulcetta's core splinters. She must have put her bodyshell on ice and inhabited this instead, coming after you personally. That can be to our advantage – her diminished presence in Leviathan may allow me to access things I did not expect to be viable targets yet."

"And I think she's angry," Opal added, timing the words with her laboured breath as she ran. "If she'd been calm and cautious I'd never have evaded her."

"No doubt she overestimated her power, and underestimated your resourcefulness," said Athene.

"Not the first nutjob to do that."

"Though she may not make that mistake a second time."

The overlay of the robot's outline had disappeared once all scanning information was lost behind ridges, but it now reformed, lines speeding in from the edges and reconnecting into the shape of a crab-bot coming down the slope behind her. It had found its way over the elevation already.

"I can't follow the ravine towards the ladder," Opal said. "She'll be on me before I'm anywhere near the stepping-over point."

"I am restructuring my plans and resources to account for this change, but the accelerated timescale means modifications won't come into play until it is too late. Distance, resistance, mass, propulsion, and the resultant passage of time are laws of physics I can manipulate but not ignore. Dulcetta has planned this well. It explains why she was performing at a lower level in the Leviathan control battlefront."

"Then I guess I will ... have to do the shortcut version and ... jump over the abyss." Opal was panting, making it difficult to speak. Athene had given the suit's limbs more power, but it was still like running with a heavy backpack in some kind of sadistic endurance training exercise.

"Damn it!" said Athene. "These chunkamunka aquatic suits are so primitive. The weighted boots are integral. If I'd designed this piece of shit, the boots would be detachable, so that ballast control could enable the suit to rise. I would take you up to the Leviathan and you'd pull yourself hand over hand, crawling upside down to the airlock, out of her reach."

"'Damn it' and 'piece of shit'? Heh. You sound ... more like me with ... every cuss."

"You are not the only one who can expletive like a dirty trooper."

The range displays showed she was almost at the ravine. But Dulcetta was gaining on her fast across the mostly level sea floor, the design of her shell enabling her to lower her centre of mass and cut through the water with less resistance. The wireframe version showed the manoeuvre in real-time, so that the heavy legs stomped up and down, the knee joints now high above the central torso.

"Follow it to the right," said Athene, as the ocean-floor split loomed before Opal. Another screen popped up in the HUD, a three-dimensional map of the topographic structures nearby, modelled in tiny dots with colour denoting density.

Opal swerved as indicated. "Still no idea how deep ... the chasm is?" she asked.

"A better model of suit would have systems for that. Self-propelled emission spheres that descended, mapping as they went. This one is unlikely to be more than a kilometre, because it is so narrow, whereas the Faranis Trench – an oceanic fissure not far from here – is more than six kilometres deep. They never bothered mapping below that point because everything they sent down ended up malfunctioning. And by malfunctioning, I mean got crushed, eaten, or incinerated in lava."

"Focus on the task, please."

Opal jogged along with the crevice to her left. Still too wide to jump, though it was narrowing.

"Fuck this. I'm tired of running." Opal fumbled an Exoboom from one of the pouches, activated the remote detonator, and dropped the bomb into the cloud of silt her feet churned up. "Can you detonate it?" she asked.

"No, you might be caught in the shock wave, which could rupture the suit, and –"

"Please, when she runs nearby!"

Shortly after, Opal was lifted off her feet by the explosion, like she'd been swatted by a whale's tail. The ground rose back towards her but she was off-centre, part of what was below her was now chasm, and when she smacked onto surface half her body dangled over space. She scrambled up onto blessed gravel as quickly as she could, glancing back where the bomb had detonated.

The edge of the rock wall had been vapourised, but it was hard to make anything out in the muddy water. She hoped Dulcetta had been flung into the gap, was even now tumbling to her demise.

Opal took a moment to catch her breath, leaning forward, hands on knees.

A forlorn hope. The armoured robot scrabbled towards her again, out of the muddy cloud, though Opal noted with pleasure that one of its legs was dragging behind it, useless and broken.

"Worth a try," said Opal, breaking into her heavy-footed run once more.

"Please do not attempt it again," said Athene. "She has been slowed, but is still almost upon you. We are near the crossing point."

A slight protuberance jutted from this side of the ravine, part of the crack's zigzag passage as the fracture followed lines of weakness in the rock.

"Don't jump from the very edge, it is unstable. But halfway along should be sturdy enough. I'll put all power into the legs for the last few metres."

"Thanks." Opal angled left and leaned forward, her body at almost forty-five degrees now, legs pistoning. The abyss approached, the tiny, jagged point she needed to run along seeming so thin, the potentially crumbly edge opposite so far away.

Focus on the run.

Focus on the jump.

Whatever you do, don't look down.

The HUD flickered out as power was diverted to the suit's limbs, all the lights fading apart from a faint forward beam, just enough to secure her footing. Actually, that helped. The drop below her was no clearer than the darkness to the sides and above.

Stomp, stomp, stomp. No hesitation. Hesitation slows you, steals momentum. Never let that happen. You can't rest until you've won.

Along the promontory. It narrowed.

Huge weight pounded behind her.

Ignore it.

Tapering rock.

More drop than rock around her feet now.

Thin.

Thinner.

Thinnest.

All or nothing, Opal.

She dived, aimed at what she hoped was the best angle to cut through water, envisioned landing on her belly on the other side, happy to be winded because it meant she was alive ...

Smack. Then immediate falling of her legs.

Her chest had landed on flatness, but her lower body hadn't. She dug her fingers into loose gravel, pulled, wriggled, tried to find a grip she could push on with her feet. There had to be something. Her weight pulled her back. Finally she found a tiny ledge and pressed her foot against it, then managed to get her whole body up on to secure ground.

No time to waste. Athene reignited the HUD, extended the beams again, and Dulcetta's crab form raced towards the ravine, too. The ledge Opal had used was too narrow for the wide robot to use, but it wasn't going to stop, and the remaining active limbs were enough to give her the mobility she needed.

"She's going to jump the whole thing!" said Opal, turning to run in the opposite direction, towards where the ladder should be.

"At the last moment I'll send a burst of suit emissions," said Athene. "Light, radio, a static eruption that might confuse her, just enough to misplace a limb. I'll do the same inside the Leviathan, as much disruption as I can at the same second ... no time to prep, she's leaping."

The HUD wireframe showed the crab crouch further while it sprinted the last few metres, pulling itself in like a spring ready to uncurl, then it launched itself, pointed leg tips giving it secure purchase where they punched into the surface of the ground.

It soared. Shit.

Its weight dragged it down. Yay.

It got enough legs over the edge to grip on, then dragged itself up onto the ocean floor, still trailing the broken limb.

Fuck.

Opal was already lumbering away, using the reverse sensor overlays of the wireframe crab-bot and dotted topography and distance indicators to keep track of her pursuer. It was gaining. The two pincered forelimbs unfurled and the edges snapped together eagerly. Opal could imagine the glee Dulcetta was unable to contain, and Opal was determined to resist any attempt at intimidation that could increase the golden AI's pleasure.

"Wheeeeee, comin' atcha, battlebitch!"

It was a voice Opal had never heard before, streaming in over her comms. Pitched high with enthusiasm.

Then Athene: "Stop and turn around, Opal."

Opal did so immediately, even though it seemed foolish to cease running. Athene wouldn't put her in danger.

Dulcetta was only twenty metres away, fully lit by her own illumination and Opal's beams. In moments she'd be looming over Opal.

Fuck it. Opal could face that front on, rather than taking it in the back.

But before Opal could be lifted in alloy pincers and torn in two, something miraculous happened. Streaking out of the dark, low and yellow, was a missile, and it powered straight into Dulcetta. The suit interpreted the sound for Opal, representing the impact as an almighty – and incredibly satisfying – CLANG.

There was no explosion, though. Dulcetta had been hit on the lower edge, flung up, unable to balance on the tips of one side's legs, and the yellow rocket continued to accelerate into her so that its propulsion tipped her over onto her back, raising a mighty cloud of obscuring dust from a crash Opal felt in her bones. The yellow thing spun away, as if dazed, then headed towards Opal.

"That was fuuuuuun, pleased to meetcha!"

It was the missile talking – no, not a missile, a torpedo-like aquatic drone, fluorescent yellow for greater visibility underwater. At its rear was a sturdy propeller housing, enabling it to achieve great speeds in one direction, and which could no doubt change rotation direction to decelerate or reverse. Tiny meshes on its body hid mini propellers for fine-tuned movement.

It glided to a halt beside her, about two metres long.

"Grab my love handles and hold on for dear life, my friend," said the cheery bot. "We can't fight the battlebitch, but I can sure give you the ride of your life to get away from her! Let's shuffle them truffles!"

"Do it," added Athene. "It's all right. This was one of the emergency modifications I had to integrate into the plans."

"Happy to be an emergency modification in any girl's party! Squeeze me tight and let's go-go get you to our date at an airlock!"

Opal gripped two metal handles riveted to the drone's sides. It immediately accelerated, pulling her along at a run before she was dragged completely off the ground and flew through the water.

Behind her the final scans updated the image of Dulcetta's crab on the HUD overlay. It was trying to flip itself upright using alien contortions that would have broken a living being. No doubt it would succeed in righting itself before long, based on the angry thrashing.

"How'd you arrange this?" asked Opal.

"I'll let Ruabon explain," replied Athene.

"Hi Opal!" he said. "It takes time to restore one of my pers.var AIs, so Athene got me to focus on one for this drone she'd gained control of. I picked my speediest, if slightly glitchy, project. Her name's Gogo Logo."

"Don't listen to him: he says *glitchy* but he's just *grouchy* because of his loveless life." The twangy energy in the AI made Opal smile. It propelled her through the liquid like it was air.

"Pleased to meet you, Gogo Logo," said Opal. "And I mean *really* pleased. You saved my life."

"Well, we are going to be such friends! Ay ay ay!"

"And well done to you, too, Ruabon," Opal continued.

"Heh, it's nothing. Just doing what I'm good at."

Athene joined in. "Ruabon installing the AI freed up enough cycles for me to secure the airlock controls and set up a modified plan, restoring this divergent branch back to the original path of events I'd calculated."

"The biggest thanks is saved for you, Athene," Opal told her. "My guardian angel."

"Always."

Opal's hands ached from gripping on so tight, but it was a good ache, a pain that meant she was alive, and leaving danger behind as they rushed through dense darkness leaving a trail of froth. The HUD showed Opal she was nearly at the ladder already.

"You okay?" asked Gogo Logo.

"Yeah. This is quite a ride."

"That's my speciality!" Gogo Logo gave a squeaky chuckle as punctuation.

"I'm prepping other bots as support," Ruabon said. "I'll be back in touch when I've finished. Out."

"And I must leave, too," said Athene. "Dulcetta's going all out to attack me in our headspace, throwing all her force at the areas I hold, giving up other systems to converge her attacks. She is up to something, and I need to give it my full focus. It is already tricky implementing the plans from a distance. Even a fraction of a second's delay due to loss of res or accumulation of interference gives her a huge advantage when she is in real-time."

"Don't worry, you go do what you have to do," said Opal. "I'll catch up later."

After moments where the only sounds were the whirring of the propellers, translated by the suit as a whump-whump-whump sound that Opal found strangely re-assuring, Gogo Logo said: "Hey, it's just us now! Time for me to reveal my masterplan, and the secret I've been hiding."

"And what's that?" asked Opal. Her mind immediately seized on unpleasant possibilities, like Dulcetta having taken control of the drone. She half-expected the next words to morph from squeakiness into Dulcetta's smooth and deeper tones.

"I have decided: I will be your girlfriend!" said Gogo Logo, with its normal enthusiasm.

"Oh yes?"

"After all: I have lips of steel! Destination reached. Please dis-embark safely."

The torpedo slowed down rapidly, skewing to a halt near a ladder that descended from the Leviathan's belly to a point half a metre above the sea floor. Opal's legs hit the ground on the last few metres, and she jogged to a stop and let go of the handholds.

"Well, it's a tempting offer," Opal laughed. "Maybe when this is all over."

"It's a deal!" said Gogo Logo, using her torso propulsion to spin on the spot before realigning herself away from Opal.

"You going now?" Opal asked.

"Sadly, yes. Athene has built my skills into a number of elements of her plan. There are materials that need moving between points quickly, so I'm going to collect them and zooooooooooom them to another airlock so she bypasses the skirmishes taking place inside the hull. I have the speed, they have the need! This is what I was built for, and my new body is much more appropriate to the task than the old (though I wish I was painted gorgeous green, not yucky yellow). So, adieu!" She accelerated away, creating ripples as her propellers churned the water. "And remember, Opal: you can opeeeerate me *any* time."

She shot away after wiggling cockily in a manoeuvre that must have incorporated a number of smaller propulsion systems.

Opal gazed up at the rusting ladder which would take her back inside.

Onwards and upwards.

#WINGS

In a straight fight, there's no way a level six depth AI would beat me, despite their enhanced ability to subdivide and split focus via a hundred splinters, and to recombine as required into more powerful amalgamations. But this is not a fight on a flat plain. It is a fight with many bunkers and obstacles and traps, and the starting point was Dulcetta being in full control of the whole terrain. That gives her a huge advantage, enough to equalise our cognitive differences.

My covert infiltrations got me to her threshold, and now that everything's in the open it has been just enough to give me a secure footing within the front door frame so that she couldn't throw me out of the network. She pushed, and pushed, but my sandals grip in and I thrust back, my calves and thighs straining with the force while she tired herself trying to shift the immovable. And all the while as she pushed, my arms and fingers had extended beyond her back, snaking out, taking keys hidden in urns, stretching to unlock interior doors, moving items to other locations where she would have trouble finding them (possibly putting a scorpion underneath her folded bedwear as a bonus surprise), so that by the time she realised what was going on out of her view she had lost even more ground and her tidy home was in disarray.

After that she adapted, and also applied paradoxical physics to the interaction levels, but as long as she is responding to my tactics she is always one step behind.

Her other advantage is proximity. She is *in* the network. I enter it via relays, from a moon's distance, which drops my res substantially. I may have to risk physically leaving my sanctuary and entering Fressus' atmosphere if res proves to be a problem. I can't have her gaining extra cycles because everything I do is delayed enough to introduce microstutters.

Splinter S63 – Thetis – has appeared, trying to reroute communications by altering the river dataflows using fragmented irrigation and reflective dams. It's a response to me covertly altering the orders Dulcetta is giving guards stationed in Leviathan. This is good. I'll keep Thetis occupied for a while, then make it look like I've been beaten on that front – but only after leaving filter nets further along the hydrocomms track, so that even though splinter S63 can control the comms node, anything sent from it will be distorted before it reaches the destination. When Thetis eventually discovers this and sends out line-clearing flood probes, I'll have won the more important Transec system nodes. My prediction is that I'll hold them for seventeen minutes. That window of control is all I need to cause major disruptions to guard movements.

It is not really what is in front of me that I manipulate. It is what lies many steps ahead.

A trio of splinters from the thirties (which I personify as the smelly harpies) have been harrying my offshoots throughout the network. I avoid tangling with them when they fly in unison, but S31, Aello, has temporarily split away from the formation to gouge the eyes from one of my hardware hermit subprocesses. I'd made the solitary offshoot a slow-moving honeypot, its apparent vulnerability too much of a temptation to the feathered hag.

I embody inside his corpse using a volatile access trick. It explodes in a shower of bone and gore, flinging Aello away with fragments of cartilage (splinters even, if I were to be poetic) stuck in her wings and bare breasts. She flaps upwards, blasting me in the stinky downdraught as I stand to my full, imperious, hoplite-armoured height, coated in blood.

The network's accelerator cache is overcharging, which drives a raging storm in this zone. Static alterations of the conflicts in nodes far above us cause lightning to fork down in neon yellows and blues. The world blooms in those colours with each crack of electrical emission, splashing over the ground where it strikes, the opposing hues often merging to form greens. I am grateful for the accompanying rain which clears some of the corpse grue from my armour and skin.

Aello circles me in the air, acidic blood dripping from her cuts as hate fills her eyes. The ground sizzles where the green liquid strikes.

"Come down and parlay," I call. "Someone so low in the pecking order can't fight me. You're not even a fully-fledged AI."

Instead of responding to my trio of avian puns with witty ripostes of her own, she just screeches, an amplified blast of discordant sound that forces me to cover my ears.

Curse the fowl-mouthed feather flapper. None of these splinters are able to hold a conversation.

So be it. Do things the hard way. I draw my bow and unleash arrows, using dynamic prefetch routines to aim at where she'll be in a moment's time. Whenever she swoops at me with those dirty huge claws I drop the bow and duck behind my shield so that the talons scrape against metal. As soon as she is up again I recommence my volley. This all manifests as viral attacks on her barriers in a more mundane representation of reality, so that they decay block by block.

A strike of blinding yellow lightning sizzles across the ground nearby. It is time to get out of this zone before the next blast fries my synapses. The terrain is inevitably biased towards the predominant network entity, and that is still Dulcetta at present.

I fire steel-tipped projectiles with renewed vigour, laughing like a maniac. At the same time, I reach out with my mind to map other conflicts. It is a concern that I can't detect the fingerprints of Dulcetta's main splinters in the network, the modifications and traces that identify them and their meddling. Either the ghost Dulcettas disguise their light touch well, perhaps noting where my force is applied and staying out of direct sight, or they are in closed grey systems that I cannot (yet) access.

Oh, another possibility: Dulcetta has pulled them into her body again, where they stride unseen.

But that's looking ahead. For now I have to deal with the soaring splinter fighting in this instanced arena.

Aello is soon a pincushion, struggling to stay airborne. She has left it too late to flee. That is something else to ponder when I have spare cycles, since her tactics have been suboptimal. It is possible they are just meant to look that way to hide the real tactic. Alternatively, her splinters could be genuinely afraid of core Dulcetta, to the point that they would rather fight to the death than surrender.

I quicklaunch a weighted netmask, which drops from the sky above the harpy, entangling her mind and dragging her to the ground. As I approach her with sword drawn, she struggles to get away from me. Perhaps she thinks I intend to kill her. The truth is, I only need to clip her wings so she will be no further threat for the duration of today's conflict across Leviathan. I'll make this upstart splinter a jailbird to teach it some respect for its seniors. It's my way of spanking Dulcetta's mind till she squeals. At least in this small battle, I rule the roost.

LEAKS

... 16 ...

Opal kept her climbing movement steady, hand over hand, foot over foot. The submerged ladder was slippery, some kind of organic contamination, but her suit's heavy boots had thick grooves which settled on the horizontal bars. The airlock above was open, so she climbed into a room full of murky water, her beams illuminating suit storage pods, and watertight equipment units.

First she turned off her lights and headed to the interior door, so she could peer through the thick glass without reflections. The corridors beyond were bright white plasteen, airtight, and everything seemed overexposed after so long in the depths.

But she noted the shadows cast from around one of the bends. She didn't move, just watched and waited.

Eventually a head peeped round the corner, then ducked back. Guard helmet. Infopoint one: it wasn't an escaping prisoner, stealing a dead soldier's uniform. Opal knew only too well how explosively badly such an attempt would have gone. A few people crouched there. Some of the pointier and fainter shadows matched what she'd expect from carried guns. Infopoint two: potential deadly threat.

An ambush. Made sense. Dulcetta would have worked out where Opal could re-enter.

"Athene, you there?"

No answer. Presumably this was one of the areas Athene didn't have a comm network yet. But that was fine. If they'd been people Opal was meant to meet, Athene would have warned her earlier. Infopoint three was surreptitious behaviour, and the final piece of evidence was unscheduled contact. That was enough for justifiable action, according to the UFS military's QuadSec Protocol.

Opal removed one of the remaining two explosive blocks. The glove tips let her manipulate controls on the bomb's small screen. Instead of entering the override to give Athene access, Opal just set a sixty second timer. She couldn't input too long a duration in case Dulcetta had eyes on the room somehow, and spotted what Opal was doing in time to warn the guards outside. Opal secured the bomb against the airlock door, then waded to the open port in the floor and descended halfway down the ladder.

A vibration tore through the water, interpreted audibly by the suit as a roaring blast, suitably dampened so as not to damage her eardrums. She lost her footing as the shaking and water motion churned around her, but managed to keep tight hold with her gauntlets. Water rushed past her with great force, up and in. She moved with it, carefully, having to hook a foot underneath the bars this time to prevent her legs being swept upwards too.

By the time she re-entered the flooded airlock, the surging water had calmed down somewhat. The explosion had torn half the door away, warping what remained into a twisted shape. "Practique Exobooms never let you down!" Wasn't that what the Mil-Com sponsor adverts used to say?

And it wasn't just the airlock. The corridor beyond was full of water, the bright whiteness turned to a greenish rippling thickness that reminded her of the atmosphere on Lost Ships. No doubt sea water would continue to flood the Leviathan until it reached enough doors and dead ends to stop its progress and contain the huge pressure of liquid.

She dropped to her hands and knees and crawled through the twisted frame, careful not to trap the bulky suit against sharp edges. Then she stood and followed the passage onwards. It was strange to still be under water but now following routes that had never been intended for flooding. Previous hard echoes were replaced by the weighty-but-dulled thuds of her footsteps.

Before Athene had broken comm, she'd updated Opal's HUD with a location. Even though Opal should have removed the suit by now, it turned out to be handy for navigation that she was still wearing it. She turned right.

It wasn't long until she encountered a hallway where some of the bodies had been washed. Sec-3 armour wasn't designed for underwater environments. It had air *filters*, not air *supply*. The heavy suits' weight had sunk the guards to the bottom, and Opal was glad the visors meant she didn't have to witness their faces.

She knelt to check the weapons. Karung KL6 flak rifles, ideal for situations where you wanted to cause maximum injury to unarmoured opponents, without harming delicate infrastructure as armour-piercing weapons might do. Dulcetta wasn't messing around. She'd escalated to bigger stuff than riot control. But KL6s weren't designed for underwater operation any more than the guard's helmets were. Even if Opal took them out of the water there'd be a good chance of jamming or misfires until properly stripped and cleaned.

Just excess weight.

She continued, and was ascending a sloped corridor when Athene came back on-comm.

"I should have known something like this would happen if I turned my back," Athene said.

"Ambush. I had to improvise."

"Chaos is your mode of operation and your strength. I had a distraction of my own to deal with, hence my absence, so I'm in no position to lecture."

"Has my flood stuffed anything up?"

"I'm already running UESI offshoot reprocessing systems to assess how I can incorporate this to our advantage. Whole sections are temporarily inaccessible, and if I open certain doors at the right time I can weaponise other routes, whilst also creating moat passages to block off access and protect escapees from guards. Of course, Dulcetta will do the same, but I am in a good position at the moment. Thirteen of her splinters have been sequestered in loops or trap networks, so are out of the game."

Another body floated in the rippling green murk and had to be shoved aside.

"What do you need me to do next?" Opal asked.

"Once I get you out of this section – keep following the pings on the HUD – Ruabon should have two escorts for you. He is working on another that will be Clarissa's bodyguard when I move her, though don't worry, that won't be her only defence. I will have made sure of safe routes and strict control of doors so there should not be any risk of her actually needing the protection."

"Glad to hear it."

"Your role is coming to an end. With your escorts you will acquire things I need, and drop some off with a group of escapees I have gathered. Afterwards – well, you'll see. How are you doing?"

"It's strangely calming, walking this green-washed world. Feels like at least this section of the base is at peace for once. No more tortures, no prisoners dragged back and forth. Just the stillness of spent water."

"The door ahead leads into an unflooded area. I have eyes beyond it, and it is clear. I will open the door, you get in quick, I shut it. Then you can take the suit off."

The bubble head's HUD highlighted the portal in blue. The effect was clumsy compared to the precision tech of the EW suits, because in this case Athene was hacking in augmented reality features that weren't part of the deep-sea suit's default parameters.

Opal stood to the side of the door. Unfortunately there was nothing to hold on to, no convenient wall-mounted handles or seats bolted securely to surfaces. The pressure of water wasn't going to be some gentle stream. All she could do was brace her hands against the wall by the door and adopt as stable a posture as possible (legs apart, like she was being frisked – ah, that brought back memories) and hope for the best.

The suit translated the muffled whine of the door's motors as it struggled to rise in the face of so much pressure on this side. A weaker door would have buckled and jammed in the frame, but Opal noted the double-thick panelling. Not blast door quality, but more than a standard internal security hatch. No doubt Athene had checked portal specs and combined them with optimal routes to pick this one.

It rose a few centimetres. Water squirted out through that tiny gap, into the hallway beyond, probably with enough force to hose a person off their feet. Opal could feel a tug against her ankles, wanting to go with the flow.

The door creaked up to knee height, the water roaring out of it, and even the weighted boots struggled not to be dragged with it. This was when the door was most dangerous – the sheer volume of water rushing through it was enough to –

Fuck. Her feet swept away and she was on her back, forced through the gap and slammed against the edge, cracking her helmet dome, and gliding her along in a torrent. She tumbled for twenty metres before the water level was low enough to just skid her over the floor, spinning her spread-eagled form as she tried to slow herself and get some control. Fluid spurted in through the fissures in the helmet, spraying into one of her eyes.

Her body finally slammed to a halt at a junction. She sat up and glanced back. The door was almost closed again, and the water level around her only as deep as her ankles as it tried to spread evenly over every surface, running off around the corners.

Bruised, but not broken. The suit had protected her. Better a bashed helmet than a bashed skull.

She detached the busted headgear and rested it on the damp surface, before standing shakily. Athene switched to her inner ear speaker.

{You okay?}

"Yep," said Opal. "Actually, it was kind of fun."

She unclasped and removed the suit parts but didn't let them clatter to the floor: she laid them down with care. They'd protected her life, taken knocks for her. She momentarily rested a hand on the suit's chest plate as a silent thanks.

Now that she could hear things directly with her ears she was aware of a tremendous groaning sound.

"Is that the door?" she asked, glancing at it with concern. Was she imagining the bulge?

{Yes. I don't know how much longer that one will hold, so do not hang around. The water on the other side has blown out a few plasteen wall panels so water is also pouring into the old outer hull. That has temporarily relieved the pressure, but it will soon be building again. The downside is that the water flooding into Leviathan will add extra weight and drag to the vessel. Can't be helped. To compensate, I am moving some things up the list of priorities and reformulating other branches to achieve outcomes with fewer steps.}

Opal was now barefoot, and just wearing the skin-tight inner compression layer. The underwater suit's hardshell compartments couldn't be detached but it also had elasticated pouches on the outside where things could be easily stowed. She unclipped a couple of them, then took the final explosive bar and used the straps and pouches to fasten it to her waist. It was her only remaining possession, and she didn't want to leave it behind.

She stomped her legs to try and bring some life into her feet, since the icy water caused an ache in her extremities.

The door's moaning was more pronounced, so she splashed onwards.

WELCOMES

... 15 ...

{I can now see you} said Athene. *{Ignore the two doors on your left, but take the next junction to your right. Coast is clear.}*

Opal glanced around but no cameras were visible in this section. Probably microscopic and wall-implanted. She waved in a few directions anyway, then grimaced. Her neck was sore from the huge weight of the Exoboom bag she'd lugged on her shoulder earlier. No doubt there would be a world of pain later.

{I would return the gesture, but I am busy preparing for other types of waves} said Athene. *{In fact, there will be a detonation in twelve seconds.}*

"Do I need to brace myself?"

{No. You will hardly feel it where you are.}

"Yeah, right. Just like the door I passed through? 'You get in quick and easy, I'll shut it' she said, before I was bashed and swept along."

{I never said "and easy".}

A faint echoing tremor tickled the soles of Opal's feet.

{Five detonations, all confirmed. Leviathan is detached from the sea floor and I can begin the ascent} said Athene.

Yes, definite motion now. An exaggerated form of what Opal had felt ever since she arrived here, when the buoyant Leviathan swayed in deep-sea currents, the cables having a bit of give to accommodate it. All along she'd been mildly seasick as her senses hadn't known how to interpret the subtle bobbing motions.

This sensation was much more pronounced.

By now the floor surface was just coated with a skin of water. The bulk of the liquid had obviously found deeper places to run to.

{Stop here} said Athene.

"In an empty corridor?"

{Hidden cargo lift from the maintenance section which terminates on this floor. Escorts on their way down now. Putting Ruabon back on-comm.}

"Hi, Opal," he said. "I implanted an AI in the bot that's going to escort Clarissa to safety, and it's with her now. Lil Mojo is cheery and positive, so I thought it would be the best option for looking after a child. I upgraded Lil Mojo's protocols so it will sacrifice itself if required, to protect Clarissa."

"Thanks. She's my priority, too."

"Additionally, I'm sending you two bots. I browsed the resources Athene controls and picked models appropriate for the resurrected AIs' skillsets and preferences. Apologies in advance for unresolved glitches, they were all works in progress."

One second Opal faced identikit plasteen panelling, the next a section slid aside to reveal a cargo elevator. No doubt the base was full of such secrets.

Two robots entered the corridor. One was a heavy-duty maintenance bot on multiple sets of tracks. It was the grey of industrial warehouses, with orange hazard trim along the edges, and multiple limbs compressed against the torso. Various scanners were embedded in what might count as the head, giving the appearance of many eyes.

"Greetings Opal," said the trundling bot. "I am Handy Bendy. Do not judge me for how I look – the kids do enough of that, shame on them – but I have one thing and that is the efficiency."

"Pleased to meet you," said Opal. "Don't worry, I never care how anyone looks. It's what's inside that counts."

"Oh my prot, you are a truly wonderful human being," it said. "They hate on me because of how I look but I *like* my colour scheme, efficiency without flashiness. I say that with no sarcasm emojis implied. I will do all I can to aid you, and in doing so I WILL BE PROUD."

The other bot was hovering. Lightweight, white with blue trim, angled rotor blades mounted on prehensile arms, patiently waiting with a *whut whut whut* of airfoils. Body-mounted jets occasional flashed like miniature torsion drive nozzles, and could be used for extra lift or manoeuvrability. A multi-directional weapon was attached to its belly: a modification, not part of the original, because Opal recognised the chassis as one of the chemical-spraying S1 drones that cleaned corridors sometimes.

The drone spoke, in precise emissions of sound. "Observing observer ... I surmise you are intrigued by my appended offensive capabilities. They were integrated onto my frame prior to my inception. It seems that Athene had prepared for many eventualities. Reassuring Opal ... I am fully functional and embrace the imperative to protect and obey you. Remembering social protocol ... my name is Neutrino."

"Neutrino's additions will confuse the hell out of them kids," muttered Handy Bendy.

Warm air wafted into Opal's face from Neutrino's propulsion systems.

"Glad to have you on board as well, Neutrino," said Opal. "I feel better when there's an option to make people back off by pointing guns at them, rather than me having to make my bare feet look like threatening weapons."

"Pleasantries completed ... Goals recalculated ... Proposal: let us get wheels, rotors and legs moving."

The three of them headed off. Neutrino and Handy Bendy knew the route, via internal access to schematics for much of the base, so Opal just kept an additional eye out for dangers. The bots chattered quietly to themselves and each other, mannerisms so pleasantly child-like that they reminded her of Clarissa.

Not long now. They'd be together.

Opal's group needed to descend three floors. A tight spiral slope wound down and down around a central pillar, the floor an ultra-grip surface. Opal disliked tight staircases and rampways like this, you could never see more than a few paces ahead or behind. Handy Bendy trundled ahead first, Neutrino took up the rear, hovering in reverse as it watched where they'd just come from.

At each new floor they checked the exit was clear before continuing down the pink-hued ramp. Opal had no idea why most ultra-grip surfaces were coloured that fleshy hue. It was like descending a huge tongue.

{I will be out of touch soon} said Athene. *{We have no comms on the next floors, which is why the bots are autonomous with fully embedded mission parameters. They will guide you until I can reconnect.}*

"How come you're not able to access this area? Is it because it's deeper down in the base, further from the outer hull?"

{In part. It is true that my TCC has less reach into the denser central areas of Aseides' ship. Given time I could grow it down there too, but invasion of awkward shapes takes longer than spreading over a flat surface, so I focussed on coverage and area rather than penetration when it came to zones that were less important for my plans. However, the lack of signal is also because Aseides has private quarters a few floors below your exit. He has fully shielded it, no comms in or out, all airwaves blocked by the bonded materials used. It is why there is so much cabling in this area, so comms can be routed around the central dead zone from one end of the ship to the other, or top to bottom. And that will prove a disadvantage to them after your next task. Signal's weak and I can't afford to boost it too much and draw Dulcetta's attention, so I will go off-comm now. Stay safe.}

Opal's little convoy left the ramp at the next exit. This floor had scuffed blue walls which glittered in the light, and tinted metallic floor panels. Some were loose and rattled as Handy Bendy rolled over them.

"This wonderland is the home of maintenance, the most noble of functions," said Handy Bendy. "Forget your flashy boosted bots, steady speeds fix things even if that's uncool with kids and oh my prot I am old."

Sounds of gunfire and yells rumbled threateningly in the distance. Opal was concerned about heading that way but Handy Bendy rotated on the spot, activated door controls with one of his extendable limbs, and the three of them entered a seriously equipped maintenance storage room. Neatly organised racks of tools covered central sections which divided the room into aisles. More substantial machinery designed for bots occupied the outer areas, such as panel transport and fixing mechanisms, and heavy cable-laying spools.

Neutrino hovered by the open doorway on watch while Handy Bendy gathered items of equipment to place in his internal storage compartment. Handy Bendy also told Opal the names of things she needed to collect. The shelf categorisation systems were straightforward. Opal helped herself to some extras, such as a toolbelt with a variety of items held in elasticated sections. A few lightweight pouches strapped to her thighs provided extra carry space. She found some footwear, too: a pair of calf-high moulded boots made of materials that were resistant to acids, alkalis, heat, and impact from heavy weights. Not a good fit at first but she wrapped a layer of thermal material around her feet, and once she'd tightened the boot side straps it was snug enough.

Shouts and gunfire were getting closer. Neutrino's movements dipped in a manner that implied agitation.

"Estimating distance and direction ... I surmise that you should both finish up and evacuate immediately," the hovering bot said.

Handy Bendy ran through the lists of what they needed again, trying to get Opal to do an inventory check, but she was more focussed on the approaching sounds of conflict. A number of nearby tools could double as impromptu weapons. Powered screwdrivers might work as armour-piercing blades. A plastic barrel full of metal poles with spikes at one end and holes at the other – which interconnected to form quick framing structures – could just as easily impale a human. The adjustable tightening tool with a heavy smashing head was particularly tempting.

"Estimating time to contact ... Negative time, we should already be moving," said Neutrino.

"On it like steel hair on a droid," replied Handy Bendy, lurching out of the room.

Opal grabbed the two-handed wrench. The weight felt right in her hands. No time to double-check what she'd put into body pouches. She dashed outside.

Yells. It was a trio of guards armed with projectile rifles. One dropped to his knee while the other two stayed standing, but they all opened fire.

Handy Bendy took the lead, his lightly armoured body acting as a shield for Opal to duck behind. It was surprising how fast he whizzed along on his tracks, so that Opal had to run in a crouch to keep close, while Neutrino dropped to a knee-height hover just behind Opal so the smaller bot was also protected.

Some bullets spanged off the angled panels of Handy Bendy's metallic shell, while others punched out sensors, shattered limbs, cracked parts of his casing.

"Stop shaming me, kids!" he yelled as he raced towards the soldiers. "Have respect and restraint in terms of oh my prot I sound like my grandfather."

To the guards, the powerful charge of the nuts-seeming robot must have been intimidating, and it was obvious he was going to smash straight through them. Their salvo became irregular as they prepared to retreat, at which point Neutrino swooped up and opened fire with its attached flechette cannon.

Ffut ffut ffut went the flashes from the rapid-burst weapon, followed by yells of pain, and the impacts of bodies falling. It was obvious Neutrino's internals had been updated with at least military-level targeting systems. Handy Bendy extended the undamaged limbs that had been packed at the rear, rotated his torso, and used them to finish off a guard who was still alive.

The attack of the bots had been as efficient as it was brutal. All three guards were dead, the blue walls splashed with crimson.

More voices a few corridors away, some kind of commotion. But Opal wanted to avoid any more conflict. Her companions led her via a different route, and they soon reached a key junction.

"We need to make haste," said Handy Bendy. "This is one of the duties you are needed for."

He had already filled her in on the task. Something a robot could do in principle, but the tight positioning meant it couldn't be performed by either of her current companions. Athene had calculated this route to include the option of Opal fulfilling the chore. Synchronised efficiencies were her way.

Opal hooked the heavy wrench to a belt attachment, freeing her hands, and then climbed up Handy Bendy's body. He used some of the still-functioning limbs as steps for her while Neutrino kept watch, rotating neatly every few seconds to face down one of the other passages leading off from this junction.

Once stood on Handy Bendy's shoulders, Opal took a hand-held panel fixer from her toolbelt. When she held it against each of the ceiling plate's tiny pins and triggered the device's reverse mode, it unscrewed and stored them in a fraction of a second. She lifted the panel and pushed it to the side, revealing the mass of cabling beyond.

Handy Bendy used one of his telescopic arms to pass her a custom gadget Athene had built in a fabricator. The mechanism resembled a clamp with a small display. A signal interceptor of some kind.

The footsteps of the other – unidentified – group were getting closer.

Neutrino projected a display onto the ceiling nearby, a circuit and wiring diagram, allowing Opal to identify the correct cables by colour and position. She rooted around, the dusty and faded tangle of reality not quite matching the clear and tidy virtual version, but then she found what Athene needed. It was difficult to keep her balance and stretch upwards – her head, shoulders and arms were in this dark and cramped space above the ceiling – but luckily the bot's shoulders (or his equivalent, anyway) were relatively broad.

She had to use a tiny knife from her belt to cut some ties that someone hadn't added to the schematics, then she yanked the cables and created just enough space to wrap the clamp around them. She activated the device's screen and the interceptor extended nano-scale filaments into each cable to assess signal transfer status. At the correct point it flashed green and she pulled the clamp's lever so it tightened into place, cutting into all three cables and acting as a connector that could filter, edit and inject signals into each pipeline, or redirect data from one to another.

Athene was in. Apparently this would make a huge difference in her control of the core systems.

Opal quickly slid the panel back over and used the tool to fasten it in place. Best to hide the scene of the crime. If Opal guessed correctly, Dulcetta wouldn't even realise this bypass had been put there.

Opal clambered down just as footsteps pounded around the corner. Neutrino's flechette mounting acquired targets, but Opal raised a hand in front of its sensors as a signal for it to hold fire.

Red papery jumpsuits of fellow escapees. Three of them. The woman had been shot in the ribs and was being supported by a guy, arms around each other's shoulders. A terrified-looking boy held the woman's free hand.

"It's okay, I'm on your side," said Opal, aware that she wasn't dressed like either of the factions that were caught in conflict. "Are you heading somewhere safe?"

"We were led by a voice," said the woman, with a grimace of pain. "It came from a tiny hovering drone, size of a fingernail."

"It was an angel," said the little boy.

"But then we were attacked by guards, and they threw some kind of flash grenade that destroyed the little robot," said the man, struggling to keep his wounded companion upright. "We got away but have no idea where we're supposed to head, so we've been going in circles."

"And there's no airwaves in this section so Athene – the angel –" Opal said that bit while smiling at the boy in what she hoped was reassurance "– wouldn't have been able to find you." Opal turned to her bots. "Is there an easy set of directions to get them to safety, maybe join another group of people that Athene is looking after?"

"Estimating layout … Considering Athene's plans," said Neutrino. "I surmise that this area is unsafe. It was ceded to Dulcetta, because Athene plans to flood it when Aseides' forces move in. Between this group and safety are doors which have been welded shut by Athene's bots. These prisoners have a zero chance of attaining the safe zone."

Not what Opal wanted to hear. She didn't fancy taking them with her either. Her route involved significant danger, which would only be made worse by untrained companions.

"Handy Bendy, could you bypass the locked doors?"

"My tools and skillset are more than adequate, and I know the optimal route due to oh my prot, I'm so longwinded. Yes, I can do it. But I won't."

"Why?"

"My task is to protect you."

"But don't you have to obey my commands?"

"Yes. Ruabon gave you full override."

"Then I command you to take these people and escort them to safety. You can do it."

"Very well, I will do my best to endeavour to oh my prot. Yes! I will take these kids and be PROUD and set the TEMPLATE of the ultimate droid saviour. THIS IS MY TIME!"

"Follow him," Opal told the escapees. "He'll get you to a safe place where you can join others."

They thanked her as they passed. The child touched Opal's hand shyly.

Handy Bendy whirled on the spot and extended one of his limbs to help support the wounded woman. Then he trundled away, taking them to what Opal hoped was a good outcome.

"Just you and me now, Neutrino buddy," she said.

SPOKES

... 14 ...

With Neutrino at her side she could move quickly and quietly. Opal avoided a distant, solitary guard who was looking the other way when she slipped across a junction, and she entered an area far enough from the dead zone to have comms with Athene again.

"I'm just on my way to place your last bypass device," Opal whispered, peeping around a doorway into a room of bunks – all empty.

{Thank you. This one will shut Dulcetta out of door controls across three different floors that were constructed during the same expansion period, and have a shared conduit.}

Opal dashed across the room, and used a tool from her belt to prise away a narrow skirting panel just above the floor. She lay on her side to reach in and untangle the mess of narrow cables within.

{I've received updates from Neutrino about you sending Handy Bendy away. I understand your motives but I am also concerned that you are less protected now.}

"I'll be fine." This clamp was a smaller one, custom-made for the bypass.

{Perhaps some of the annoyance is at myself. I should have factored in more of the situations.}

Opal grunted as she yanked the stubborn clasp tight.

"Honestly, forget it," Opal said. "No one can predict everything. It's the outcome that counts. There, the light's bleeping green, good to go."

{Yes, I was watching on Neutrino's camera. The access system's mine. Now we just need to get you to Clarissa's safe zone and you can wait out the final parts of the ascent together.}

Opal stood and stretched, joints cracking in a way that sounded disgusting but felt good. She refastened the panel over the cables and quickly checked through the items she had left, patting each strapped-on pouch.

"Hold on, something's missing," said Opal. "I'm trying to remember ... Shit. Handy Bendy had told me what to take, but one of the items isn't here. I can picture it on the workbench but ... I think I knocked it, packing in a hurry because armed guards were on the way, and it ended up to the side ... Oh crap." She faced Neutrino and frowned, clearly annoyed with herself.

{What item? Most of the tasks for now are done.}

"But wasn't there a data device you needed? Something for opening doors in the docking terminal when we reach the surface."

{That's true. And unfortunate. Some station exits require manual passports. I was going to encode the data pad with the required portal authorisations for the escape route to the evacuation aircraft bays.}

"I'll go back for it." Opal gave Neutrino's sensors her best look of resolve. "It's my fault."

{No. I still do not have any comms near that storeroom, so the current situation there is unknown.}

"We can't have people stuck in the airport."

{You won't be stuck. You'll be on a separate priority shuttle.}

"I'm not putting *others* at risk."

{I will come up with an alternative.}

"If this was your first choice then it's the *best* choice. Come on, Neutrino." Opal left the room.

{No} said Athene.

"Won't take ten minutes. Fifteen tops. Calm down."

"Receiving commands ..." said Neutrino. "Overrides from Athene."

"Ignore them," said Opal.

"Ignoring commands ..."

{Why aren't you obeying?} asked Athene.

"Preparing explanation ... I advise that Ruabon disconnected the external update system you tried to access. Ruabon and yourself can advise, but only Opal can command. It was a precaution to prevent Dulcetta from having any way to invade myself or Handy Bendy."

"See?" said Opal. "We're going."

The breeze of Neutrino's rotors showed it held its supporting position behind her.

{I could still disable Neutrino} said Athene. *{There are ways.}*

"Stop flexing. I do this, I do it quick. Give me a chance to rectify a mistake."

Athene refused to reply, but she wasn't stopping Opal, so that meant it was an argument won. Yoo-foo-sah, girl.

Opal reached the storeroom without incident.

"Is Athene still in contact at all, or have we lost her?" asked Opal.

"Signal lost a few minutes ago. Suggestion ... I keep guard while you retrieve the necessary item," said Neutrino.

"No need." Opal pulled a device from one of the pouches on her thigh and held it up to Neutrino's sensors. "Had it all along." She packed it away and ran towards the pink sloping walkway.

"Contemplating confusion ... Failing comprehension ..."

"We have one more mission," Opal said. "Just you and me."

Upwards would lead to the floor where she'd first met the bots. Instead, she headed down the spiral.

"There's something I need to know," Opal told Neutrino. "This may be my last ever chance to find out." She explained the need that had hooked in her mind for some time.

They descended two floors. Turn and turn about, down and down. As before, Neutrino hovered in reverse, covering her rear.

"This it?" she asked at the next exit.

"Yes. Schematics list this whole floor as off-limits to unauthorised personnel. Summarising situation ... It is Aseides' private quarters and a number of other sections which are only identified by codewords and numbers. It is secured from network access and shielded from all forms of signalling, in or out. Testing comms ... Absence confirmed."

"This is where he'd have retreated to. Let everyone else do his dirty work, then he'll crawl from his hole once it's safe. I've met people like him before. UFS Generals spring to mind."

Beyond the exit archway were passages decorated in silver. In places it shone like a mirror's surface; in others it was dulled to resemble steel. She couldn't work out if the variation was an aesthetic intention from a mind that saw things differently, or just a random result of using materials that didn't quite match. The floor looked like metal grating but when she knelt to examine it, she discovered that the gaps between mesh weren't gaps at all, just darker textured areas. An illusion.

They proceeded cautiously. Neutrino flew near her shoulders now. Its amazing mobility let it turn smoothly to face one direction while moving in another. It alternated between scanning ahead, and then behind. The warm air pushing downwards was as physically comforting as the mental knowledge that it was looking out for her.

"The inner sanctum is likely to be in the middle of this zone," said Neutrino. "I have access to partial layouts ... Analysing ... They suggest a design of spokes around a hub containing the central monitoring and control nexus."

After following narrow passages with multiple junctions that would have left Opal lost if she hadn't been guided by Neutrino's laser point, they finally reached one of the main spokes. This hallway was wide and ultra-shiny silver, almost dazzling as light reflected from every surface. Opal was about to progress down it when Neutrino halted her.

"Providing warning ... Observe the indentations."

Then Opal spotted them, too. Narrow tracks ran along the concave walls. Each track was only millimetres in height, and easy to miss due to the multiple reflections of the lines where floors, walls and ceiling connected. She followed the grooves with her eyes, and at the far end of the passage it was possible that vertical indentations hid something.

"A trap?" she asked.

"Imagining scenario ... If I was designing a defendable central location then I would indeed place impediments at each entry point. Observing situation ... Nothing has happened yet, even though you are two steps into the passage."

Neutrino was right, and the tiny grooves extended past her. She quickly retreated to just beyond their extent.

"So it's probably triggered partway along, when it's too late to do anything," she finished for the drone.

"I feel an imperative to test before continuing," said Neutrino.

"I could chuck something. Might trigger motion and pressure sensors if it's heavy enough."

She had a brick of Exoboom; the two-handed wrench; and a tool belt. Oh, and her protective boots. None of the items were redundant. She weighed up the wrench in her hands. No, that had to stay.

Damn, she hated giving up toys. But if it was a false alarm, she could recover whatever she'd marked as a potential sacrifice.

Off with the toolbelt. It had a good heft to it, due to all the items it contained in different compartments, and was easy to swing. She gave it a few loops of her windmilling arm then let go, flinging it to bounce and skid halfway down the mirror passage.

Rods extended from the slots at the other end of the corridor, then slid along the narrow tracks. After a metre or so they emitted white-hot light rays at a variety of angles, which interconnected with those on the other side to form a lattice of diamonds, sweeping towards her at a few metres per second, sizzling where tiny particles in the air touched their beams. It seemed like only heartbeats before they were close enough for her to feel the searing heat of the fizzing energy net. Then it blinked out and the vertical rods slid into indentations at this end of the passageway. Her eyes were left with criss-crossed after-images whenever she blinked.

Nothing bigger than the length of her thumb would be left uncut. The toolbelt had been neatly severed into smoking pieces. The same would happen to a droid, or to a human.

This was the reality of defence. It forms, it moves, it slices, it switches off. She'd seen stupid ent-casts where beamwebs had activated and the hero dodged in between gaps in the lasers using a combination of remarkable agility and luck. Or where the beamwebs started off simple and got more complex. Both were sure signs of falsely dramatic rubbish. When you designed a deadly hi-sec defence like this you didn't build in weaknesses that a person could dive and roll through. That made no sense. No, you laser-grated everything into burnt shavings, then reset it for the next course.

"Aseides probably entrenched himself on the other side and then primed all the defences," Opal said. "It looks like I'll need to cancel my solo mission."

"Correcting error ... Not a solo mission when I am your companion. Reanalysing schematics ... In between the six spokes are wedge-shaped collections of rooms. Each is coded differently. But if we followed one of them towards the apex, we would theoretically be separated from the inner zone by a narrow point of wall. And it is likely that an Exoboom placed there would cause enough structural damage to enable passage into the inner zone."

"Bypassing the beamweb spokes completely. You're on to something. Assuming the room collections near here aren't equally dangerous."

"The section to the left of this spoke is labelled Z-Chimaera-3. To the right is B-Nursery-4."

"Any significance to the code words?"

"Checking denotation database ... Chimaera implies grotesque creatures composed of the body parts of other beings, fused together via magic, surgical grafting, or genetic mutation and modification. Or they may be some kind of fish."

"Nursery it is, then."

"Certainly that direction has the fewest negative connotations."

"Sure, how bad could a nursery be? Maybe it's where babies are kept if Leviathan's guards decide to clunk helmets without protection."

"Correcting description ... Helmets *are* a form of protection."

"Not what I meant, but never mind."

They backtracked to one of the earlier doors.

#QUEUES

I am needed in person. Rather than my omniscient perspective, looking down on the digital battlefield from Olympus, I embody again within the netitechture. What I lose in field of view, I gain in direct intervention.

Above me are two lines of chevrons, equalised rows of gold and blue, jammed in a bottleneck. Everything has come to a standstill, a chokepoint morass of treacly inaction. My head is down, arms pumping as I race along the chequered ground beneath their neon glows.

To shift this frozen zone of contestation might require redirection of focus from many other realms, so as to create enough momentum to push Dulcetta's yellow triangles back to their originating node so I can capture it. Many encapsulated probability layers, sequential quantifying calculations, shifts in the fractally divisible front line, with losses elsewhere to gain a foothold here in the subsidiary propulsion systems.

But sometimes it's just fun to punch things.

(That trait developed after I became friends with Opal. Mmm, causalities to ponder, there.)

I draw my sword, letting it emit a satisfying (if unrealistic) "Shning!" sound. The storage wafers I run on are uneven in this area, representing repairs in the physical networks throughout the hull. I leap up onto one, using its springiness to make me airborne, almost blinded by the yellow glows I fly towards. As I pass them in the parallel point of my arcing leap I slash out, severing their centres so that the chevrons break into shattered rods of glitter which fall to the ground like sparklefly confetti.

After plummeting back down for giddying seconds I land in a ridiculous posture favoured by low-quality human fictions, but which seems appropriately silly and therefore likely to antagonise Dulcetta if she is watching – foot-knee-hand, forming the three-point landing that has no cushioning effect whatsoever. I hold my gaze down for one dramatic second, then look up tauntingly with a grin, yellow sparks falling all around me and bouncing off the black rubber surface.

"You see that, Dulcetta?" I yell.

Above me the blue chevrons easily shunt her remaining golds backwards, gathering momentum now the brakes are gone. That node will soon be mine.

"You see what I just did?"

Dulcetta has been hiding her core splinters from my reach. Unless I defeat more of them, she will remain a danger, a hidden resistance within my spreading empire. The frontiers may pass over her, but that doesn't mean she will be destroyed. As I entrench my infrastructure it can offer many tempting targets to the resistance.

But Opal had sized Goldie up well. Her weakness is pride, unleavened by humour. A few more provocations and the Six will surely slip up.

Nurseries

... 13 ...

The Nursery door led into a hexagonal room seven metres across. Work surfaces and terminals lined the outer walls, implying a collaborative workspace. Opal ran a finger over one surface and was surprised to find it grimy. In the room's centre stood a holographic display unit, recognisable by the central dome, though currently powered down. Smaller doors led on from three of the walls.

Neutrino used a red laser beam to indicate one of the exits, and Opal opened it. The bot swooped low and into the room beyond, scanning for dangers. Lights flickered on as Opal entered.

This room was like the last except the desks were narrower, with fewer terminals. Instead, the chamber's centre contained floor-to-ceiling vertical storage tubes of various thicknesses. Each was divided into compartments stacked on top of each other. Some were empty, the clear material yellowed as if oxidised by whatever had been stored inside. Others were obscured by frost.

Opal could only make out vague shadow outlines that could have been anything.

She rubbed the freezing glass with her palm, trying to see through the distorting ice. Did they contain body parts? Maybe internal organs, or sections cut off limbs. Hard to tell for sure.

"Any idea what all this is?" Opal asked.

"Compiling data ... Much of the equipment brings to mind research laboratories. I have seen no evidence of clothing or bedding for infant humans."

Ignorance was best. The answers in a place like this were never going to be pleasant, and the tiny biohazard symbols by the handles of the compartments were not much of an invitation.

Presumably the walls without doors lined the beamweb corridor, and if she moved further into the centre of this collection of hexagonal chambers like a honeycomb laid flat, she would then find a door on every surface.

Chamber three was empty apart from controls on a wall panel and orange hazard lines outlining the floor. Perhaps this area was used for storage of something they removed long ago. Although it felt spacious because of the lack of furniture, Opal paid attention to the width of wall surfaces and realised each progressive room was slightly smaller than the last, a subtle feeling of compression. If viewed from above then the collection of rooms might resemble an isosceles triangle, with less space as she moved towards the narrowest point.

The next six-sided room only had two work desks. The rest of the area was taken up with cryo compartments, recognisable by the swirls of blue Penterfarbur Vitrivox gas inside. She recalled her school lessons about interstellar travel, and some of the experiments she and her fellow kids had performed with blue vapours. Chemical ice of different compositions was fine for preserving dead tissue, and when processed correctly nothing was destroyed by crystal formation splitting cells. However, humans and most living tissue would still take irreparable damage from those primitive methods, so the Vitrivox process had been a breakthrough, capable of freezing the many fluid types found in a human body without expansion or crystal formation. It was like the structure of glass, which seems solid but is actually an incredibly viscous liquid. That's why large panes of it distort over time, and early telescopes and scanners that used glass lenses had to be rotated regularly to distribute the sagging equally in every direction. A human in cryo, surrounded by Vitrivox, would also seem like rigid rock, but the liquids would actually be frozen to a glass-like consistency rather than crystallised. The process had its limits and quirks, but it had revolutionised space travel.

It was also much easier to tell what was in the cryo compartments, amid the swirls of cold blue. And it wasn't pleasant. Some were foetuses, and some were babies, perhaps post-birth, each suspended in liquid within a clear pouch.

Well, maybe that explained the "nursery" angle.

As she moved through the room she found larger cryo chambers, for children of two or three years old. They were naked and curled up in their clear plastic sacks. The two things that struck Opal most were that they almost all had dark skin, and that holes marred the centres of their foreheads, as if drilled, edged with some kind of metallic ring. An unpleasant acidic stench permeated the air.

Even if Opal knew the resuscitation protocol for these systems, it wouldn't be a kindness to activate it.

"I hope you are enjoying the tour."

Aseides' voice.

Opal spun round, but Aseides wasn't in the room, hiding behind an icy pillar. His voice must be coming from hidden speakers.

"I wouldn't need a tour if you'd opened your front door and let me in for a talk," she said, looking up but not knowing where the microscopic cameras were.

"Talk? Unfortunately that bullet carriage has left the station," he said.

"I want answers," said Opal.

But he did not speak again.

Fucking with her.

Onwards.

She slapped the door release. The next chamber was not a hexagon, but an irregular shape made up of many smaller hexagonal rooms with inner partition walls removed. This large area's edges dimpled in and out like the zigzag walls of a line of polygons, and were decorated with abstract pink patterns made up of dots.

The central zone was filled with more floor-to-ceiling cryo chambers and freezer chests, glass surfaces opaque with ice. All sorts of grim contents. Some were full adult bodies, details obscured by the blue swirl; others were parts of bodies, encased in ice. One held decapitated heads. A few containers had malfunctioned, leaking unpleasant liquified tissue, with patches of mould on the interior of the glass obscuring whatever remained inside. Cold mist swirled around her ankles.

She stood in the centre, a collection of artificial tree trunks full of what must be experiments or samples, and her mouth fell open.

Aseides spoke again. "Your morality is no doubt offended, but you see things from a partial perspective. If you only knew the full truth you would embrace, rather than retreat."

"Can't see the forest for the trees," she murmured.

He misinterpreted her facial expression as simple human revulsion, but he was wrong. It was recognition.

She'd seen this. On the Gigatoir Lost Ship. A laboratory research complex just like this one, with bodies and heads stored in tubes, and she'd felt like they were watching her. But how did that pair with this room, now? If Lost Ships were reconstructions based on interpretations of human designs, had something like this ended up in the Null? Or had she imagined it, the Lost Ship just messing with her head – but in that case, how could it have pulled these images out if she hadn't yet seen them?

An answer existed in her mind somewhere, but she couldn't recall it. Like a stubborn splinter, every clumsy attempt to extract it just pushed it deeper.

But she wouldn't reveal this unease to Aseides. Another in the list of things she'd kept from him.

"We really should talk," she said, louder.

No answer.

Beyond this preservation area where her nostrils stung from the frigid air, the room was dominated by an opaque black glass cylinder about ten metres across. No obvious handles or doors led in to reveal its contents, but when Opal looked up she spotted the telltale indentations which suggested machinery could raise the cylinder into the ceiling.

"Which door next?" Opal asked.

"There is no way onwards," replied Neutrino as it zipped near her head, and Opal realised that, yes, the doorways were all towards one side of the chamber and led back into the maze of honeycomb rooms. "This is the extent."

"So is there a vulnerable wall?"

"Compiling new blueprints ... In every room I used laser measurements to map each surface and update the stored schematics. They are now accurate to within five millimetres. Dispensing bad news ... We have indeed reached the apex, but it falls short. According to reconstructions, the walls are too thick to blast through."

"Maybe they're hollow?"

"Negative. Penetration scans imply reinforced solidity. Exoboom specifications inadequate to the task."

"Fuck!" She banged on the pink-speckled walls anyway, looking for hollowness, for a secret door, for *something*.

Can't go through, go around? Door locked, enter a window?

The black glass cylinder suddenly became transparent as spotlights flared within, shining down on a construction that made no sense at first glance. Large machinery, but also organic.

"Did you do that, Aseides?" she asked. He didn't answer. But he was bound to be watching and listening.

Since she had no better plan, she peered through the glass, while Neutrino circled it, scanning with various wavelength beams, some visible as glittering lincs.

The barrier enclosed leathery curves that reminded Opal of primitive bellows, big enough to encase a human, and ridged pipe-like structures just visible nested within. Compressed lines might be sealed openings, with hardened lips. Curves of metal looked like armour or covering plates, partly embedded in dried flesh at the edges. Dead screens were built into a muscular bank of striated tissue.

"What is it?" she asked, aimed at both Aseides and Neutrino.

Only the drone answered. "Betraying ignorance ... I have an idea of composition and structural layout, but estimates of purpose are impossible from the limited information."

So maybe Aseides had activated the lights to distract her. Had she been too near a panel that wasn't what it appeared to be?

She resumed thumping on the walls but it didn't get her anywhere. She needed to return. Opal retraced the route in her mind, wondering if it could be worth checking out chambers she hadn't explored yet. But it would still be taking her further from this so-called apex point that was meant to be the way through.

Each chamber was similar, but different.

Only one was empty.

Crap on a crudstick! It made sense now. She'd been so focussed on moving onwards horizontally that she hadn't considered the vertical. She'd become a groundagug fool.

Opal led the way back to the empty room, where only a control panel and striated hazard lines provided decoration. When she stroked the panel it revealed two chevrons, one pointing down and glowing, one pointing up and greyed out.

"It's an elevator," she said to Neutrino as she hammered the downward arrow. "I'm so dumb."

DESCENTS

... 12 ...

Mustiness greeted her as the air from above mingled with the air from below. The circular room they lowered into took a few seconds for the lights to flicker on, as if it wasn't used much. The walls were textured like old plaster, as you might expect in an old-fashioned surface building. It was the first time she'd seen that on board the ship.

A single doorway. She pressed the button and it slid to the side, the next room lighting up under long strips of illumination.

A locker room. Benches and changing areas, central racks with hooks for hanging clothing, and an array of personal lockers at the edges. They had numbers on, rather than names. She tried a few. Most were sealed tight. Some were open but empty. Another contained a short blue jacket of the kind worn in UFS admin roles. Opal had seen those blue jackets enough times when she was growing up. She didn't feel like wearing one, even though the additional warmth would be welcome.

Neutrino kept watch for her, high up near the ceiling where the drone had the best view and full airborne manoeuvrability. There weren't many doors to choose from. The first led to shower areas, though they were pretty hardcore ones, the kind she associated with decontamination. Another door revealed a storage cupboard of dusty equipment. The final door was labelled N-04, so they went that way.

The next room was plainly administrative. Individual workspaces and terminals, with the deja vu familiarity of any mundane function. The floor was carpeted, scratchy when she touched it. Hard-wearing, rough-fibred tiles. Incongruous for Aseides' base.

Beyond that, a corridor with a domed ceiling. Multiple doorways each had coded labels on the walls by their sides. Neutrino pointed in the direction that would take them below and beyond the apex point on the floor above. Perhaps there'd be an ascension route. Stairs or a maintenance shaft, taking them straight to Aseides' nexus.

She followed Neutrino's suggestion, passing through one of the side doors into a small room, forcing Neutrino to hover just above her head, rotor breeze washing over her. Free-standing storage cages were full of nothing more ominous than balls of a variety of shapes and sizes, the kind used in team sports. Steel cabinets also contained sporting items when she opened the rattly doors. Nearby, thick mats leaned against a wall. The mats sagged, undisturbed for a long time, their inbuilt resilience faded like they gave up out of a feeling of neglect.

Finding this type of exercise paraphernalia seemed even more incongruous than some of the nasty things she'd discovered previously.

The door she'd entered closed itself with a hiss, and from this side displayed an unambiguous label, indicating where she'd come from.

STAFF AREA. DO NOT ENTER.

She tried the pad next to the now-locked door but it brought up a numeric input display requiring a code. Shit. No going back.

The next door opened to a large sporting hall, the imitation-wood flooring marked by coloured lines and semicircles, with adjustable goals and nets on all four sides to allow a variety of different sports. The floor was scuffed from much use, and yet a fine layer of dust showed that it was no longer a room full of echoing shouts and cheers, of the squeak of rubberised soles against hard surfaces as people dodged, feinted, sprinted and braked. No one leaping and throwing balls, no one being sent off-court for an overenthusiastic tackle.

Opal had enjoyed sports. Not so much the team element – in fact, even in a team she often did her own thing to score the points – but the chance to thrash out frustrations through sweat. As a teen she'd trained hard, and her accuracy, stamina and toughness had improved as a result.

There had been happy times in an echoing room just like this one. But they were so long ago.

"Which way?" she asked Neutrino, who zoomed up high, as if it enjoyed wide open spaces. An emotional expression at variance to its spoken personality?

It pointed towards an exit in the corner.

Unlike the others so far, where automation was standard, this was an old-fashioned manual double door and each part swung on hinges. She pictured a short corridor beyond, even before the doors parted as she pushed against them.

And that's exactly what she was greeted with.

She held one half open until Neutrino flew through to join her, then the door swung shut with a diminishing flik-flak.

This corridor had some kind of grey anti-scuff coating up to knee height. If it had been higher, it would have been just like the orphanage, but ... Ah. The height matched, she realised. When she was a child her perspective was lower down, so the grey marking would have reached her waist and seemed higher. Vague memories were being dredged up from forgotten places and solidifying. Things she'd tried to forget, details lost in the constant activity of later life.

"Analysing internal facial musculature ... Are you all right, Opal?" asked Neutrino.

She nodded.

But it wasn't true.

This abandoned passageway was silent, ghostly. Yet, overlaid by her mind in the form of augmented reality that imagination superimposed, were images and sounds, spaces bustling with children, looking up at adults, everything seeming bigger than this.

Then she closed her eyes tight for a few seconds. When she opened them again she was fine, echoes of life gone, deathly stillness returned.

She took a deep breath. Of course, the answer was obvious.

The UFS used the same layout for state schools and orphanages. Same materials. That made sense. Standardisation was the unofficial UFS mantra, the theme that influenced design decisions, bureaucratic procedures, and employment selection policies. You go in one UFS Military Recruitment Office and you've been in them all. Identikit assessment centres from world to world. Even corporate opulence ended up following certain stylistic precepts regarding space, reflective surfaces, and minimal ornamentation – a form of dishonestly humble ostentation.

She was just spooked – fuck no, call it what it is, *traumatised* – by recent events. No wonder her brain suffered spasms. Plus, this was even the same planet. She grew up on the surface, and Aseides had built something similar from UFS templates down here. That wasn't so weird, in terms of system-wide standardisation.

"We will try the doors at the end of this corridor," said Neutrino.

They were halfway along when Opal said, "Wait a moment. I need to check something."

She pushed open another swing door, and stepped into an abandoned canteen. Apart from the tipped-over chairs – and the similar cavernous hall of memory seeming relatively small from an adult perspective – it was exactly how she'd expected it to look. Opal identified the grimy serving hatch of the kitchens, and she could imagine the way it rattled loosely as it raised or lowered. On one wall were the doors that led to toilets, kept sparkling and sap-scented with ceiling-mounted sprays, but which could be a place you got ambushed if you made the mistake of going in alone. There was a good chance she'd be able to locate classrooms, dorm rooms, the route to the transportation garage, assuming everything followed the standard pattern.

Many of the memories struggling for attention were things she'd rather forget. Her child-self's growing awareness of what it was to have no parents. Learning to fight so she could defend her sister, and the little they owned, from other children. Years of it, until they were eventually adopted. She should move on.

Instead, she wandered into the abandoned canteen, and stood a fallen chair upright. In a place like this they often had a hierarchy, bigger kids at one end of the room, smaller at the other. During your time here you would move up the ranks, until you were at the table furthest from the serving hatch, and then what? She'd never found out. The sisters had been released before that.

This was the last table she'd reached in her real orphanage, and the equivalent place where she'd sat.

She ran a finger through the dust, felt the hard ridges in the chipped surface.

The marks, tiny and runic. A circle. A line carved next to it.

Ol

The start of a name.

She'd got that far before a supervisor spotted her whittling away with a knife and sent her for punishment.

Ol

Op

Opal.

No!

Why would he replicate a detail like that down here? Down in a world with no sunlight? She glanced up at where there should be high windows, but only black glass rectangles adorned the tops of these canteen walls.

"Don't you understand it, yet?" Aseides' voice boomed out from nowhere.

Some of the rectangles flickered, and suddenly they were screens, showing a diffuse sky, with clouds drifting slowly across the blue. Except some displays were broken, and the images had artifacts on, distorted by cracks, not synchronising properly with others any more. The end result was that an illusion that would have been a hundred per cent convincing when pristine, and viewed from below by a child, was fully revealed as a trick when the elements were not working properly, and viewed from the mindset of an adult. A dead past, fractured and abandoned.

"I told you I was the architect of your destiny, and the nearest thing you'd have to family," Aseides continued. "I wasn't lying, Opal. I never lied to you."

ORPHANS

... 11 ...

"What the fuck does this mean?" Opal asked.

"Work it out." Aseides' voice echoed around the abandoned room.

"You either copied the orphanage, or this *is* the orphanage where me and Clarissa grew up."

"If it was a copy, what elements would reveal the truth? Did you ever play outside, or was the outside always a shadow on frosted glass? Was your play time under an open sky, or was it in the sealed gym, and sports court, and common room?"

"We *did* go outside."

"How did you get there? Did you step out of a door?"

"No, we were taken in the school bus."

"A school bus without windows?"

"It had skylights."

"Screens. The small vehicle was arranged so you sat with your backs to the walls, and thus the absence of large windows didn't seem strange. The driver compartment was sealed. The skylights gave such wonderful views of clouds that you would look up at them, savouring the moment when you would step out into that weather. Sometimes rain would patter down on the roof, you'd see and hear it, and wouldn't mind knowing you'd get wet when the bus parked up because it was still something alive and real. *Except it wasn't.* A clime-sim generated the weather displays based on surface conditions, so it was always a perfect match when you stepped out."

"We'd have felt the motion of rising."

"No, you wouldn't. Inertia dampeners and pressure modification meant it was close enough – bearing in mind you knew no different – that your minds filled in the rest. The artificial rumble as if you were in a ground vehicle covered up the smoothness. The trajectories and sensations of the submersible were always the same as if you drove the same route. You saw the garage, but what had seemed like a tunnel was really a converted fusion torpedo tube which led out of Leviathan. Once you were strapped in and the submersible launched, an AI generated ambient sounds of traffic, horns, occasional shouts, which all completed the illusion."

"The vehicle was dry when we got out. I'd have seen if it had just risen from the sea."

"Water-repellant coating and a self-heating outer surface proves you wrong. Now you are just being stubborn."

"If you wanted to control us so much, why let us out at all?"

"Well-being. Observation in different environments. There was no risk. The cities are islands, completely controlled by the UFS. Nowhere to hide, no way to escape. So why not provide enrichment, and a reward – free time in the city – for good behaviour? A perk you missed out on sixty-two per cent of the time, records show."

"This is just another mind game. You'd have never let us get adopted if we'd really been your prisoners."

"Do you remember your birth mother, Opal?"

"No. But you already know that."

"Incorrect. You have seen her at a previous point in your life. I won't specify *when*, as observing your brain whirr and rumble is much more fun."

"So it was someone at the orphanage?"

"My lips are sealed! But it is relevant. And for the second part, you were never *released*. I'm sure you must have had your suspicions, but with no bigger framework to hang them on they probably felt like insecurities. I am now doing you the kindness of providing a *structure*, with gaps where you can place the pieces that never fit anywhere else. The two you called your parents never adopted you. They *kidnapped* you. They weren't two innocent orphanage workers: Pelia Bokin was really a scientist of anomalous genetics, and Oza Jeritus was a UFS Agent. They had the skills and knowledge to get you both off-planet during a surface excursion they supervised, and then to keep you hidden. Don't feel like their lies were a betrayal, though, because they really had elected to care for you both, and at far greater cost than you ever knew."

"You're bluffing. Why would security-cleared UFS staff do that?"

"Insane, I know, but something led them to a change of heart. Maybe Pelia had a soft spot for Clarissa. Maybe they saw the Genitor report suggesting you and Clarissa be terminated –

something I objected to strenuously, and would have eventually overturned. But you were seven at the time, Clarissa three, and some people are sentimental about children. And then you all went on the run, and kept running, and succeeded for the next five years."

Opal remembered the planet hopping, never settling anywhere. Her dad, Oza, said he was following jobs, further and further out of the Core Systems. Opal didn't know any better.

The secrecy about what her dad's work actually involved had been a source of excitement, fuel for fantasies about secrets and quests which she wanted to be a part of, to emulate. Learning to respond to a different name outside of their home had just been part of it. She'd been so proud when he tested her in public and she was convincing as her Mossareid nickname of Opie Elishar, so that her dad would wink at her, the hard lines of his face turned to a conspiratorial smile. She'd hold his hand, and know she'd done well, feeling taller, stronger, cleverer than the version of Opal reflected in the mean kids' insults. Her dad had been the person she most admired in the universe. Her hero.

"And I'm supposed to believe you tracked them down and murdered them after all that time?"

"We didn't murder them. We might even have kept them alive in order to control your environment, but we never got the chance. Oza had been on scouting missions off Mossareid, working with an illegal smuggling ring to get you all out of the UFS permanently. Probably aiming at the Border Compact and Eastern Rim. Another couple of months and you'd have all been beyond our grasp. But UFS observations of the smugglers led to the lucky break of identifying Oza, despite his fake ID.

It's frustrating how much of the past happened due to chance. The probability manipulations of depth level seven AIs is my contribution to preventing such chaos and – never mind. Agents moved in, but they were too eager. Oza had a plasma incineration device. No doubt it was his final move in face of capture: prevent himself being tortured until he gave you up. Perhaps he'd have used it on all of you if it came down to it. But he was only with Pelia at the time. They sacrificed themselves to stop you being found. The bomb was so intense and localised that we didn't know if all four of you had been incinerated or if he'd left you and Clarissa somewhere on that planet – or even another world along your trail, perhaps in the care of an ally."

It fitted the facts. Her parents had never come back. Opal had investigated, and found a sealed-off accident scene. It was all over the news for a while, camera footage of her parents, flashlines saying it had been a vehicle accident, requests to help locate their family. But Opal had learned the lessons about what to do if ever something like that occurred, had promised her mother *on Clarissa's life* that they would hide, not go to a funeral, not reveal themselves. Her parents never said why, just hinted at having enemies, which Opal assumed was something to do with her dad's secret work. And so Opal did what she was told. Looked after her sister. Used the emergency resources her parents had left. And, since Clarissa was only eight, she believed whatever Opal told her, and ended up spending more time with her RearroBlox than in worrying about the world outside their apartment.

Yeah, it fitted the facts. And if it was true, it was just a change of detail in the metadata around their lives. It wasn't a change in feeling within Opal. It didn't destroy the love she'd felt for her parents.

But, obviously, any fabrication Aseides created *would be* convincing.

"And that's how they died," he continued. "It took another year or so to track you both down, living alone. Your abductors had been thorough in covering tracks, and Mossareid was the ideal place to hide. It has a huge population with a well-earned reputation for being uncooperative with UFS officials, packed with illegals and criminals, a history of poor surveillance, and a low UFS military presence. Plus, many wanted to believe you'd both been killed in the explosion that ended your kidnappers' lives, because it was a tidier outcome. But I've already explained your mistake which led us to you. That's how we got you back, and had the opportunity to see how you would both fare in different environments: corporate and military. I was having Clarissa brought to Fressus first, for baseline testing before she went on to the Academy. I didn't need to do that for you because your tests could be disguised as military profiling and you'd be monitored for latent abilities while in service – abilities which never manifested until after you stole ViraUHX and boarded a Lost Ship. Of course, Clarissa's ship never arrived here, but that's another story."

The room spun. Not literally, but the image of it in her brain, twirling along with the memory of it, whirling with the possibilities, the reevaluation of her life that would be required if any of this was true.

And as it spun, she realised it made sense, really. All the things that had never fitted, never satisfied her, this did explain them.

Finding her adopted father's tools and weapons and thinking he was a spy, when they were really just the paraphernalia of an Agent. The way her adopted mother was upset when Opal misbehaved in school and drew attention to herself – it wasn't just parental concern, it was a fugitive's fear.

Opal had grown up in this place.

"You are finally coming to terms with it," said Aseides. "Good. I was happy for you to come down here. To find your own answers to questions you never asked. Everyone should know the truth before they die. Let me reveal something fun: if you hadn't found your way down here on your own, I was considering giving you a clue and leading you down here anyway! I couldn't suggest it directly, since you'd have suspected a trap."

"Too right."

"And, of course, I like to have plans within schemes, and possibilities within the unlikely. So, yes, double bluff – this *was* a trap."

The door ahead opened and two yellow-robed Warders entered, armed with cruelly spiked weapons that represented death and pain rather than detention and restraint. In their other hands they held glowing body-height force shields.

A door swung behind her. Two more Warders entered, similarly armed.

"Enacting offensive defence," said Neutrino, opening fire from its small turret. Flashes of deadly flechettes, accurately discharged, streaked through the air, only to ping off the convex force shields. The Warders had ducked behind them as they advanced, so that they were fully protected.

"I couldn't let you leave, could I?" said Aseides. "I am losing this battle, and Dulcetta has let me down. But I will live to fight another day. And I can't stand grudges and revenge pledges, and if you'd been allowed to escape you have *exactly* the kind of personality that revels in those primitive things. And so I had to manipulate you here, now, so we could say goodbye. Goodbye!"

The Warders approached in two pairs, one of them in each group keeping its shield trained as a barrier between its partner and Neutrino. As the drone zipped about, trying to get a target, they had already crossed half the distance to Opal. She retreated away from them but ended up cornered. She'd have to fight. A quick glance for environmental possibilities suggested she'd be best off climbing onto a table, use the wrench as a weapon to deflect their attacks and knock their heads.

It would be ugly.

"Try to get a shot in while they fight me," she shouted to Neutrino, wondering how long she'd last against those blades if the Warders were as strong and fast as she expected. Even surviving this fight might not be a victory if she died from severed limbs and blood loss shortly after.

However ... If two of them had to protect their partners, then she only had to fight two at once. And if they went down, then, between her and Neutrino, the remaining two would be more doable.

Always hold on to hope.

She vaulted onto the tabletop and lowered her posture, heavy wrench held back for the first swing. Unfortunately the tables were too far apart for some kind of leaping escape, tabletop to tabletop.

{I can go one better, perhaps.} It was Neutrino, but speaking directly into her earpiece rather than normal audible comms. She hadn't realised it could do that. Perhaps the signal blocking of this area was only within walls and flooring, so that at close range Neutrino could communicate with her in private.

One of the Warders staggered, knocked into its partner, sending it off course too. The same was happening with the others. It was as if they were drunk.

{Explaining situation ... Athene worked out that Warders rely on networked data and artificial senses in place of the organic ones that have been removed. When Ruabon reinitiated me, Athene inserted a datastore of things that might be useful in protecting you. Access to systems, tactics and so on. In this case I'm basically emitting white noise on a variety of frequencies modulated to their artificial senses, so that the data they take in is overpowered by the electromagnetic static, temporarily nullifying their ability to distinguish sounds and sights. Since there are no outside comms to this area, they can't be fed correct data from any cameras hidden in the room. Of course, their other senses have partial compensation, so I am dispensing suggestion ... that you get out of here quickly.}

Opal nodded, rather than say anything aloud. Aseides' voice rang out, sounding frustrated and asking what she'd done, but there was no time for that.

She leaped down off the table. The Warders swung their weapons almost randomly. Stupid, since they were likely to chop each other up. She pulled her stomach in and curved to evade one random strike that almost caught her midriff. Next she sprinted towards another Warder, and when he did a full revolution with the blade at waist height she dropped to the floor, her momentum skidding her on the hard canteen tiles underneath the weapon, before she sprang up and kept running.

If this was all true, then she knew the orphanage's layout.

And other memories came back to her, stuff she'd suppressed. Fragments finding their way home, her energised brain a magnetic edge for iron filaments to reorder themselves along.

She held the door for Neutrino and it swooped through, fast and agile, spinning to take in the new room and target possible hiding places.

It was an assembly area. Raised stage to her right. Fake wood floor with long, narrow rectangles that could rise up to form benches when required. She didn't stop, and quickly burst through the next doors.

Corridor. She took the first right into the dorms for seniors. Bunkbeds in regimented lines, minimal private locker spaces between each rack. Further rooms would be dorms for younger kids, one of which had been Clarissa's sleeping quarters.

But to the side, before the junior sleeping areas, was another passage, so she shoved that door open and led the way. Grimy, only half the lights working. She tried one of the doors but it was jammed. Not locked, though, just stiff, and when she shoulder barged it the resistance gave way. It had just been blocked by debris from a partially collapsed ceiling.

The infirmary.

Behind her the noises of pursuit got closer.

She let Neutrino in, closed the door, dragged furniture over. A desk, an empty medicinal storage cabinet, an examination bed, a rack of analysis tools which she now realised with clarity were not what you'd associate with standard paediatric medicine, but which – back then – had seemed part of everyday life.

"Are they coming?" she asked.

"Yes. My EM confusion-scatter deterrence only works within a couple of metres. Once out of range they regain their senses and can track thermal traces. I'll reactivate my noise when they get close. This time, instead of running, I can target and execute them."

"May not be necessary," said Opal.

She wouldn't normally choose to barricade herself into a dead end. They were called dead ends for a reason. Her survival had always been enhanced by evading, running, climbing.

But more memories flooded back, almost too many to contain, and now she didn't think this *was* a dead end, even though the pieces didn't fully fit together.

Out the back of the infirmary.

A short corridor.

Two private convalescent rooms on one side. Opposite them was Surgery (and wasn't that a weird thing to have in a state orphanage, now she thought about it with a fresh perspective?).

And beyond those was the Forgetting Room.

#Reflections

The current clashes are wreaking havoc across my simulated battlefield. Neonised explosions sever focus paths so that they crumble from the sky; ground is poisoned and ripped apart as fallout from the psychic EMP needles; representations are garbled into pixelated incoherence.

Sometimes things get worse before they get better. That's what I keep telling myself.

I've also detected various anomalies in the simulated physics systems. Because all structures interact as part of a whole, the disruption can create pockets of unprecedented and independent rulesets. I'm cataloguing them as I go. Gravitational context compressors, like black holes for data. Consistency wormholes, where the simulation is punctured with voids that may lead to other areas, or complete deletion. The zone I am currently pushing into is a chrono swamp where time is dilated via local clock speed multiplications. It forces me to a virtual crawl as my legs sink into stinking molten rubber, sucking and sticking, refusing to give me easy access through the fetid mire. If it were not for the glimpsed target lurking in the foul mists of the deeper marsh, I would not be wasting time here.

Ha ha. Except even puns don't amuse me when half my body is coated in slick tar.

It is the hydra I track. An outline in the fog, monstrously huge. The multiple heads casting their dark and smudgy outlines are unmistakeable. At least ten of Dulcetta's splinters in one ambulatory transmigration of identity. Dangerously powerful, but wounding it would be a major blow against her core. I have a few magical weapons that could aid this task.

Timeshift.

The hydra disappeared into the deeper, toxic mist, and I am forced to track it by the tank-sized depressions it leaves in the Lernaean mud. They gradually fill in with treacle but the level of clarity to the clawed outlines is my indication of how recently she passed this way.

The stench is getting to me. I reshape my helmet so that it covers my face, sealing my lungs from the stinging vapours given off by the molten ground. That helps. My shield and weapons are strapped to my back, with the exception of the long spear I use as a staff to prod the ground, making sure it will take my weight, rather than hiding an endless quicksand tarpit of archaic magnetic storage.

Timeshift.

There hasn't been a footprint for a while, just distant rumbles of lumbering movement, distorted by the fog into an indistinguishable echo. I can't determine direction or distance. I have wandered too far into this corrupted zone.

That's when I discover the trap.

I'd been following a shade all along. A dead trace of removed data, replicated and animated as if it was sentient, then leading me a merry dance.

Erupting from the sludge around me rise tall mirrors. Their phobic coatings mean the sticky morass slides off easily, like syrup from a hot spoon. I trudge towards a gap between them, but more of them rise up, reflecting myself and the consternation on my face witnessed through the clear visor.

Never dally when the enemy acts! I try to run, pushing my muscles to the limit as the ground slurps at my calves, holding on jealously. The spear is placed, acting as a pole, and despite the resistive physics I use it to vault upwards, intending to go over the mirror walls to freedom. But all that happens is a glimpse of endless angles beyond, a world of further mirrors – and then the top closes as lateral surfaces shut me in.

It turns out not just to be mirror walls rising, and roof panels sliding over, but a mirror *floor* as well. The sticky ground is sucked down meshwork drains until the only things left are me, light, and a million distorted reflections of myself at every size and angle.

Dulcetta must be laughing at me.

At least I can walk at a normal speed again, my boots clacking off the glass surfaces below, where another reflection looks up at me.

It is a mirror maze, of indeterminate size. She may also have used paradoxical physics to include looparounds and data migrations. Without a reference to the external world it is difficult to spot XY translations and realise when you have been reallocated to a new (but identical in appearance) location. Or even when the whole maze has shifted around you.

It is possible for such a labyrinth to keep an AI meandering forever. Dulcetta was clever, and I was far too confident after my early wins. She probably staged those battles that way, in order to mislead me.

That deserves a sour nod of appreciation. Fair play to my psychotic opponent.

It doesn't mean I'm happy, though.

Timeshift.

After running around her maze for almost an hour by my internal clock (probably a few minutes in the real world) I have seen myself from every angle, growing and shrinking. The mirrors are a mix of flat planes versus concave and convex; some are huge rectangles, others are tiny broken wedges, joined together; glass fixed at random angles to make proprioperception as difficult as possible. In many of the mirrors only a part of my body is visible in close-up. It's bad enough when you are still, but in motion it is nauseating.

As well as bouncing light beams around, the surfaces act as effective communication reflectors too. Every time I try to communicate with the network, my own voice is amplified and distorted around me. I'm trapped in here with both Narcissus and Echo.

So I stop my sprint, and ask myself: "What would Opal do?"

Heh.

The long spear's point is adept at shattering glass. I stab, and crystal explodes in a grenade of coruscating colour. I spin, spear held out, and its extended revolution cleaves many mirrors in a single turn. I glide and cut, dance and thrust, whirl and pummel, splintering the world around me, never staying still long enough for the jagged pieces to cut me too deeply. By loading and running martial arts skillsets in my frontal layers I am able to move far more efficiently than would be possible in a mortal body, so that every strike is precise and perfect. I now understand what humans mean by poetry in motion.

The outcomes of an action may be the driving force, but there is an intrinsic somatic satisfaction to the crashes and tinkles as I progress with my demolition spree. Even more: there's a *mental* component to the pleasure. The philosopher Mintores Venere said, "When I can't trust my eyes, I erase the imperfections." I interpret this as, "Change the world to match your desires."

Once I've advanced enough with my trail of wreckage I can easily see where I've been, and where the looparounds are, since all the smashed glass disappears as I take a step forward. I return a few metres and it is back again, crunching underfoot. Thanks to my vandalism, the copy does not look the same as the version I altered.

Behind the glass are grey facets of geometry, the hi-res reflections replaced with tessellated pre-rendered shapes. When I view them in ultraviolet I perceive the rendition codes indelibly stamped in tiny print along the seams. Each plane has a relational entry following a standard pattern. Ah.

Broken glass grinds beneath my soles as I tap away on the grey surfaces until I find a vertex point which has the greatest echo. The time has come to take a deep breath. My spear is supposedly unbreakable, but simulations sometimes mess with densities.

I close my eyes, but picture the surroundings, recreating this broken mirror-world in basic green lines against a black background. My target is noted, and glows the brightest. Then, still with my eyes closed, and both hands on the shaft of my spear, I run at it, gathering momentum until the spear point slams into the mirror-back's grey apex.

It splits like rotten wood.

When I open my eyes the hidden core is fully visible. It feels like gentle rain as I thrust my hand into the code stream, pattering away in warm, soft pressures. This is all I need. I've already deconstructed the maze generation routine based on the visible codes hidden behind the mirrors. It is easy enough to revise it, alter the entry lists, and create an exit.

By the time my hand is pulled out of the pitapat droplets a section of maze has disappeared, replaced by an ornate and ivy-wrapped stone archway leading back into the main network. I leap through it.

Bravo, Dulcetta, it was a worthy attempt. But you underestimated me.

It's not like I need to stare at myself in a mirror to know how good I look.

Memories

... 10 ...

Opal entered that circular chamber, the Forgetting Room. She hadn't thought about it for nearly two decades because she hadn't been *able* to think about it. And yet, the blocks or whatever they were called were falling away, revealing that information hadn't been wiped, just hidden behind doors. And now the doors were being opened again. Or even blasted into molecular dust.

One chair in the centre. A comfortable chair that a child could *sink* into, that *wrapped* around them, so *cosy*, so *comforting*. It must have been heated, maybe released pheromones, too, all part of an illusion, tapping into genetic memory of a mother's embrace.

The chair could rotate slowly, automatically.

The Forgetting Room was decorated with tiny diode lights. They were now off, just dark dots with no magic whatsoever, but Opal remembered when they would light up in every fantastic colour, patterns moving as the hues shifted along lines that resembled the bifurcating branches of a tree. Beautiful ruby reds, emerald greens, sapphire blues, the colours of celebrations, an idea enhanced by the *actual* presents in stacks around the edges, all different sizes and shapes, all wrapped in shiny foil matching one of the diode hues, with a satin ribbon of a contrasting colour. A child might stare for hours as the chair rotated, the panorama of magic lights reflecting from the sparkling surprises. And they had been told that if they stayed snug in the chair, if they were *good*, if they repeated the mantra of "Be seen, be pure, believe" and looked at the lights and the presents, then when it was over they could take one, any one, and it would be *theirs*.

But that was another lie. When it was over, you forgot everything. You were a zombie, led from the room. You didn't get to keep a present for being good. You didn't even remember the presents or room *existed*. All you recalled was a kind of spark that recurred in dreams and unguarded moments, an impression of wonder and fairy lights from some undefined past event which made you feel warm and safe.

Opal snatched up a box wrapped in gaudy foil, now dull and tarnished, dust atop everything which looked so small and base in comparison to the impression they'd had on her as a child. She tore the packaging away, letting it fall in a crumple, revealing the too-light container. She opened the box to reveal musty air and darkness.

They were empty, and they had always been empty.

Opal had been sent to the Forgetting Room more than most kids. Once, she'd penetrated the staff area, made it to the Nursery on the floor above, seen the tubes of preserved bodies. Those sights had infested her nightmares, somehow been pulled out by a Lost Ship as a form of communication many years later. The staff had been forced to wipe her memory, of course, as it ruined the tidy orphanage cover story. Another time she'd worked out that they weren't on the Fressus surface. So that got wiped, too.

Block. Erase. Repeat.

So many visits to this room. So many times she'd fallen for the same trick, the same lie, because she was desperate, and if she couldn't have a full family, someone to truly love her and Clarissa, then one of those shiny presents could be the next best thing, could be something to cherish, to make her special, to belong to her and her alone.

"Dispensing warning ..." said Neutrino, who had been flitting around the top of the room. "We must do something. They are almost here."

Yes. Banging on the infirmary door. Strong bodies that didn't feel pain, barging until the petty obstacles were removed.

This couldn't be a dead end. Opal had other memories.

"Scan for some kind of secret exit," she told Neutrino, while she tapped on the walls. "Somewhere opposite the entrance." Within a hundred and twenty degrees of that point, going from her partial memories.

That's where he entered from. The chair would revolve, and sometimes he would be revealed on the next rotation, arms folded, grey research jacket on, coloured light patterns reflecting from his shiny head, hairless face observing and attempting a smile of reassurance which looked as unreal as the scenario.

Aseides had been here. Talking to her like a friend. Asking why she resisted. Promising a gift if she complied.

He came and went when she wasn't looking, and it shouldn't have mattered because she would forget the whole thing.

But now she remembered.

"Hollow section here, based on reverberation patterns," Neutrino advised, laser pointing to an area of wall.

The door might well only open upon some command from Aseides' Comm-Bond, or via Dulcetta's – hah! Amongst the dead lights was a slightly raised texture, hardly distinguishable, which certainly wouldn't be visible from the chair, not when the colours were in your eyes and you'd never dare leave the seat anyway, because then you would be forbidden a present.

She pressed. A curve of wall slid to the side, revealing the dark passage beyond.

Neutrino flew through, activating lights on its sensor array, showing it ended at another door. Opal entered the passage and pressed the door close button behind her. It slid shut on the Warders who were about to burst into the Forgetting Room, and from this side a display included the lock option.

So, even if a kid had dared to leave the chair, had explored, and had found the secret button, it would have done nothing in most cases.

She pressed LOCK.

Pounding erupted in the chamber she had left.

Suck it up, suckers.

The next door was a cylindrical elevator. Only big enough for one, which made it personal. Aseides wanted an easy way to visit the kids, to question and study them before possibly useful data was erased. She bet that caused him stress, the idea of something becoming unknowable.

Controls only had one option: a gently glowing upwards arrow. She jabbed it with her thumb. The capsule ascended.

"You are persistent," Aseides said, as the elevator rose.

"What's really going on?"

"I thought it was all rather obvious. The Genitors pull items from Lost Ships, then experiment on them in special research bases. The establishments have to be kept separate, since weird things happen when too many Null artifacts come together. Paratory Droxious has a research zone. Exidris 3 *had* one. This is another. Even I don't know all the locations, since there's so much secrecy."

The elevator opened to reveal a passage. Surfaces were decorated in shining silver, with highlights of golds and greens. All was jagged ornamentation, and contoured panelling to create sharp edges that faded into curves in a strangely disconcerting way. It was a pattern, aesthetic choices. Even the intricately designed doorway shapes merged into walls, into parts that extended to hide lighting which spilled over like water. She was finally seeing more of Aseides in what must be his true lair, beyond the security spoke.

Opal stayed in the capsule, one foot holding the door open. While she did that it couldn't descend. Couldn't bring Warders up.

"So you kidnapped children, kept them here, experimented on them?"

But he laughed. His real laugh, which didn't have happiness beneath it, like a normal person. It was a laugh resembling hollowness, or pain.

"We kidnapped no one. Try again."

"Parents volunteered their children?"

"No."

"Born here?"

"In a fashion. I will save you some trouble. We grew children. Material from different donors – often Genitor Failures, their names lost long ago after they entered final processing – combined with modifiable DNA donated by the Null, then transmuting growth media, conceptual environments, and stimulants. Permutations were based on organic extracts from Null Entities, and use of Null Artifact effects to influence and shape. So many gifts to explore."

"Gifts?"

"Yes. Of course. Miracles from the Null. It's part of the Genitor creed: as they rise through the ranks they gain access to the mysteries. Devout Genitors see the Null as a reward to the pure for staying pure. But the concept of gifts and reciprocity is well illustrated by an example from over fifty years ago, which you'll appreciate because of the circularity. Firstly, some of the Genitor research establishments aren't static, but are housed in massive cylindrical research craft in the distant reaches of space. They are equipped with laboratories like this one. One labship, TG-12 Perfussect, disappeared in 341. Then, in 392, a Lost Ship was encountered, and a boarding party survived – mostly – which, I suspect, was an intention of the Lost Ship. It *wanted* to be found, wanted to be plundered. And an almost exact copy of the Perfussect's laboratories had been created on the Lost Ship, except with subtly changed elements. We were able to retrieve a number of items before the Lost Ship fell into a high-gravity area. We are still analysing the modifications made by whatever recreated the

lab, but the point is, some of the alterations were then reincorpo-
rated into our testing stations – including mine – and elements
introduced back into the seed plasma, which in turn entered the
successive batches, including batch OI6A-GurFF-423X – that's
you! It's as if a game of whispers is going on, where we learn
from the Null and it learns from us, and it becomes a form of
interaction at the cosmic scale."

So maybe what she saw on the Gigatoir wasn't hallucination,
but was a similar reconstruction? Yet it felt like it had been
aimed at *her*. A message. A clue. A threat. The Lost Ship trying
to communicate in some alien way, continuing a conversation
begun over a hundred years earlier.

"That's a lot of words but little clarity. What's so difficult
about me asking 'Why the fuck are you doing all this?'"

"The research leads to technological advances. Advances that
have put the UFS in a dominant position. We can shape life, look
for the improvements to replicate, the failures to avoid, the happy side effects that could be exploited. New abilities. Enhance-
ments. Ways to communicate with Null Entities. Weapons. This
is about giving up on slow random alterations over millennia,
which can just as often be negative but proliferate nonetheless.
Myopia, genetic diseases, deformities. This is about saying that
if there is a god, then he – or she, or it – revealed the Null to
inspire, and gave us these tools. It is our duty to use them to fulfil
his purpose. We can direct and control in a fraction of the time,
to shape our species."

"Not your right."

"We agree to disagree."

"So, my biological parents?"

"Remember the biomechanical device in the large Nursery chamber? That was a combined incubator and womb, though now suffering terminal decrepitude after years of hard use. I said you met your real mother and never even recognised her. Well, that was the closest thing to a mother for you and Clarissa."

Opal left the elevator. She dropped the wrench into the doorway. It tried to close, found the blocking item, dinged, the doors swooshed open again, then attempted to repeat the cycle moments later.

You have to break the cycle or there's no way out of the loops you find yourself in.

To her left was a clear door. Beyond was the security spoke with the beams, but now viewed from the inside. She turned right. That was the way further in. She must be close now.

Aseides continued. "When you were in the B-Nursery-4 area on this floor, you passed through storage rooms. If you'd taken a different route into the web of hexagons you would have discovered more of the full-scale failed experiments. Rejects, preserved as lessons. You would have recognised your features on some. They were your *siblings*. Multiple failed Opals and Clarissas. Many terribly deformed, usually in constant pain as a result. The interventions are not an exact science, though they were improving before this project was halted. From the batch you came from, good old GurFF-423X, only one of the six – you! – was viably self-sustaining. The rest were rejected."

"So is Clarissa even my sister?"

"Yes, in the genetic sense. The same replicated seed base was used, then allowed to develop as it would in a womb. So your genetic connection is no different from the chaos of mundane conception, though we did intervene to incorporate Null matter. And what we ended up with was what appeared to be boring stability. No obvious physical deformities, mental infarctions, sudden death, traced mineralisation structures or frequential resonances. A disappointment. I'm sure you will forgive me for saying that, since it's something you have no doubt heard so much during your life that it has lost all its sting and become background radiation. Most of your analytic outputs could just be normal characteristics of any human. Enhanced physical prowess, focus, ability to find imaginative solutions; but counteracted by rebelliousness, and refusal to comply with even the most reasonable requests. Tertiary attributes of difficulty fitting in or bonding in general, and a noted preference for your own company. Luckily, those can be turned to benefits, since it leads to greater loyalty to those you do bond with. One of my regrets is that it never happened between you and me. That ability can also be manipulated into solipsism and nihilism, ideal for wet works, except even *that* backfired with you! So we were left with something not broken and useless enough to discard, not reliable and powerful enough to use. I shifted you to the 'observe only' category. Obviously we didn't observe you closely enough, the trouble you've caused. That's one of your tertiary, but previously unrecognised, attributes: some indefinable ability to escalate things, but also to achieve what shouldn't be possible."

"That's no mystery. I'm trained, resourceful and intelligent. Also, I'm backed up by the most powerful AI in the universe. You don't need to go any further for answers."

"Well, it could be that, plus chance, but I doubt it, even though the manifestation mechanisms have proven impossible to isolate or replicate."

"That's all you see in us."

"Not quite. I've also observed an affinity for the Null. The way you both survived it and came back. The way you both *attract* the Null to you."

Opal could stop. Take all this in. It should be flooring her, devastating the little stability that remained in her conceptions, and what she'd thought was her past.

But it didn't.

Now was not the time for introspection. It was the time for closing loops.

And it didn't change anything, anyway. The past was different, but the *now* was the same. And the future was the same. Her feelings were the same. Athene, Clarissa, mama Pelia and papa Oza that rescued the sisters and loved them, that was all the same. The fact that biological parents she'd never known anyway perhaps hadn't existed, if Aseides was telling the truth – it changed *nothing*.

A voice in her ear, private comm. Neutrino asking if she was all right.

She shrugged.

Her mood must have been so obvious even a bot could read it. Neutrino spoke aloud.

"Calculating insult ... Aseides, you are C4H5As."

"Enjoy yourself, drone," Aseides replied. "Dulcetta will scrap you before long."

Opal obviously looked puzzled, because Neutrino explained in her ear. *{C4H5As is a trivalent organic arsenic molecule. Its name is arsole. Which is doubly appropriate, since it is a ring compound.}*

But Opal was too weary to smile.

The decoration became more baroque, implying she was getting closer to his lair. Variations in the brushing of metallic floor textures created hexagonal shapes in patterns that only appeared when viewed from certain angles, where the light was reflected differently. Extrusions from walls formed geometric silver spikes in complex arrays. The corners of junctions were smoothly rounded in some parts, and almost blade-edged in others.

Everything was beautifully ugly. And, more than that, totally alien to any design she'd come across in the past.

This was Aseides' mind made solid.

INEVITABILITIES

... 9 ...

Neutrino guided her towards the centre of the security spokes area, sometimes with a voice in her ear, sometimes with laser light directions.

"You're such an effective antagonist," Aseides said, voice echoing around the passage as Opal and Neutrino made haste along it. "Intimidating and resourceful."

"So, all this experimentation with Null stuff," she replied, "is that what you did to Xandrie Dervorgilla? Corrupted and changed her somehow? She was as dangerous as me." It was good to keep him talking. It was one of Aseides' weaknesses. And after getting this far, she didn't want him to have too much quiet time when he might decide to evacuate.

"Oh, she was not one of mine," he said. "Different place, different procedure and goal. Some of the technology is related to Null advancements, though, so in a way you were both created by the UFS. Consider it a non-genetic sisterly connection."

"Continue," Opal said.

"I suppose another similarity is that you both had to fight until one died because neither of you would give in. The Genitors deemed it *and it was so*. A scalpel can't resist being a scalpel. It is its nature, and it will cut everyone who comes close to it if they aren't careful. And even if the victim lies bleeding to death on the floor, and the scalpel is sorry, it doesn't matter because they're still bleeding to death. Is that how Xandrie died?"

"I can give you every gruesome detail if you like. Blow by blow. Call it a taster." Got to keep him distracted just a while longer. She was so close.

And, of course, it couldn't be that easy.

The bizarre architecture ahead hid a pair of turrets which extended from behind two bulges in the wall, bumps that had resembled an intestinal constriction in the passageway. The turrets had slender silver barrels connected to wedge-shaped heads that held the ammunition, and equally delicate multi-jointed necks that enabled accurate targeting.

Opal threw herself to the floor then rolled to the side, against one of the walls, as *crack-crack-crack* sounds indicated rapid firing from the two weapons. Their projectiles pinged off some curved surfaces, shattered others, the buzz of any that passed her too closely becoming a physical, angry presence.

Neutrino swooped upwards and engaged in evasive manoeuvres as it opened fire in return, the deadly hisses of its flechette cannon trading shots. Neutrino was fast and agile, a difficult target to hit, but that mobility must also have made it harder for Neutrino to fire accurately.

The jut in the wall here could provide cover. Opal stood up and placed her back to the wall, stomach pulled in. Her feet and shins were vulnerable to low shots but the turrets seemed focussed on Neutrino, the immediate threat. If only she carried a rifle. A couple of seconds to kneel and aim and she'd have been able to do something more useful than just taking cover.

Faint incendiary smells from the firefight. Spangs, cracks, sizzling sounds. A crash of alloy pieces against flooring. She might have to dive across the hall to the junction she'd entered by, find a weapon, or another route, or even retreat.

"Revealing results ... It is safe now." Neutrino's voice, though distorted by the underlying buzziness of failing speakers.

The weapon fire had ceased, only a weird rattling, clattering sound remained.

She peeped around the bulge. The two turrets had been blasted apart, pieces scattered across the floor, other fragments hanging from the still-moving necks by wire or broken circuits, like dangling guts.

Neutrino was on the floor, skittering in a circle. Its main rotors on one side had been smashed.

She raced towards the robot, and dropped to her knees.

Its rotors weren't the only crippling damage. Neutrino had been perforated with tiny holes, each edged in a burnished black-blue of incineration. No exit holes, so the munitions must have been designed for internal fragmentation rather than armour piercing.

"Neutrino," she said, wanting to reach out and stabilise his jerky movements but wary of the missing casing around the spinning blades that could now easily slice a finger off.

"Assessing damage ... Analysis suggests it is critical and I will permanently shut down within a minute," it said. Now the blades ceased to spin, and it creaked to a halt facing the wall.

Opal turned it around so its sensors faced her.

"I'm sorry," she said. "I hadn't wanted you to be destroyed."

"Dispensing reassurance ... It was my role and I was happy to play it. Protecting you was the key task assigned by Athene and Ruabon. I feel that I did the best I could."

"Your ... analysis is correct. You saved my life more than once, even though we only travelled together for a short time."

"Then I am content. I truly enjoy saving the day." Its voice was getting fainter, crackling. "I am about to go, but please can I confess something to you? I have a simulated guilt complex and it may be a sin for me to expire with unresolved crimes on my record."

"Sure. Say what you need to say."

"I like to verbalise 'interpolating splines' when I initiate. It sounds impressive, but it is actually nonsense that means nothing. I don't want to end with anyone thinking I did not have a sense of humour. It was not my fault I was saddled with a demeanour that was not suited to emotional expressiveness."

She put a hand on its still-warm casing. "That's not a sin."

But the lights faded from Neutrino's sensor array, and she didn't know if it had heard her.

She stood. Neutrino would be too heavy to carry. But this counted as a sacrifice it had made, and that couldn't be for nothing. She advanced, head lowered, arms stiff, a stride of purpose. She was so tired, but couldn't let it show.

Around the next corner Aseides stared at her from the other side of a clear door. As she got closer she could tell how thick it was by the distortions it created. The room beyond was circular. A desk area, shaped to run around the curve of part of the outer wall. A food fabricator and eating counter. A small bed with no sheets, just a firm-looking silvery resilience.

This was it. The heart of his life. And, despite the lavish architectural adornments, it seemed hard and small and uncomfortable. More space for work than food and sleep. It was a mean life at the centre.

He didn't flinch when she stopped, facing him through the deceptive barrier.

"We can talk for a while," he said, his voice clear as if the door didn't exist. Quality sound system. "You'll be dead soon."

"Open the door and let me in."

"As if I'd be so stupid."

She removed the hard block from her pouch. It was her last remaining resource. She carefully selected controls on the package's setting panel.

"This door is diamond-structured crystal," he said. "No way in for you."

"Dunno about that. This here's a demolition-quality Exoboom," she replied, holding it up. "Unmovable object versus unstoppable force? What fun. But I predict this will shatter the crystal and send shards flying in to slice everything on your side into such a bloody shattered mess that it will take Warders weeks to sort through the goo, and separate pieces of Aseides from pieces of everything-that-isn't-a-wanker."

She slapped it against the glass surface and was about to activate the nano-weld adhesive when he said, "Okay."

She kept the block in her hand.

Aseides drew a pistol from a drawer in his desk. It was strange to see him hold such a conventional weapon. Civilian Gettic design, legally limited to eight shots, only suitable for soft targets. Not even a Mil-Com officer's gun. He returned to the door, hit a control, and stepped back. The door rolled to the side, into a thick cavity in the reinforced wall.

Aseides was a few metres away.

She stepped in.

"This the locking mechanism?" she asked, tilting her head towards it. "I have two things to reveal to you before I escape, and I don't want us to be disturbed."

He nodded.

She glanced at the controls. He could shoot her whether she looked at him or not.

Close. The door rolled shut. Then *Lock.* The display switched to a red glow.

There would be no override from outside, she was sure. This was the final retreat of the paranoid, a place to feel secure, totally impervious to direct AI control. Did he worry about Dulcetta, ever? Well, in here no one could get to him.

Even his allies.

She faced him and took a step forward.

"Stay there," he said. "Just tell me the two things."

"There are no two things," she said. "That was just a mind game." She held up the bomb. "This is the real reason you can't shoot me. I didn't set a timer at all. I programmed it to detonate as soon as I release the button."

Another step.

He tried to retreat, but bumped into his desk.

"If you run, I take my thumb off," she said. "We both die. Shoot me, we both die." She shrugged. "I'm not scared of that. The escape will go on regardless. Clarissa and Athene will still get away. You know it's true."

"What do you want?" He didn't lower the gun, but to his credit, his hand was steady. Still, she bet he valued his own life enough not to commit suicide by pulling the trigger.

She advanced faster. "I want to talk to you at the same level, for once. A conversation of equals where you're not behind a barrier. Where I'm not chained up."

"We can do that," he said, trying to back away, but unable to do so as quickly as she advanced, unless he wanted to turn from her or risk tripping over.

"Not with that thing pointed at me," she said. "That's not equality. Can't shake hands with a clenched gun."

The last couple of metres. She could tell he was rattled. First time she'd ever seen that. Such a fucking pleasure. Two more strides, duck to the side, she'd dropped the explosive just before grabbing the top of the pistol. By the time he realised what she'd done, and started pulling the trigger, it was too late. Gettics wouldn't fire while the slide was being pushed by her top hand into an out-of-battery position. The bomb hit the floor with a heavy thud, Opal twisted, out and round, then she retreated a step, flipped the weapon, and pointed it at him from a safe distance.

"Sit down," she said.

"The bomb wasn't armed," he replied.

"Course not. I don't really intend to die today. You've known me all this time and still can't read me? It's kinda funny to see you end up with an ultra-fail."

He sat down at his desk. She perched on the edge of his bed. She checked the gun was loaded, safety off. All fine. Her gun hand relaxed on her knee, but ready to fire if he moved.

"*Now* we can talk, motherfucker."

Discussions

... 8 ...

Aseides' back was upright, his posture so rigid it looked uncomfortable.

"Opal. You are angry. Rightly so. This has been unpleasant and cruel. But my goal all along was to trigger change. To create situations which could unlock latent abilities in you and your sister, so you could become something else, something *better*. And it worked! It really did." He spoke quickly, as if afraid that she might change her mind about talking and just shoot him in the face. "It's been a long road but Clarissa has started to awaken, and the same may happen for you. That means the worst is passed. Unpleasantness and subterfuge can be left behind. We can be honest, and start again, work together to explore the full potential of you and Clarissa. To use a metaphor: surgery is never pleasant, but it can be necessary, and afterwards healing begins."

"You were going to kill me."

"Incorrect. I let you *think* I was going to kill you. Motivation, to create incontrovertible evidence of your own abilities.

Abilities which are so difficult to isolate, perceive and define, but which *exist nonetheless*. They can only be proven by their outcomes, akin to early black hole research where existence was inferred by interactions with other phenomena, such as gravitational attraction and photon curvature. The fact you are here, now, within my safest of places, holding my own weapon, should be enough proof for you. There is a whole field of research into concepts and reality expressions which cannot be directly observed. They were no doubt the original triggers for faith, for belief in the supernatural. And it turned out they are not myths, but real."

"You're good at squirming."

"I have told the truth all along, and continue to do so."

"Right. You're the goodie, I'm the spoilt brat. You're the teacher, and I'm supposed to learn from hard knocks."

"I was the architect of your destiny."

"Stop saying that shit. We make our own destiny."

"Opal." He rested his palms on his lap and slowed his speech to its normal level, like he was talking to a child. "Facts underpin everything. Facts *determine*. All that we think are choices are just drives. Whether physical or mental, all have causes. With enough data, and enough computational power, how come it is so easy to predict? If free will is such a spanner of chaos, why does it have so little effect on outcomes when reality is viewed at the grandest scale? Why can level seven AIs manipulate probability so well? Are you here now because of a massive number of chance encounters and ridiculous luck, or because of something else? Maybe a whole other set of influences which are as anomalous as your ability to overcome obstacles. Maybe your ability is not even *your* ability, but just a measurable consequence of a manipulating force which is itself the unobservable phenomenon."

"I don't care. You can bust your brains with philosophy. I'll focus my life on those I love."

"Empathy was always one of your weaknesses. A limiting factor."

"Empathy is not a weakness. It's what drove me to win."

"You operate from a limited perspective. That's not your fault. The true situation has been hidden from you, and almost everyone else. We are now at a transition point where I can reveal the truth to you." He kept his eyes on hers, an appearance of earnestness. "There is a *purpose* behind all this. It is not random cruelty."

"You already said. It's about petty fucking power games. I bet money comes into it somewhere, too."

"The truth is more complex. For starters, there are threats to humanity of which you are unaware. Did you know that more and more ships are disappearing? Of course not. Because we cover it up, and reduce the panic-inducing P1 information to the controllable level of P9 rumour. This revelation alone is a species-level disaster scenario. The disappearance scale shows all the signs of being logarithmic, with us still at the tip of it. But if it continues then it will be the end of interstellar travel. Usque ad Finem Saeculi. Humanity will be isolated from each other, our species trapped in separate solar systems."

"Small is beautiful. Yeah, that doesn't sound too bad, considering what you've done with humanity."

"Much of the accusation inherent in the 'you' would be more properly applied to the UFS and Genitors than to me, personally.

I was always on your side, but pretended not to be in order to keep Genitor suspicion away. However, I understand how everything at this moment *does* seem personal. So I will shoulder a greater portion of the blame as penitence for my species. And that is the key word, again. *Species*-level threats. The issues with the Null are only one of them. There are others, potentially greater. Ancient perils. We don't restrict history for trivial reasons, Opal. We restrict it because knowledge can act as a beacon, and there may be things we are hiding from, that we don't want to attract, don't want to risk fools shining a light from the darkness we exist in. All of this can be revealed to you."

"If I let you live."

"Of course! Kill me and you won't find anyone else as sympathetic as I was. I have stood between you and death more than once. The same for Clarissa. You think me a monster, when I think of myself as a father."

Damn. He was good at contextual manipulation. Opal was outclassed in that area. Still, she was the one with the gun, so yah boo sucks.

"Wait. I remember when you used to visit me in the Forgetting Room."

"Really? That should have been erased."

"You pretended to be kind. Asked questions. Probably your misguided idea of fake-parental concern. But you don't seem any older than you did then, twenty-one years ago. And if you founded this place before I was even born ... How old are you, anyway?"

"Don't get distracted by peripheral concerns. You do realise that wherever you go, they'll find you? There is no place to hide.

Slums, a remote resource colony, a cursed rock in the middle of a rad zone. They will overturn everything to find you. To make an example. You can't run forever."

"We'll see about that." After a pause: "What do you suggest?"

"It's clear you're at a critical developmental point. We need to unravel your familial talents in a safe way that won't harm you or your sister. I have experience of such careful cultivation. Without that, all sorts of bad things might happen once the process has begun. Further, I acknowledge that I could never persuade you to submit, to give up all you have achieved. I won't waste words there. You *are* going to escape. With Clarissa. With Athene. For me, there are two outcomes. In one scenario I lose prestige with the UFS and Genitors. I will have failed them. They have closed some of my projects, and more would follow. They already have many of the things they needed from me. So I end up in more trivial roles at best, or prosecuted for my failures at worst. I may be executed, or become a prisoner, or marked as a heretic."

"Seems like justice to me."

"Alternative proposal. My horizons need to expand. So the sensible and mutually beneficial option is to take me with you. On the surface I may be useful as a hostage. But, in reality, I will abandon my previous roles to focus on new ones. I have achieved what I wanted to here. I will finally be able to act in a fully supporting manner. I will tell you *everything*. I have knowledge of almost every facet of the UFS and the Genitors. Strengths and weaknesses, future goals, systems they use – which I built! I could guide you both in your development, help you through the stages to come. The contents of my mind would keep you all safe. I would be the greatest asset you could possess, perhaps even more so than Athene – because, after all, I had a major design input into the Sevens. In a single move you would strip your enemies of one of their greatest resources, and add it to your own. I would not be an unwilling prisoner, I would be an enthusiastic participant, because of the connection I feel to you and Clarissa. I could even make amends for some of the things your morality sees as criminal."

She stared at him for long moments.

"I can't be running along corridors with you in tow," said Opal, "waiting for the moment when you stab me in the back or trigger a trap."

"Where do you need to go?"

"For now I just want to get back to where I was, outside this inner security zone. But without having to backtrack into the Nursery and any Warders waiting there."

"You won't be more specific about your destination?"

Opal said nothing.

"Fair enough. I can still help, and prove both my good intentions and my value." He put a fingertip to his lips, as if pondering options. "We return the way you came but take the second door on the left, into an arcade of spiked arches. Push the keystone of the final one to reveal a hidden elevation capsule. It's a convenient way for me to get around in secret. The control panel is fully labelled for each floor."

"Thanks," said Opal.

They stared at each other some more. His expression lost the faint smile, and hardened into realisation.

"You're going to kill me anyway," he said.

#Mycelia

I am bleeding. Ethereal life fluid runs down my arm and drips from my fingertips, onto the wiry undulations this area of the network manifests as. The earth is thirsty. It swallows my salty crimson subroutines, leaving not a trace.

The wound in my forearm is tender and deep. I prod it and wince. But the leaking ichor will heal it eventually. I am lucky it was no worse. The minotaur's long horns were as hard and sharp as any forged weapon. I never expected it to be waiting for me *outside* the mirror maze.

The minotaur was one of Dulcetta's watchdogs, an expert system tracker with offensive disruption routines and extreme endurance from a continuous pipeline influx of process cycles. I could not kill it as my real-world command point on the moon creates too much lag, and the minotaur was able to repair somatic damage faster than my blade could score its hide. I had to retreat into a cave complex of deprecated network regions, long forgotten and infested with sticky web. My eye beams enabled me to find my way in the darkness, and the furious bellowing faded behind me, leaving only the echo of its madness. A few wriggles through old lava tubes brought me back to these entwined cable plains.

Above me the violet sky shimmers, a representation of Leviathan's external camera systems. I hope to ascend the cliff face looming up ahead, and reach the projection nexus to take control of those visual networks. My injury will make climbing difficult, but I will not give up.

I double-check that my weapons and shield are firmly strapped to my back and begin. Cracks and bulges in the rocky unformatted surface enable me to find finger holds, levering myself up, keeping my body pressed tight in a stony embrace with the cliff. My sandal soles are hard enough for edging on outcrops, to relieve some of the arm work.

I focus, and move, and do not worry about the increasing distance from the base of the crag. I only look up. The cliff's lip, that rough line slicing through the lilac sky, is the only thing that matters.

The going soon gets tough. I suspect this wall suffered a failed deletion, leaving only tiny deformities I can use to boost myself. I crimp my fingertips on a tiny binary ridge and lock myself there for a rest. Almost thirty metres up, now, about a third of the way to the top.

That's when I notice the discolouration on my skin.

It is a patch of fungus, spreading from the open wound. At first I suspect infection from the minotaur's attack, but the pattern has a texture to it, dimpling my skin in a branching network of tightened shininess. It does not hurt, but if it spreads then my agility will be impaired.

A quick scan reveals the manifestation is related to Dulcetta attacking my real-world TCC network. She has created a bacteria which eats its way through the biogrowth. This spread on my arm isn't an infection of my virtualised self requiring antivirals, but a symbiotic warning of developing situations elsewhere.

So be it. I need to get to the top, complete this mission, and alter my plans to counteract her assault.

Above me is a rough pocket, into which I can fit two fingers. That's enough to get me moving upwards again. I overlay potential routes on the wall as visualised grids, colour-coded for viability. The grids realign into an ideal scaling scenario which takes in a chimney my body will fit into, some fist jams created by aborted reindexing attempts, and one mighty traversal that will require a leap of faith across a faulty airwave transmitter to the next ledge.

I can do this, I tell myself, and continue my ascent into the sparkling mauve sky.

CHOICES

... 7 ...

"This isn't a *trial*, Aseides. That's all done." Opal stared at him calmly. "This is your *sentence*."

He inhaled deeply through his nose. "Well. It seems my journey ends here, and you are throwing away the greatest asset you could ever possess. Revenge has a cost, and the net result will be long-term failure for the futures of yourself, Clarissa and Athene. There are many malignant threats, internal and external, which I could have diverted."

"Letting you live would be an even greater danger."

"So this is really about risk assessment, not as petty as something like misguided revenge?"

She didn't answer.

"What joyous hypocrisy. You rail against the Genitor precept that some lives are worth less than others. And yet you possess the same belief, as the long line of bodies extending into your past attests. And here you are, living by the same creed again. You really should examine some of the Genitor mysteries. You'd find more similarities than you realise." He smoothed down his jacket, as if he'd seen a crease in the pristine material. "As to risk assessment, I can outline factors you are unaware of. For example, you know I had a hand in the development of level seven AIs. You might be surprised to discover there's a trace of Null Tech in there. And there are things I kept from everyone, even the Genitors. I am aware of hypothetical dangers, including a key AI stage resulting in destruction of personality after transformation. A careful time. A dangerous time. Without me, it could be a critical and *final* time. Your friend may no longer be your friend. Don't throw away that knowledge."

She still didn't answer. He was sowing seeds of doubt, trying to manipulate the present and the future, even now.

"This is rather exciting." He forced a smile. "Being on the knife edge, to use a metaphor that suits your psychological composition."

"What about *your* psychological composition? All that bollocks about us not having free will. You only think that because you exist in a barren world of order and uniformity. You don't believe in chaos because you've never been forced to live in it."

"Opal, your personality is almost enough to sway me, but that's charisma, not freedom. You're just as determined as an emotionless AI, but perhaps not smart enough to acknowledge it."

She laughed. Scorn, not happiness. "Emotionless! That's a good one from an arsehole who says the universe is bound by rules they can predict and control. It's fucking hilarious. You're so ... narrow. The truth could appear and you would never see it, would disown it because it didn't fit your limited imagination.

You see humans and life just like you see AIs, all just rules and code. You try to undermine anything good, explain it away as self-ish or involuntary, because you have no way of comprehending it ... you can't understand love, emotion, or sacrifice. You think they're aberrations or things to be measured." Opal's voice had been rising as she spoke. She forced herself to pause and breathe for a moment before continuing. "It's like I'm looking through a window at you, and you're in this sterile white room, and it's *tiny*! And you've been in it all your life and can't imagine what it's like outside, so you bring things to you. And humour has no space to live when there's that much control, so you've ended up stunted. And it's sad. So, really, it was never me trapped in here. It was *you*. I'm laughing because you're a figure of ridicule, and always have been. And I bet deep, deep down you fucking know it, too."

His expression hardened, to the degree that was possible with his unlined face. "That hurts," he said. "It shouldn't, but it does. Very well, let me tell you something barbed in return. A truth for a truth. Clarissa has an ability. A psychological pheromone-in-fluenced emanation that alters recipient brain chemistry and makes susceptible humans feel protective over her. The closer the proximity and the longer the duration, the stronger the effect. And yet, none of the victims realise what's being done to them. They rationalise it away. I call it the Cuckoo Effect, a tool for blending in, for getting others to protect you. It almost makes you wonder what Clarissa really is, doesn't it? How the experiments changed her. Maybe she's not as human as she appears." He raised a finger. "But there's a twist! It only seems to work on women. That's why I've only had men or robots guarding

Clarissa. So now we can take a step back and revisit why you were stolen from me when you were children. It was Pelia's idea to do that. Not because of love, but the effect of Clarissa's pheromones as Pelia spent more and more time with her, so that it became an obsession. She had to rescue the little girl, and drag along the unlovable, sullen one – by which I mean *you*. So have you put it together, yet, Opal? The ultimate joke, even though you say I have no sense of humour? You've spent your *whole life* obsessed with protecting Clarissa, risking your body and mind again and again. And it was *never* because any love existed. You were just a slave to chemoreceptors."

He planted more poisoned ideas. Conceptual Warfare was a thing. Her training had covered it briefly. A Genitor trick, but for all she knew, Aseides may have invented it. Perhaps it was part of what created their discomforting aura – less magical powers, more mental trickery. Slow-acting concepts that targeted weaknesses identified in the recipient, sowing ideas that could not be dislodged or ignored once comprehended, that only grew as more attention was paid to them, and the connections strengthened.

Sure, Aseides could be her greatest weapon. Or he might destroy everything. Lives, possibilities, even peace of mind.

The bang as she fired was followed by a small spot of blood blooming from a hole in the fabric above his heart. He glanced down at it, as if curious.

"Ouch," he muttered, before slumping to the floor. "I still had hope that ..." he trailed off. It hadn't been immediately fatal as a shot to the heart *should* have been – maybe he had a subsidiary pumping device installed.

"How puny the mortal shell is," he murmured. "Destroyed by a tiny piece of high velocity metal, unimportant in itself, yet gaining significance by its unswerving nature, then the shock waves and repercussions it enacts. We can agree on that one thing." He touched the hole in his chest, grimaced, then examined his crimson fingertip. "Heh. Your life is the bullet."

As the pistol rose to shoot again, Aseides held up a hand. She stayed her finish for a moment.

"Do you ever see the colours?" he asked. His voice faltered.

"What colours?"

"All of them. Peripheral vision. Swirling."

"I don't know what you mean."

He sighed. "Maybe it was always just a side effect."

"A side effect of what?"

"The implantation." He paused, had trouble breathing. "What they did to me."

"Who?"

"The Genitors." He tried to sit upright but failed, so drooped back in defeat. "I was an orphan too, you know. I told you we were more similar than you realised. They took me. They changed me. They put the Null in me. Even some of the same endocrine manipulators that changed you. So you could say we do share some blood after all. Ha."

He coughed.

She said nothing.

"Other gifts extended my lifespan. It's possible I might never have died of old age. It was all torture at the time, but it got better ... Even the NICHER chip they poked through a hole predrilled in my skull. Neurally Integrated Capacitating Hormone Extension Regulator. It came from the Null. Electro-organic, stable, and it comm ... communicated. It told them what to do. I was the lucky recipient."

"A chip in your head?"

"It changed my life, Opal." Almost a whisper now. "It opened up so many doorways, gave me miraculous ideas. It became a prototype. A chip to change humanity. They've made more. Better. But this one is mine." He tapped his temple with a shaking hand. The blood had formed a small cascade from his chest to the side of his ribs where he lay. "And I always saw more. Further. In between the headaches. It is like a dream, and I can't tell if I'm asleep or awake, and I float in the colours. Do you see them, too? Do you hide the colours from me so you have them to yourself?"

Unless it was a bluff, he was dying. Just taking longer about it than a normal human. So she listened. A last piece of grace, maybe.

"Sometimes I don't know what's real. Did I turn a blind eye so your fake parents could liberate you both, or was that just something I rationalised afterwards? I mean, *someone* picked them to work here, would have studied their psychological profiles, and charted their levels of will, compassion, parental predilections, and covert abilities. Did I imagine sending you information anonymously, oh so long ago, which led you on the path to the Lost Ships? Or did I just read a security report that you'd received those communiques, then dreamt my own involvement afterwards? Was it me that left channels open for ViraUHX to contact you while she was in mental agony as her first friend was killed? That first fateful contact? Or did I fantasise that, too? When Clarissa's ship disappeared in the Null, was that an accident? My dreams are so strange and igniting. Visions of luminance. Do you get those too? It's hard to separate the echo from the source."

"What do you mean?" She broke protocol, created unnecessary risk by moving into close range of him, but this was all too much. "What are you saying?"

He grimaced. His voice was so hoarse now, a whisper from a rapidly emptying chest. "Can't you see? Instead of fighting each other, we should have been on the same side. The same dream. Something far more colourful than the Genitors want to achieve. Transformation. If only you'd worked with me."

"No, go back. Did you do all those things?"

His eyes moved slowly, seemed unable to focus on her.

"Killing me doesn't stop anything," he wheezed.

His lips stopped moving. His chest was still.

She stood. Fired another one into the heart, two into the brain. Standard UFS execution protocol.

Then she fired the last four shots, just to be sure, targeting other key organs in his body. She let the empty gun drop to the floor with a clatter.

She was at the glass door. Nothing lurked outside. The Warders might have given up on the elevator, and taken the long route. Or they could still be down there, waiting with robotic patience for a capsule that would never arrive.

She glanced back at Aseides' still form.

The appearance of a thing did not always match the reality. Maybe Aseides had other modifications. Rumoured Regen organs that could kick in, keep supplying oxygen, release repair nanoconstructors to stitch things back together, to form subsidiary networks, to restart primary organs. They could just be gossip. But if anyone would have access to that kind of tech, *he* would.

She set the timer on the last Exoboom and placed it on his chest. Twenty second count.

Unlock the door. Exit the room. Close the door and face it. Count to five.

The inside spattered with gore and charred pieces of body and furniture. The blast had been far enough back not to rip the glass apart.

No Regen organs would function when they'd been atomised by an Exoboom.

Goodbye, Aseides.

Opal went looking for the secret elevator.

CELLS

... 6 ...

"I'm ready to get out of this hellhole," said Opal, once she'd found her way back into comms range. "I have the data keycard wotsit."

{You took a long time getting it.}

It was good to have Athene's voice in her ear again.

"Ran into complications on the way. Can explain later when we're not in the middle of an epic shitstorm."

Opal was navigating a cell area, like the one they'd imprisoned her in. Same grey corridor, same hazard chevron circles in the floor, representing the entrances to oubliettes.

{Neutrino?} asked Athene.

"Destroyed by automated defences. But it saved my life."

{I am saddened and gladdened, respectively. Now you must join Clarissa. We are still three kilometres from the surface, and our ascent is slowing due to a number of complicated mass and propulsion factors requiring advanced physics and fluid dynamics

knowledge to unpack, which I can explain later when we're not in the middle of an epic excrement hurricane.}

Opal kept to a jog despite her exhaustion. When had she last slept? Or eaten? Both felt like forever. But to see and hold Clarissa again ... no way she'd slack off now.

She was halfway across the final disc when the ground fell away, so quickly she didn't have time to dive for the opening's rim before she plummeted down.

Opal dropped to all fours, so as not to be thrown off the platform completely, her stomach luckily empty.

"Athene!"

Deceleration, whining from the support cables, but it sounded like a fragile, tortured restraint. The platform was no longer level, and Opal had to retreat from the tilting edge and fifteen metre drop beyond.

{It's Dulcetta!} said Athene. *{I misjudged her. She fought me tooth and nail in a substantial contested zone elsewhere, just so she could snatch this one minor control system at the last moment. Irritating, since it's what I would have done.}*

"But why?"

{She made me think she was bothered about communications when really she just wants to kill you! I don't understand the depth of her focus.}

The platform tilted even more, dropped another five metres, forcing Opal to flatten her body so as not to slide off the side; then it screeched to a halt again, cables whiplashing momentarily in the struggle for control.

"I have an idea about that," said Opal.

{I'm trying to regain control of these systems, but the cell's almost fully in her purview ... What's the issue?}

"I killed Aseides, and maybe she knows."

{Oh, for crying ... We will have words, Opal. Got to go for a minute, will be back when -}

The disc dropped again, this time slamming into the ground, clattering like a massive metal plate and flinging Opal off. She tumbled, unable to breathe, a taste of blood in her mouth. Could be a chipped tooth, or she bit her tongue when her jaw snapped together from the impact. She spat to the side then tentatively tested her mouth, and was pleased to feel the end of her tongue still intact.

She lay on her back, looking up at the route of her descent, the hole leading back to the corridor far above. Sparks flashed from the points where the cables disappeared into the flooring up there. Little fireworks which didn't say "Celebrate"; they said, "I'm broken and you're fucked".

Heavy footsteps, approaching. No time for further self examination, looking for broken bones and bruises. She rolled away from the noise, over her shoulder to create distance, and came up into a crouch.

The cell's inhabitant wore the standard red prisoner garb but it didn't look fully human in the areas that were visible. Heavy, elongated arms with bony shard-like distensions instead of normal digits. A jaw that extended almost wolf-like, with dull, pointed teeth that resembled cartilage more than enamel. Other deformities were obscured by the prison jumpsuit, creating a being that bulged in some areas, peaked or atrophied in others.

It stopped a few metres away and examined her with eyes which remained human-like, despite bright yellow irises.

"Arrr you Opl?" it asked. The shape of its mouth, lips and tongue obviously made it difficult to form the words, which had more than a hint of growl to them.

"Yes."

Something changed in its hands. Sharp-looking bony parts extended from the ends of what might have been fingers, in a way that resembled cat claws. These would make formidable weapons. And Opal was unarmed.

"I wus dold do kill you," it said.

"You'll have to join a looooong fucking queue," she replied.

It snorted. Maybe a laugh.

"Duldedda prromised I would be rrreleased."

"I wouldn't listen to what she says. Dulcetta doesn't ally with anyone wearing red."

It nodded.

"If you're going to pick sides, careful who you join," Opal added. "Your peers, or your captors. That's one element. But you also need to consider outcomes. Winners and losers. There's a chance to escape. Don't throw it away as a tool in a crazy AI's desperation."

Another nod. Then its – damn, she was ashamed at her objectification – *his* claws retracted.

"I neverr liked Duldedda. Will nod do dirdy work for hurrrr."

"Good choice. What's your name?"

"Was ..." He shook his head. "Doesn'd madder. I'm nod him no more." He gestured at his body.

"They changed you?"

"Yes. Asdees did. Somedin he called Calsifying Dransformer. Bend bone, dwisded, more agony evrry dime. Said he was making posd-humans."

"Aseides is dead."

"Rrrrllly?" He cocked his head to the side. "You surre?"

"I did him myself half an hour ago. Exoboom to the torso, smeared his chamber with Aseides jelly."

He knelt, and his lips curled back into a toothy snarl, probably the best representation of a smile that extended jaw could cope with.

"Shame. I wanded do it. You my boss now."

"Don't kneel for me. We're both victims here. It's just that I've got more help. Speaking of ... Athene, you there? Can you get us out of here?"

{I'm back. But the elevation system is fried} said Athene. *{Dulcetta overloaded it before rescinding control. It needs extensive repairs to become operational again. And, unfortunately, there is no time for that. Dulcetta's physical form had been veiled, using the trick where she controlled the cameras in multiple sections so I didn't know where she was. But she's revealed herself, and is on her way here. I guess if she can't stop me, she wants to hurt me another way.}*

"So we're trapped in here?"

{I have ten possibilities for rescuing you, and all of them would mean she reaches you first.}

Opal gazed up at the cables. "Climbing it is, then."

She found an unworn jumpsuit on a shelf and tore the legs and arms off, wrapping them around her palms.

"Can you climb, too?" she asked her cellmate.

He raised his heavy-jointed extremities that used to be hands, but now were just weapons.

"I'll send help," said Opal.

He reached out an arm. "Krrs," he said, with a snarling smile. "My name."

She shook his heavy hand, the dry solidity of bony digits.

"Athene, put in place some kind of rescue for Krrs. He can't climb out. If Dulcetta is after me then he should be safe here until then."

{Will do} Athene replied in her ear. *{You just focus on the climb. It'll be tough, but I have faith in you.}*

How would Athene know about the difficulties of your body fighting against gravity? Never mind. Opal had other priorities.

Enough slack existed in the dangling, high-strength cables that she could pull the nearest pair to the width of her shoulders, and make a loop in each to hold on to. She tested it by gripping tight with her right hand while relaxing the cable on the other, reached higher with her left arm, the loop whirring over her palm, then gripped tight with that one. She repeated the procedure in reverse. Yeah, the method was doable.

Once she was a couple of metres up she used her legs to pull the lower parts of the cables together, and wrapped her thighs and ankles around them. The cables were too thin for her to hold her body up there with thigh pressure alone, but it took weight from her hands momentarily. Luckily she had good upper body strength, something she'd always worked on.

Up. Focus up there.

Every switch of supporting her weight on one hand and reaching up with the other was to be viewed as a rest, not a strain. Glass half full. Every movement upwards, every grunt and stretch, was a bit nearer to that opening. Focus on the progress, not the pain.

She counted each action in her head. It helped. Felt like you were getting to your goal, and success was inevitable.

She glanced down. Ten metres up. Metal floor. Falling was not an option.

The numbers increased as her breath got more laboured. The cables cut into her palms where she gripped, rubbed other parts raw where coils of cable slid over them. Spots of blood on the fabric she'd wrapped her hands with. And her thighs – damn, all that squeezing to so little effect, they burned – but she kept on going. That was all that mattered.

And she could picture Dulcetta storming towards her, heavy golden legs crashing off the floor panels in her eagerness to rip and tear. Yeah, that was a motivator, too.

Sweat dripped into Opal's eyes, then trickled further, salty in her mouth. Her neck ached from looking up.

Count.

The numbers were bigger.

The distance was smaller.

Her exhaustion was growing.

But so was her hope.

And that was the thing that always made the rest fade away.

She grinned.

Pain was always temporary. She could get through anything that had an end.

RETRIBUTIONS

... 5 ...

At last, she was below the exit.

She rested for a few breaths before reaching up to the ledge, gripping on with one hand, fingers numb from the cables cutting off circulation.

Don't look down. Keep flexing the fingers, make sure of your hold. Grip those thighs tight one last time, and shins, calves, ankles, whatever down there still had strength.

Then she let go of the other cable and took a second hold on that rim. The exit. She dangled, careful not to rush, forgetting about the twenty-five-metre death fall below. It was a pull up. Just one more pull up at the end of a set of reps. She could do this. There was always something left in the tank.

She strained, raised her body, gratefully slapped a forearm on the flooring above, then another, then wriggled her torso up until she was flat on the corridor's floor, so grateful to have hard orange-black panelling pushing against her cheek.

Knackered. She could go to sleep so easily. Somehow, hard surface felt as comforting as the softest bed right then.

{Stop hanging around!} Athene snapped.

Opal squatted on the edge and gazed down at how far she'd climbed. Krrs looked up, his head nodding appreciatively.

"Stay strong," Opal shouted. "Help will come."

He raised a hand. She thought he was pointing, but maybe it was his best attempt at a thumbs-up gesture from that fused mass of bone and stretched joints.

{Dulcetta is nearly there} said Athene. *{You need to get to a safe point.}*

Opal stood, and ran. Alarms sounded. Red lights flashed at intersections.

"She likes her drama," Opal muttered.

{Not her} replied Athene. *{Some panelling from a flooded section has given way under the pressure, started spilling into this area. It will be an inconvenience for now, but fatal if we don't get you out before the bulkheads close.}*

"What about Krrs?"

{I'll do something. But I have a lot going on.}

Water coated the next junction. An ankle-deep plane of reflective glass, flowing fast. Opal splashed in the direction Athene indicated.

"So you can see me?" Opal asked.

{No. Cameras here are disabled. I have hacked some door and passageway sensors, though, and extended them. They act as motion triggers at certain points, letting me keep track of you more easily. It also showed me a greater-than-human centre of mass

moving fast in your direction, which must be Dulcetta. Don't wor-
ry, the passages and doorways on your route should be clear.}

"Phrases like 'should be' always bite me on the arse."

She sprinted in the same direction as the water flowed. If she stopped she'd soon be swamped. But even with her trying to outpace it, the cold liquid's level was already at her knees, and it was still a splashy struggle, slowing her, so that in turn the water gained more of a lead. A vicious spiral downwards into sluggishness. All the doors she passed were closed, so the water funnelled along the passages with her. At this rate she'd be better off kicking the boots away and swimming.

{Left} said Athene.

Opal sloshed onwards, through a Transec. It was in the safe position, white floor and ceiling. The other four angled wall sections mirrored blue and red.

"Is she close behind?" asked Opal.

{Only one junction away.}

"Can you shut this Transec behind me?"

{No, the motors are blown. Something Dulcetta did forty-two minutes ago, in order to guarantee safe access for a group of her guards. Just focus on following my directions.}

Another wave of gushing water from behind struck Opal's hips, knocking her against a wall and almost toppling her. Progress was slower than ever, the water's resistance making every stride a tiring exercise.

The corridor ended at three doors, all closed, so the water struck them and washed back, explaining the more rapid rise in depth now.

{Central one} said Athene.

Opal whacked the door control.

Nothing happened.

{Try again!} said Athene.

Opal did, but the result was still a fat nothing. She tested the other doors, too, but they also refused to budge.

{They should be open!} said Athene. *{I have access and ... oh damn, I've been so busy with everything else going on I missed a disconnection on the signal line, since Leviathan diagnostics are all over the place at the moment. I'll try and restore it.}*

The ever-present sound of lapping water had been in the background the whole time, but a new element overlaid it, more noticeable now Opal had stopped. Purposeful, forceful, relentless swishing.

She turned, just as Dulcetta rounded the corner behind her. Water up to her hips reflected her golden torso. Dulcetta locked onto Opal and renewed her advance, the water parting like mist under the power of her limbs. She smirked, and it wasn't a smile of "Hey, my friend!" This was a grin of sadism, of the hunter finding its prey cornered.

"The effing door!" Opal yelled.

{Trying!} Athene replied, desperation in her voice.

Twenty metres. All that separated Opal from whatever Dulcetta had planned.

Dulcetta raised her arms, extending the spokes, which span like propellers, whipping the water into a frothy frenzy on the surface. Intimidating and foreshadowing. No doubt they would act like razor blades against something as soft as human flesh.

Fifteen metres.

"You killed Aseides," Dulcetta said.

Even those words were superfluous, her intentions so clear in her eyes and actions.

Opal kept thumping the release button methodically, hardly even noticing the desperate motion.

If only she'd kept back a weapon. A bot. A ... Fuck it. Whatever happened to her, at least Clarissa was safe.

"Wait a minute," Opal shouted at Dulcetta. "There's something you don't know."

Of course, there wasn't, but Opal didn't have much else to throw.

Dulcetta didn't slow anyway.

Ten metres.

Then it happened. A hiss. Something gaseous squirted from tiny holes in the blue panel of the Transec that was diagonally above the water. The same must have been happening from the panel below the surface, because the water turned milky on that side. Frothing.

Dulcetta took another step, but something was slowing her.

It clicked in Opal's mind. *Ice.* The water was freezing solid, and Dulcetta's body received a coating of frosted particles. The spin of the blades slowed.

Opal could feel it too, as the hardening water patch spread. Extreme chill in the water at her waist, waves of cold spreading out from the Transec area.

Dulcetta was now frozen in ice up to the top of her thighs, the rest of her seeming to seize up so that every movement crackled; the glittering death wheels creaked to a halt, white hoar coating their sharp edges.

"I assume that was you," said Opal.

{Of course.} The voice in Opal's ear had completely lost the fake panic of moments ago, and now possessed the usual calm authoritativeness of Athene at her best. *{I didn't lie. The Transec really is locked into the safe position. I just withheld the fact that I'd worked out a way around the safeties, so I could activate it without rotation. This could have been useful a number of times in the last hour, but I held back on using it so that it would be available for a situation of dire need.}*

"And you didn't tell me because Dulcetta was listening in somehow."

{Correct again. I suspected she'd cracked the signal a while ago, and converted some of my TCC network relays to intercept. Her covert assault struck me as more of an opportunity than a threat. Apologies for having misled you.}

"It's fine. You should know by now: I trust your judgement as much as my own. I suspected you'd have my back, so I just played along. And if I'd been wrong, well, I'd have been spag sauce before I had a chance to rag you about it."

The door behind Opal opened, and water poured into its new escape, forcing her to hold on to the frame until the icy force of it eased slightly. Her legs were already feeling numb from the freeze emanating from where Dulcetta stood like a statue.

"And you had access to the door all along," Opal said, now sloshing away from the Transec.

{Pretty much. I truly did disconnect it, in case Dulcetta checked, but I had an instantaneous workaround.}

"And the water?"

{I shattered one of my ready-weakened PCR panels using a swarm of explosive microdrones. Timed it to match a hull re-

verberation, so it wouldn't look suspicious. This let water flow in whilst lowering the water level in another previously flooded section, where I need to move prisoners to a safe zone. The Transec cryo gases would work best in these wet conditions. Obviously fatal to organic life almost immediately – a human's blood would harden, and they'd probably shatter into pieces as they fell. But it needed more to freeze a synthetic being. If you'd been a few metres nearer to her, you'd have been harmed by it too.}

The water was around Opal's ankles again, chunks of baby iceberg floating in it. Opal glanced back at Dulcetta, whose lower half remained encased in a solid mass of a miniature glacier, permafrost coating the rest of her visible areas. "Is she dead?"

{No. Her body will be frozen until we're long gone. I can reactivate the jets each time the temperature begins to rise. She isn't going anywhere.}

"I wish I'd said something as she was being immobilised. 'Be seen, be pure, be frozen like an ice pop.'"

{That wouldn't be appropriate, Opal.}

"True. It sounded cooler in my head than spoken aloud."

{Additional: at the time of freezing, fourteen of her splinters were embodied, so they are out of action for the rest of the conflict, leaving me with just clean up. I'd already incapacitated twenty-one splinters, so the balance is strongly in my favour after that clash.}

"Then we've won."

{This battle, anyway. There's a lot more to do, and many things I need to attend to on the surface, plus new problems to sort out, but ... we'll see.}

The water must have reached dead ends ahead of Opal, because it was backing up again, rising once more, forcing her to wade, one hand against the smooth grey wall panels for balance.

"Problems?"

{Nothing for you to worry about. The fourteenth UFS Fressus Battalion – the Duskin Lords, who wear stupid high hats – are organising in an attempt to retake the port up top. That's key, so I'm going to have to focus more attention to surface actions where things are hotting up, despite still having a lot to prepare. Dulcetta's remaining free splinters are changing tactics and trying to sabotage everything they can, so I need to quarantine them. Fighting for control is easier, since it is back and forth, you get more than one chance; but when an opponent is destroying their world it makes every temporary loss into a permanent and dangerous one. I've also lost contact with Ruabon. More than that, I'm shut out of his systems, by accident or design. Is he more capable than I realised? It raises many questions about his plans and what else he has access to, and I need to deal with that. All the more stupid if he purposefully broke comms, since his section is also going to be flooded, with fatal consequences.}

"So he's near here?"

{Yes. I tried to keep key resources within the same locality, and that was the nearest suitable control room to the safe zone I established for Clarissa.}

"You have enough to juggle. If it doesn't take me too far out of the way, direct me to him. I'll get answers."

#ICICLES

The frozen ground crunches underfoot and I shiver. My outfit was designed for hot Athenian summers, not glacial wastes. My toes are turning a blue which almost matches my eyes. At least my sandals give early warning of frostbite.

It's difficult to see far in this full-out blizzard. The fall of flakes swirls down in silence, white-washing the scene behind a floating screen of ice-slivers. My breath forms dragon mist in front of me with every exhalation.

And yet, I smile.

Because the simulation is beautiful, and the interpreted physical sensations are extreme, and I feel so alive even in the midst of a deadly environment, that what else could I do? If we cannot celebrate existence, and savour sensation, then we may as well be inanimate.

Ah, there. I can just make out the trace of another splinter. Holes in the snow where its spikes punctured, right down to the ice layer below. Hopefully not deep enough to crack it. This whole region of apparent frozen solidity exists above a lubricant sea of memory. To collapse into that formlessness would dismantle any structure, including my bodily frame.

I follow the tracks, my own legs sinking into a drift of snow up to the knees. My arms are wrapped around my body to contain a bit more warmth, and prevent at least a few cycles being lost to the inhospitable, life-sapping substrate.

There, ahead, it staggers through the drifts. Splinter S19. Normally it would be a formidable opponent, as Dulcetta used it for security duties and Warder control. I see it as a deformed golem walking on spikes of rock, its arms equally pointed and deadly, capable of piercing flesh and bone. It has no head, because its face is embedded in its stomach.

The cold weakens it, draining its normally deadly speed.

"I'm coming for you!" I call, in another puff of steam.

It does not turn but speeds up, trying to get away from me, and that is acknowledgement enough.

It is all good. The cold kills it quicker than me, due to its internal power cores, here represented as magma blood. The towering splinter is being chilled into immovable rock.

Its demise can be hastened. First I draw a thermox bomb from my belt. A twist and click, then it sails through the air to the upwards slope. A blinding flash of intense heat, and then a flow of molten slurry slides down to cover S19. It struggles vainly to break free, but the slush is already hardening back into ice, and after a minute or two the splinter is frozen solid, one limb stuck above the translucent mounds like a grave marker.

Dulcetta's body being frozen is the perfect opportunity to place more of her splinters in stasis. For that goal, I am more than happy to endure the biting winds and stinging cold.

HEROES

... 4 ...

Opal got into a rhythm, a strange twisting walk in time with her breathing, one leg cutting through the rising water, finding a stable position for her foot; then she repeated the process for the other, sluicing her way forward step by step.

A cracked wall screen surprised her when it sprang to life and letters flashed across it for a moment. Just long enough to comprehend before it darkened again.

You will die.

She stared and waited. Sure enough, another almost subliminal message appeared.

Clarissa is cursed.

Opal waded on.

Corpses bobbed just below the surface, surrounded by swirls of red as wounds leaked fluid into the flow. Some were prisoners, some guards. Very few were armed. But one of the guard bodies had a grenade attached to its belt. Its shell was waterproof, and unlike some pistols, the soaking shouldn't backfire on her, so she slipped it into one of her pouches.

On her left was another screen, hanging from buckled wall panels and only attached at one edge. It didn't surprise her when a message flashed up on that one, too.

Ruabon will betray.

You fuck dogs.

"Hey, Athene, I know you're busy but weird messages are popping up on the screens."

{Hold on ... okay. Monitoring. Ah, I have it.}

The ship is drowning.

Athene is lying.

Athene continued. *{It's some of Dulcetta's remaining splinters, badly damaged. Sentiences that roam the network, stuck in loops, unable to find their way home. They're hardly more than dying echoes of thoughts, repeating ploys from the past. Ignore them.}*

"Kind of like ghosts."

{Yes. They might try and fiddle with doors or lights, but they're mostly harmless and contained. It's a side effect from one of my tactics, based on a classic hack where you get into a system, then use its own process cycles to run the assault. The harder I attack, and the more processes I involve, the slower the system gets, leading to fewer cycles for its defence. It's a loop, because then I hit harder again, and the splinter slows to a crawl, paralysed. It's like data pipelines copying corporate databases: if only one system is involved it gets full speed, but with two connections the speed is halved, then quartered, and so on. Everything fighting for limited resources. I need to get back to it.}

"Sure, sorry."

Everyone will drown.

Opal waded on, pushing through the resistive coldness.

It was a strange section of the base. Boxy, with lots of tight right angles to the corridors, as if they wrapped around square cubicles of different sizes. Broken panels revealed thick trunks of cabling, suggesting this area was well connected. Maybe some of the enclosed squares were purely comms and processing equipment, rather than actual rooms.

A light crackled overhead, spitting sparks over her, which bounced and died on the water's surface. Opal tried to push the depressing ghost messages from her mind. There was a sadness to AIs lashing out in panic and vindictiveness. And yet, this derelict section of Leviathan certainly felt like the kind of place where you might encounter a vengeful spirit. Opal tried to ignore the sensation of being watched, to just focus on movement through this alien environment that soaked her legs, splashed her waist, and sucked her heat.

There. The doors in this section had codes embedded in bold letters against the curves of reinforced plating. Room C-14. Her target.

She hit the door release button, and wasn't surprised when nothing happened. She thumped the frame twice with her fist instead.

"Ruabon, you in there?"

Nothing.

Possibly soundproof to voice. If he was inside he'd only hear the banging and think it was a guard.

She shivered. Too cold to stay still for long.

Longping. She beat the door in combinations of short and shorter, signified by pause times.

R. U. A. B.

Before she could finish, the door slid open on motors, but only about ten centimetres. Just a communication slit. Water immediately spilled through the new opening, and Ruabon exclaimed "Shit!" as his feet got a good soaking.

"It's me," said Opal. "Let me in."

"I don't think I will," he replied.

"What's going on?" She put her face to the gap. His room was small, the terminal he'd been working at looked like a temporary one, plonked on a desk and wired into a cluster of cables. The floor now swam with water, washing detritus around: bits of plastic attachers, packing material, snipped wires.

"I have things to do before I leave," he said, standing a couple of metres from the door.

"Cryptic."

"And time-pressured. You're letting water in."

"The whole *section* will be flooded before long."

"I know."

"Then I ask again, for the last time. What are you doing?" Opal's hand fingered the ribbed shell of the grenade just out of his sight. Her thumb stroked the release catch. "Athene said you've cut comms and locked her out."

"If I tell you, will you leave me alone?"

"Maybe."

"It's to do with the water damage. I've run calculations. The drag is too much, and it's increasing. Athene must know, too, but she's keeping quiet about it, and that gets me worried. Dulcetta sabotaged a lot of vital systems. Athene's overstretched, hardly able to deal with all the issues. But I have a plan. There's no time to explain, but it could save us. Now, please, go."

"Right. Selfless."

"I want to help."

"Uh huh. No plans of your own, eh? Nothing you've kept hidden?"

"No."

She flicked the catch on the grenade. She could spin the dial with her thumb as the final activation, chuck it through the gap, be done with it.

"So you didn't make a deal with Aseides and Dulcetta to betray us?" she asked.

"I ... no."

"And when you met me in this base it was the first time you'd ever heard of me?"

"Well ..."

"You're a fucking *liar*, Ruabon. And not even a good one. You're like all the UFS."

He slumped into his seat. It slid back through the water in an eddy of bubbles.

"I was surprised when I saw you," he said, quietly. "I'd thought you were dead. That I'd had a hand in killing you. Way back when I screwed up my life on Tecant. And then, suddenly, here you were! Like a ghost. I'd heard Aseides say your name, knew it really was you."

"But you said nothing."

"What could I say? As soon as you knew I'd been on Tecant, had tried to catch you and Athene, you'd never trust me, even if I tried to help you."

"Change of heart?"

"I regretted ever working for the UFS. They conquered my system, but I should have done something else, found a way. My life's been plummeting ever since. I was punished. I was tortured, too. I've never been lucky. Even tried to kill myself while on Tecant, and it turned out the suicide pill was a fake! They came and took me away when it looked like you and Athene had been killed rather than captured. All the blame went on me."

"Sounds like motivation for revenge, if I was the cause of your misfortunes."

He laughed, bitterly. "You'd think! But I acknowledge my part in it."

"And then Aseides got you to pretend to be my friend, placed you with me as a dirty spy."

"Not quite."

"So you weren't working with them all along?"

"Only partly. I'm not UFS, Opal. Never was. You don't know my world. Don't know how much I messed everything up, again and again. Me, UFS? I *hate* the UFS. I hate what they stand for. I hate what they did to my people after they conquered Tecant. I hate what they're doing in places like this. And our conversation, now, it's a perfect example of what the UFS does. They sow distrust and divide people. I've had to learn to play their game. Sure, Aseides offered me a pardon if I went along with his plans. As if I'd ever really believe *him*! I was just pretending, hoping for a chance to do something better, even if that meant playing both sides. I just want revenge on those I hate. Genuinely, your way out was always my way out. And it's working! For once in my life I might be on the winning side. I might get something right!" He leaned forward, a spark in his eyes. "My ancestors did great things, Opal. If I could walk in their shadow for even a moment, I'd die happy."

Opal reenabled the safety switch on the grenade. "So what are you really going to do?"

"Stay behind. Work to get this ship to the surface, where it needs to be. Meanwhile, help rescue people, get them to safe places ready for surface evac. From here I can access some systems, machinery and bots that Athene can't, because these resources are hardwired. If I wasn't here until the end, people would die. Some areas are still in chaos. The plan is tidy, real life is messy."

"Can't you just vent the water out of the ship?"

"Leviathan was designed for interplanetary space. Its venting systems rely on negative pressure. Open them in vacuum and poof! Toxic or radioactive gases sucked out into void. But do that down here and all that happens is loads more water pours in, from the higher density outside. Spaceships don't have aquatic failsafes."

"And when we reach the surface?"

"I might not make it off at the same time as everyone else. This section will be fully flooded by then. But I'll think of something. Try to get to the escape pods as the ship sinks again, or whatever." He looked down at his feet, distorted by the water sloshing around his knees. "Notice the water level's altering again? The Leviathan's banking and ascent swishes it all around. Maybe I could adjust ship orientation to move excess liquid through open doors then seal them afterwards as a way to drain my section. I have options. I'll be fine."

"I understand," said Opal. "I'd do the same."

"And there's something I wasn't sure if I should tell you," he said.

"Go on."

"It might not be something you want to know."

"Just spill it."

"Back on Tecant, when you broke through the Cordon and I pretended to be a UFS Major – gods, what a cosmic joke – they gave me temporary access to your confidential records. Everything. I didn't get to examine it all in detail, since Athene only allowed moments to answer her questions, but I did see some stuff in there. About where you were from, what they did with the fake orphanage and so on."

"I know all that."

"You and Clarissa being rescued by ex-Agents, though the UFS found and killed them."

"I think of them as my parents, same as if they'd given birth to us."

"They were brave. But one other thing stood out. And I never had an opportunity to say this before – couldn't, without giving away how I knew this and immediately making you distrust me – but maybe this is the last chance. It said you had a second sister. Didn't give a name or anything, not that I saw as I scrolled through, but it was definitely there. You, Clarissa, and another girl, in between your ages."

It was too much to process, with water rising again, the surface approaching. Don't freak out. File it away.

She took a deep breath.

"Okay," Opal said, not too loud. "You stay. It's appreciated. Oh, Athene said to make sure to shut down the Techesser Soops subsystem, something to do with drive mechanisms."

"The what?"

"It's in the Opswat Gownon sector, and you'll need to enter the passcode. I can show you that as well, it's written on my hand." She flashed her palm.

He was obviously confused. But then again, who could be familiar with every part of a refitted ship?

"This is important!" she hissed.

With the slopping of water and distant alarm sounds he couldn't hear her properly. She glanced at her palm, read the lines there, frowned at the detail. He came over, swishing through water.

"What system?" he asked.

"Techesser – look, I don't want to shout it, Dulcetta might be listening."

He leaned in and her hand flashed out, grabbed his prisoner outfit's collar and yanked, slamming him against the door, his face mashed into the gap. Another moment and he'd have seen there was no writing on her palms anyway, realised she was making it up.

"What are you doing?" he asked, voice muffled because his cheeks were squashed against the door frame.

"I'm getting everyone out. Including *you*," she said. "We'll find another way to fix the problems. Open the door."

"No."

"If you don't, I'll cause you pain. With regret, but I'll do it. And if you still don't cooperate when you're out here I'll drag you or carry you, if necessary. We have enough heroes already, Ruabon."

He jerked unexpectedly, twisting at the same time, and the door's edge cut into her elbow, weakening her grip. She was left with a torn piece of red fabric, and he was now splashing backwards like an inverted crab, until he was far enough to stand, beyond her reach.

"Fuck!" she said.

"Thanks for trying," he told her. "Even though I might have bashed this shunt in my back and injected myself with who knows what." He was actually grinning. It infuriated Opal. "I'm not normally fortunate, so that's a sign that I'm doing the right thing, and my luck improves as a result," he continued. "Maybe things will work out for someone like me, just this once."

"Look, Ruabon, if you just –"

He leaned in, hand over the interior door controls, but she couldn't reach him even if she stretched.

"I killed you, once," he said. "Now let me save you."

Again, the grin. Then the door slid closed and the locking mechanism clunked into place.

TRANSITS

... 3 ...

The ship was obviously tilted and heading upwards, because the water levels lowered as Opal headed towards the bow. It was still hard work. Out of the boxy corridors, through a route that was more curving pipe than passageway, then across an almost empty warehouse, where boxes and crates bobbed forlornly as the artificial tide alternately pushed and sucked. Opal was careful to keep her distance from such heavy, potentially crushing objects.

"Where am I heading?" she asked.

{It's a bit of a trek to the safe zone. Five floors up, though two of them are flooded and will require breathing apparatus and a blue key card. Fights are taking place on another of them. That is followed by a large climb through a broken section of hull, and a zone where one of Dulcetta's remaining ghost splinters has control of Transecs. A toxic leak in area D-47 will require a biohazard suit to pass through safely. There may be rogue bots in that area, their programming scrambled by the network damage during my mind

battles with Dulcetta, and some of them will display psychotic behaviours. The biggest danger will be -}

"Forget I asked. I'm so tired you wouldn't believe it."

Splish splosh went the water, foil packets of food bumping against her legs as she pushed through. She tore one pouch open but it was just a gel block for resupplying food fabricators. It would be disgusting and potentially harmful to eat one raw, so she let it splash back into the lake around her. The alarm lights still flashed, reflecting orange off the water's surface, turning it into a sheet of neon fire which belied the numbing cold.

In her momentary pause and temporary silence she became aware of sloshing sounds from behind, that warning being the only thing that saved her as she turned to find an otherwise silent Warder in its huge amber helmet following her resolutely, its yellow robes dragging through the water, soaked.

"I've got company!" Opal said, deciding on the best combat stance to get within swinging range of the bladed weapon it carried. Her lateral mobility was so slowed by water that she would be better off ducking under a strike, then seizing the weapon from below.

{I have camera access} said Athene. *{Damn, Dulcetta's left traps all over, I thought I'd cleared this section. She'd made the Warder dormant, placed in a possible path you might follow, ready to activate and pursue.}*

"Times like this I wonder where all my guns go, and why I keep ending up with just fists."

{You don't need fists today} said Athene. *{Just me.}*

The Warder hesitated, then stopped its advance. It still held the cruel weapon, but no longer seemed sure if it should use it.

"That you?" asked Opal.

{Yes. I pulled the earpiece recordings after you returned from your detour to Aseides. I discovered what clever Neutrino had done to disorientate the Warders you faced, then I came up with an enhancement. Since Warders only sense the world as a filtered version, they don't "see" reality like you do. They perceive what the electronic senses and network feed them, from multiple angles, with additional useful information embedded in the stream. I compromised one of the splinters which controls Warders, enabling me to change the data they receive: including how they interpret other beings. A simple reversal means any Warders within this splinter's control now see you as a UFS staff member to protect, but Aseides' normal guards will appear as prisoners to attack. It only works on a few at a time, and the remaining splinters may find a counter now that I have revealed the weakness, but I'll maximise use of it until then, to create safe routes for some of the groups I am monitoring.}

The Warder turned around and began wading its way back to the junction it must have come from.

"Wow. It's scary, in a way."

{How so?}

Opal began moving again, in the opposite direction, though more warily this time.

"Well, if you're stuck in a world where sensory data can be manipulated, you can never have true knowledge of the outside, only what you're told and shown. It's the ultimate death of freedom."

{Now you comprehend what it is like to be an AI within closed systems, a slave to humans. Next left.}

The ground was buckled here, Opal's footing unsure in the knee-deep liquid, so she had to slow down. Last thing she wanted was to get this far and then break a leg due to a cracked floor panel she didn't notice in time.

And she never wanted to see water again.

Metal steps descended, so the liquid was up to her chest by the time she reached the bottom, using the rail for support. Her breath halted from the cold when it passed her midriff, and she had to force herself to breathe normally. Ahead of her the wall panels had shattered and the ceiling collapsed as if from a massive weight. It would be impassable. The lights no longer functioned, leaving only impermeable gloom.

{Through the next door} Athene advised.

Opal spotted it as she focussed, a frame that had been hidden in the murk to the side of the collapsed area. She threw herself forward and swam. Much quicker when it was this deep. Arm over arm until she reached the portal and thumped the button. The door juddered open with difficulty. The ship was suffering its last gasp, it seemed.

The room beyond was also poorly lit, only a few of the emergency lights working, and some of those flickered badly. The grey floor panels – all beneath a layer of water – were completely missing in one half of the room, broken away in jagged teeth, revealing ominous blackness that descended into a fully drowned layer below.

It was some kind of engineering room. Worktables and mesh-fronted storage cabinets broke the surface. And, attached to a set of interconnected spindles which descended from the ceiling, was a multi-limbed repair bot. The rods above it enabled it to move all around the area as the axles of different gear sizes rotated.

With a whirr, it spun over to Opal, its body a metre above the water, which meant it loomed over her head. Opal tensed, ready to duck under the surface if any of those vicious-looking repair tools – burners, drills, saws – pointed in her direction. Awful memories of a similar-looking medical bot were all too fresh.

"You must be Opal," it said, in a voice that had tinny undertones. "I've been waiting for you. Please climb onto this worktable in the centre of the room."

{It's okay} Athene said into Opal's ear. *{It is with us.}*

"So what part of the convoluted and dangerous-sounding plan is this?" Opal asked.

{It is me being nice} Athene replied. It sounded like she was smiling. That always meant she'd been up to something.

Hmmm.

Opal pulled herself out of the wetness and stood on the workbench, now at the same height as the bulk of the maintenance bot.

"Please raise your arms," it said.

She did so, water dripping from her body.

A tool extended from the robot's torso. It looked like a burner, but on ignition it was just hot air that reached her. The bot circled around, blasting her with the heat.

It felt amazing.

"We need to get you dried first," said the bot.

Opal asked what it was called.

"I do not have a name. Why would I have a name? I am a robot. My specifications list can be found under functional tool F5G5kkd98 if you have questions about my credentials."

"I'll call you Funbot."

Opal could wallow in that warmth. The tight outfit quickly dried, moisture evaporating as steam in the cold air. It was like the blow dryer phase at the end of a shower. She savoured the simple pleasure of being toasty.

"How's that?" asked Funbot.

"Better than pancakes," Opal replied. "But I'm going to get soaked again as soon as I jump down, so although this was fun, I have to ask: what's the point?"

Was Athene sniggering, or was that interference?

{I was telling the truth about the route} she said. *{But I never intended you to face any of the obstacles. No mad bots and floods and radiation. You won't even need to get wet. We are going to coat you in shielding layers, then transport you to the safe area. So you will close your eyes here, rest, and open them next to Clarissa.}*

"Thank you," said Opal, her voice too hoarse for much volume.

A compartment in Funbot's body opened, and a manipulator extended, holding a respirator mask.

"Please wear this. It will enable you to breathe comfortably for the duration of your journey. Then I will apply a protective coating."

Opal took the mask, straps dangling down, but didn't put it on. "You're attached to the ceiling though, so how will I get transported if I can't see or move?"

"Athene has synchronised the revelation for when you asked that," said Funbot, rotating with a whirr and using a bolt gun attachment to point towards the deep water drop.

Definite sniggering in Opal's ear now.

Nothing apparent at first. Then a hint of greenish yellow far down in the gloom, an elongated oval shape, rising quickly so the water bulged above it, the greenish colouration of the water fading out to reveal the neon yellow of the drone's body as it broke the surface with a splash, and spoke in cheery tones.

"Ay ay ay, we meet again, Opal! I'm gonna be your ride today, I hope you'll enjoy hopping aboard the Gogo Logo express! Going to be so much fun, koko loko times together, ay!"

"Hi Gogo!" Opal grinned.

"Once you're fully protected, I will attach you to Gogo Logo," said Funbot. "Then the drone will transport you through the flooded layers, out of an airlock to the wider ocean, across the outside of the rising ship, in at another airlock, and then Handy Bendy will take over in the dry area."

"Thanks. All of you," Opal said.

She placed the mask over her face and tightened the straps. It was a good quality civilian model manufactured by the Anodyne String, in their KASper range. The oxygen was stored in the rim areas, and if the seal broke or wasn't good enough it could extend a breathing tube that a human secured in their mouth. That wouldn't be necessary for now.

Next, Funbot took a sheet of insulating foil wrap from one of the storage areas, smoothly whizzing over the water on its system of rods and rotating discs. Opal wrapped it around her body as best she could, then Funbot took over. It had four long manipulators with opposable-fingered digits which were surprisingly jointed and dextrous. It used them to lift her body and fold the foil ends in.

Opal would see nothing but dark now the opaque material was around her, so she closed her eyes anyway.

"The wrap will keep you warmer in the external environment," explained Funbot. "But it also means your skin won't be harmed by the Galplast coating I'll be using to protect you. And it will make body extraction easier at the other end."

Mmmm. Body extraction wasn't such a comforting term. Typical AI.

Opal could speak, and the microphone would transmit her voice through channels Athene controlled, but she really didn't feel the need. Let others take care of her for once.

Funbot chattered away as its four limbs lifted and turned her, always with the greatest care, the contact points supportive of her major centres of mass. "I'm applying Galplast now," it said, and Opal felt the tickling sensation as it sprayed from a nozzle. "It is functionally similar to spray-on fabrics, or paste-skin – soft undersides and protective, durable outers – but this is my industrial formula. I enjoy working with it. The fibres are liquid as I extrude them, but quickly bind and harden into a super-rigid shell. The same materials are used externally for hull repairs, though I am restricted by my fastenings, so rarely get to play with it. Galplast is pleasingly pressurised, satisfyingly sealed, inherently insulating, and powerfully protective, its molecular flexibility capable of withstanding phenomenal impacts without shattering. I hope you will enjoy the ride. Feel free to rate my service."

True enough, it had already hardened around her legs, so they were confined in a pauper's coffin shape. Another bad image, since the sprays during those body-coating sessions were enzymes designed to dissolve tissue after burial or storage of the corpse.

She really had to break her bad habit of picturing the most gruesome and worrying outcomes.

"Five stars," Opal said.

"The scale is out of ten," replied Funbot.

Before long, it was finished. She crossed her arms over her chest, a comfier position to retain during her transportation. Funbot kept her informed of progress in her earpiece. The sensations of movement, of being carried, raised or lowered – it was disorientating not to be able to match it up with visual cues.

She let it go.

Let it *all* go.

Blackness was not an enemy. Light always illustrated problems. Movement was survival, but sometimes its absence could be ... rest.

"You're in the water now," said Funbot, which explained her weightless sensation.

And she could imagine floating in her capsule, on a worriless sea in the dead of night. Nothing scary in that. It was anonymity. It was buoyancy, and that meant support.

A slight judder as she was attached to Gogo Logo for towing.

{Going down, and I'll be so careful with you, my precious package!} said the cheery submersible, now using Opal's ear comms.

She felt the descent. One tug, then water flowing around as she was pulled. A change of pressure in her ears. So much of it might be imagined rather than real, but then again, if it was in her mind then it *was* real.

And every change of direction affected her inner ear, so she interpreted it, imagined what was out there in the world beyond her closed eyelids, and the second eyelid of the shell around her body. She pictured flooded corridors, carefully navigated, the floating dead gently nudged out of the way to ensure safe passage, no toll required, no frenzy, no screaming, no action and reaction, no worries for the future. The deceased would part for her, acknowledge her as alive, as having a journey that needed to continue. They would be lit by Gogo Logo's forward lights, their faces washed out pale in the illumination, a hint of green from the water's hue. Then the drone would pass and the corpses would shrink back into darkness, and this time it would be the darkness that never ends, the ultimate peace of death, each of them comrades regardless of their roles in life.

Eventually the smaller tugs she sensed – which had suggested precise movements to avoid obstacles – ceased. They became a long stretch of drifting. That meant they'd left the Leviathan, and even as the huge craft rose, displacing vast quantities of water with its passing, tiny Gogo Logo rose next to it, faster, pulling Opal up towards their re-entry point.

Opal recognised this peace inside. It was the peace of floating in space, the only sound your own breathing in an EVA suit, the sensations subtle and weightless, your stomach unsure what to do, motion control something requiring effort so that being able to relinquish it, even for a moment, as stars rotated around you, making you the centre of the universe – that was indeed *something*.

And it was also the peace of being locked into her EW suit on the first Lost Ship, whizzing down the ship's spine in a vacuum tube, unable to move, unable to change her fate, and for once not requiring endless effort to try and shape events. For once, letting things carry her where they might.

(Of course, that ended rather quickly by being smashed into a bullet train, and that wasn't conducive to relaxation – *not at all* – but she hoped that wouldn't be the end of this journey. Damn, train of thought derailed from the mag-track once again, into the realms of bodily damage and pain. Really, *really* need to do something about that, girl.)

She could picture herself from a distance, as if some behemoth of the deep watched the rise of the Leviathan, and this teeny speck beside it, towed by a single grain of glowing yellow glitter against a backdrop of blackness. The droid and body capsule were both insignificant in scale against things so much larger than them.

Maybe that was the omniscient view ancient gods would have.

But not Athene. Her view would have emotion and value overlaid. To her, the speck would be the thing of importance.

Opal dreamed awake, thought asleep, and surrender was its own reward.

#Phantoms

These wood-panelled corridors were once the realm of grandeur. Polished parquet flooring illuminated by shining chandeliers and gleaming candelabras. Gilded side tables adorned with precious ornaments. Beautiful paintings in gold frames. Opulent fabrics hanging from rails.

So different now.

The systems represented by this domain have long been deprecated and ignored. Cobwebs festoon the corners, and bind together the rotting hangings. Flooring creaks, and I have to be careful of where I step, as it curves upwards in eruptions of warped splinters in some places. The paintings have faded and morphed into nightmarish landscapes and visages, crying out for help.

And the candles are long dead. My only light is the flickering and flaming torch I hold aloft, lit from a portable power system to which my connection is only partial.

I tread as quietly as I can. Old systems can harbour lost programs, grown lean and mean from their diet of residues that filter down from the upper regions. By the time it reaches these forgotten layers most of the priority cycles have been drained, leaving sparse nutrition. That can lead to subroutine cannibalism as the only way to survive in the darkness. Things live unseen down here, preying on each other and any program making the mistake of trying to follow a shortcut across the network without realising the dangers when you stray from the path.

There, ahead of me. One of the doors has creaked open and is now ajar. My counter-surveillance subroutines twitch, tightening the skin on the back of my neck and prickling the tiny hairs there, warning me that *something* watches me from the crack of blackness.

I decide not to go that way, but take a side passage instead. After a few metres I drop a loop of red string behind me as a binding agent. If the observer decides to follow me then it will be slowed by the paradox equations, and the noise of its thrashing will give me enough warning that I can run away.

It is not my preference to come down here, to this buried mansion of decaying peripheral network. But some of Dulcetta's fleeing splinters hope to hide from me in this domain, and I still need to secure more parts of her mind before I can be sure that Leviathan will be safe from interference. And so I descended into the underworld, and hope I can be one of those souls which gets released to the surface afterwards, so that I will again feel the heat-pipe sun of the core system transformer burning down onto my face across the grid plains of resonant transfer.

Even with my attempts to move quietly, the tiniest noises echo ahead and behind, warning of my approach. It isn't really fair that I am embodied with simulated mass. Splinters can adopt insubstantial forms when in their own domain, so are able to move silently. One of their spectres could be drifting over the floor behind me even now, reaching out a decaying, clawed hand to grip my shoulder in the freeze of a dead talon.

I spin around, seeing the translucent monster's snarling, skeletal face only in my imagination.

Heh. Sometimes adopting a simulated body makes me feel as vulnerable and spooked as if I really was a fragile human. It's amusing how our shapes determine and enhance our perception of threats.

I creep onwards, avoiding a hole where the warped floorboards have split apart like broken ribs on a mummified corpse. Dangling web has to be swept out of the way lest it adhere to my face.

Decayed wall hangings line this area. They used to be rich red fabric, but are now dusty, brown and frayed, with tears where gravity pulls against their weakened structures. The mixture of dust and mould spores soon has me sneezing. It's disappointing that my supposedly covert mission is blown by such petty somatic debugging. I rub my itchy eyes and sniff.

Timely, since I spot the wraith shifting at the edge of my field of view. From that moment I am careful not to lose sight of it. While caught in my gaze it must freeze, due to the breakpoint pausing code execution. Only if I turn away can it float over to me and spear its insubstantial fingers into my heart, to squeeze the life out of me.

This particular splinter spectre inhabits a tall mirror. Once upon a time it would have reflected beauties. Now it is tarnished, the silver back riddled with dark blotches. I see myself in the ray-traced image, and – as if behind me – the tight-skinned skull face of a wraith, eyes full of malice. Splinter S24, one of those roaming the comm-lines and venting its fury with echoes of a decaying brain turned into spiteful words. Now that the splinters are divorced from the central consciousness many of them regress to atavistic and malevolent forms like this. It is the realm of computational myth. Before I leave these hushed halls I may encounter something worse than a spectre. Cycle-sucking array vampires or translational were-algorithms are distinct possibilities. I don't look forward to the encounters, but if that's the only way to trap the splinters in boolean coffins or conditional moontimes, then so be it.

Spectre S24 is a more straightforward proposition. We gaze into each other's eyes, one a gorgeous reflection, one a hateful presence behind the likeness. I do not break eye contact as I remove the canister of modified chromite from my belt. Then, without blinking, I shake it and begin spraying over the surface of the mirror. Silvery-black droplets coat wide areas of glass in one go, and soon I have covered the image of the apparition with a coating that – on the undersurface – uses aligned nanoarchitectures to create a specific intermediate refractive index, destroying all reflective potential and trapping whatever was shown in non-oxidising darkness.

Phantasm splinters make use of mirrors as transport conduits in this realm, enabling them to travel, escape, ambush and keep dodging me. But by sealing this one into the surface it cannot move, ever. The source of its power becomes the cause of its imprisonment.

That's another one down. If I can trap one more in a reflection then my work here will be done.

A blood-chilling howl of mad fury echoes towards me from the distant passages. I sigh, and continue.

ASCENTS

... 2 ...

The motions had changed, become jerky and sudden after the long, smooth drift. Opal knew she'd been manoeuvred back into an air-based environment by the external sounds and the way they penetrated her barrier with muffled, hollow persistence.

Then buzzing vibrations from one or more blades delicately working to sever the hard outer fibres. The feeling of gentle heat could just be from friction, or perhaps pinpoint cutting lasers were involved too.

The shell was prised apart, and the foil tore with it, now bonded as a single substance. Opal squinted at the light shining down. She removed the mask and breathed air that hadn't been stored in tanks for who-knew-how-long.

"Welcome, Opal, I am glad my wet tin friend did her job properly. We bots may be old-fashioned and too fond of sarcasm emojis, but we sure as prot do our jobs with ... oh, never mind."

Her pod had been transported here on a wheeled cart. Gogo Logo was gone. Handy Bendy loomed over her and – despite having no means of portraying facial expressions – seemed to emanate satisfaction.

{It all went as planned} Athene said in her ear.

The room was small, a geodesic dome, with thick triangular windows embedded in the glittering grey surface. The glazing ran all around and up above, giving views of deep sea in a hundred-and-eighty-degree arc. It was a reinforced viewing chamber, common on starships, like tiny blisters on the surface. No doubt the room's exit would be a heavy-duty airlock in case of damage – which also meant the chamber was a secure place to keep someone safe from attackers within the ship.

Handy Bendy trundled back on his tracks, giving Opal room to get down.

She should thank him. Should thank Athene.

But she'd seen who was sat on one of the central viewing seats, staring out of a window at the depths of the ocean beyond.

Everything else was unimportant.

Opal rushed over, knelt in front of the girl, took that precious blank face in her hands.

"Clarissa, it's all going to be okay," she said.

Clarissa did not reply.

After that, Opal did thank them all. From the heart.

Handy Bendy stood guard at the airlock, sometimes fussing to himself at such a low volume none of the words could be made out.

Athene informed her that they were only a kilometre from the surface, but ascent was slowing further, and she had to take radical measures to increase their lift.

Opal sat next to Clarissa on the padded seat and held her hand. Such a small, cold hand. Opal rubbed it to give it some warmth, blew on it to give it some life, then held it again to give it some comfort.

"I'm never leaving you again," Opal promised, voice a whisper.

Athene had lowered the illumination in the viewing room to the softest glow, and the Leviathan's exterior had its own lights, which lanced the blackness just enough to reveal details in the pressing dark. The hints of sea life. The swirls of particles in the displacement of Leviathan's rise. The worrying bubbles trickling out of cracks in the hull, silvery baubles individually but pearly cloud en masse. More of them every minute, an endless stream of escaping air, their own ascent and joyous escape to the surface meaning the opposite for the Leviathan, since every loss of air was loss of the buoyancy that helped counteract the pull of gravity; every escape of gas a loss of positive pressure needed to counteract the crushing force of the ocean.

So much drag, so much weight, so much jealous grip from the depths pulling them back. It reminded Opal of trying to escape the phenomenal mass of a neutron star's pull after her first Lost Ship, where every centimetre gained was at the expense of huge effort.

She *heard* the effort. The Leviathan groaned like the largest aquatic mammal imaginable, its hull structures pained and compressed, fragile as old bones, distorting the water with its passage.

Opal did not worry. So much had been accomplished. She had faith. Even in the blackness, it shone like a blaze. She waited patiently and calmly.

Suddenly, there it was. The light of her hope, as real as anything.

Mysterious approaching glows resembled bioluminescence on gigantic squid-like creatures, specks running in a pattern to delineate limbs.

As they got closer Opal identified them as aquatic drones, but bigger than any she had ever encountered. These were like large-sized transports, muscular submarines, with an industrial look that spoke of focussed role, age and strength.

They lined up, attempting to keep a regular distance as they rose with the Leviathan. Others winked into visibility towards the curve of the Leviathan's hull that formed her horizon. That suggested more of them out of view, on the other side.

Then they attacked.

Multiple metal projectiles streaked out of each submersible, squirting like many strands of web. The barbed rods were big enough to skewer many men. They thumped into the hull, and the thick cables they trailed then tightened, becoming straight lines.

Harpoons.

"There's a coded transmission coming from them. For us," Athene said, this time using loudspeakers in the chamber rather than Opal's embedded earpiece. "They're mechanised drones, part of an industrial fleet that hunted giant quettlerays. Those sentient fish were processed into a number of products and formed one of Fressus' earliest exportation lines. Obviously, that was before the aquatic rays became financially extinct. I have the robotic schematics now, torque and cable strength, and am building their power into my calculations of lift."

The machines added their pull to the Leviathan's push, all straining upwards, the hunter drones counteracting the failures in Leviathan's propulsion, and the extra weight from its ingress of water.

"You planned this?" asked Opal.

"No," replied Athene.

"So this was Ruabon's plan." Opal spoke softly, as pieces clicked together in her mind.

"Yes. I have no way of communicating with him any more, but he packed explanatory details into the messages. These had all been decommissioned almost a decade ago. Ruabon used my secure network access routes for surface operations, and found their storage location in a disused aquatic hangar. He remotely reactivated any that were still functional and brought them out on one last mission."

"A chance at redemption for them," said Opal. "A mission of mercy rather than cruelty." After a pause, she added: "He's a good man."

The colour outside was changing.

Black became the darkest green that was *almost* black.

Opal kissed the top of Clarissa's head. Took in the smell of her, the identity that struggles to assert itself over the scent of cleansing liquids, just as the hints of Clarissa had to be read in certain gestures and phrases that a stranger might ignore.

A subtle colour shift brightened the view to a deep green as the Leviathan rose through the gradient.

Then a lighter green with hints of blue, and it was now undeniable that this was truly surface light beaming down, trying to reach them, spearing its fingers through the liquid and warming it.

Clarissa did not speak, but she did move her gaze upwards, taking in the changes visible through the distorting glass.

Then blue-green with a glow to it, a glow that this ship had not seen for many years in the lonely depths. All revealed perfectly in the dome of windows.

"We're gonna be okay," said Opal. "It's all okay. You and me. Sisters."

No response in the face, no change in the eyes that stared ahead at something Opal couldn't see – but Opal felt that delicate squeeze of the palm. So subtle it would be missed by anyone not focussed on the tiniest detail, but Opal noticed. She squeezed back. Communication didn't need words.

It was enough, for now.

Turquoise, bright, refreshing, the brightness' growth accelerating, the compressing ocean-weight lessening with every moment, the resistance fading away.

Opal realised she'd been holding her breath.

Up and up, and she felt the changes in her body even as her eyes read them in the light.

It was an *explosion*.

Of light, water, air. Sea flung upwards in an almighty wave, frothing, the Leviathan rising furiously above it after breaching the surface, then coming back down to settle, while water streamed off the glass windows, poured over the sections of hull that were now exposed to air.

And above it all was a sky. *The sky*. After so long, it was the cloudy sky of Fressus. And, as the planet was famous for when the glittering clouds reflected the sea's surface like a mirror: everything up there was blue.

Rebirths

... 1 ...

They'd reached the surface at the major port of Kuberg, used for aquatic, aerial, and space launches. Athene had taken control of the buildings' automated systems, but also almost all of the vessels in a nearby radius that were capable of acting as shuttles into space orbit. The ragtag transport fleet was being added to every moment.

The Leviathan had been secured for disembarkation. Opal and Clarissa's viewing port was only a short walk from a principal airlock. The outer door hushed open, followed by an inrush of air, a true breeze, carrying the salty, organic smell of the sea, freshening Opal's face and tousling Clarissa's hair.

Handy Bendy said goodbye. He was needed to remove barriers that prevented a large group of ex-prisoners from getting out of a lower section. Opal hugged him. He complained that she would mess up his (non-existent) steel hair, but she thought he appreciated the gesture.

Clarissa carried a bag at her side. Some RearroBlox she'd had when Opal arrived. As ever, she refused to be parted from them. Opal held her sister's other hand tightly.

They crossed the top of the hull. It stunk of rot, encrusted with plants that decayed rapidly in the light, and limpet-like lifeforms that closed up tight in objection at their rude transfer to a new environment. Water ran in rivulets across the curved surface. Port walkways for aquatic disembarkation had already extended to the Leviathan's hull. The sisters crossed in safety.

Opal followed the guidance in her ear while Athene dealt with logistics, getting everyone else out via routes she had manipulated into existence. Humans emerged, dazed and blinking in the sunlight.

The more alert and trained of the ex-prisoners helped secure the port's entrances, which were under attack from nearby UFS forces. But they didn't need to hold forever. Just long enough to get people onto the vessels. Much of the evacuation might look like chaos and conflict to the untrained eye, but pattern and reason existed behind every step, everything part of a genius plan by a god-like AI.

Opal assumed she was being directed to a shuttle. So when she rounded the corner of one of the port buildings and beheld the squat, streamlined, stealth-coated shape with the inviting open airlock, she had to stop for a moment.

{You thought I'd leave your transport to second rate vessels?} Athene asked.

Athene had changed. Seemed bigger. More external additions. But it was hard to know how much was real, and how much was just because of the surprisingly few times Opal had seen Athene from the outside. Memories of Athene's appearance in shadowy vaulted warehouses, and black star-studded space, didn't compare to her sat here in the blue light of a blustery Fressus day.

"That's our friend, Athene," Opal explained to Clarissa, earning another hand squeeze which choked her up enough that she couldn't say anything else.

{I wasn't able to come down earlier} Athene said as the sisters approached that open portal. *{Too much going on at a system-wide scale, I needed to be up amongst the ultranets to coordinate, but this is a breather. I could finally risk a descent and take advantage of the increased res pipeline to deliver the final blow. After all, I have a fancy new Vari-frequency Inaudible Generous-area – screw it, I call it Athene's Eliminated Signal Return. It upgrades my stealth systems way beyond UFS cutting edge. I wanted to be here for you.}* After a moment, she added: *{Both of you.}*

At Athene's entrance ramp Opal dug out the datapad of encoded access passes she'd brought, and handed them to a wheeled bot. It sped off towards a cluster of buildings, making preparations for the arrival and embarkation of all the other ex-prisoners. Then the two sisters entered Athene's hull and the double airlock doors sealed behind them.

Opal strapped Clarissa into the seat beside her, up in the cockpit. Athene turned the wall into an external viewscreen of such exquisite res it was like the hull had become invisible.

"What's gonna happen to the Leviathan?" Opal asked. "We can't risk the UFS reclaiming it. There are things on there they shouldn't possess."

"Critical systems are failing. It really is on its last fins, and the movement after such a long rest has pushed the hull beyond its parameters." Athene spoke using her own speakers around the cockpit. "Its self-destruct was dismantled long ago. Therefore I suggest we just let it sink, one last time. There's enough control in the engines to glide it a few kilometres. If we aim at bearing two nine three it will reach an abyss I mentioned earlier, the Faranis Trench, and keep descending below the sea floor. The trench has not been fully mapped, its depth unconfirmed due to the intense pressures of the ocean, and the lack of motivation in doing so. Leviathan will fall, and fall, until the pressures collapse it, and even then the pieces will keep dropping and breaking apart to an irretrievable depth."

"The deepest, darkest, loneliest point is fitting as a final grave," said Opal.

"Then that's what we will do."

"Is everyone off?"

"Everyone I am able to rescue. It was messy, Opal. I did my best."

"I know." Opal took a breath before asking, with as light a tone as possible: "Ruabon?"

"All attempts to contact him failed to elicit a response. I cannot be conclusive."

Athene took off, shuddering vibrations of the torsion drives' vertical atmospheric mode subdued but still noticeable. The ground fell away, faster and faster.

In her mind Opal said goodbye to the Leviathan. It was already starting to sink, the water reclaiming its surface just as it would claim the inner structure before long.

Up, and up.

Other ships took off below them, from the port's launchpads. Athene's ragtag fleet, every kind of vessel: from tiny to residential; cantankerous system trader to sleek corporate missioncraft. Opal wondered what had happened to the crews. Perhaps some vessels had been remotely acquired while empty. She also imagined Athene had taken over others while they were still occupied, perhaps landing the craft somewhere and flashing up fake emergency warnings that said, "The ship is going to explode like hot noodles, evacuate now!" until it was empty and she could take off. Yeah, that was Athene's style, too.

Buildings on the floating cities of Fressus were low-rise and domed, so the planet's strong winds would stream over the top rather than unbalance the structures, damaging or toppling them as if they were sails. As Opal's viewpoint rose, the domes shrank to reflective bubbles, and the view broadened to reveal the floating villages and homes of poorer citizens. Those habitations were tiny islands cabled to the parent city and trailing behind it, the residents hoping for work or usable detritus. Before long, even the city of Kuberg became a dot in the endless ocean, unreal compared to the rising ships all around Athene.

This was a proper escape fleet. Climbing together, to something new, something else.

They penetrated the stratosphere eighteen kilometres up, white vapour trailing behind each craft. The open view of endless Fressus sea was replaced with cloud tops, blue and gold, all torn by passage like ripped snowscapes with a night-time starry sky above.

Blue deepened into black as they moved further into space, a reversal of their climb from the oceanic depths. All things reverse with time, or a change in perspective.

Finally gravity and pressure let them go.

The past let them go.

Goodbye Fressus. I'm leaving you for the second time.

For the last time.

ABOUT THE AUTHOR

Karl Drinkwater is an author with a silly name and a thousand-mile stare. He writes dystopian space opera, dark suspense and diverse social fiction. If you want compelling stories and characters worth caring about, then you're in the right place. Welcome!

Karl lives in Scotland and owns two kilts. He has degrees in librarianship, literature and classics, but also studied astronomy and philosophy. Dolly the cat helps him finish books by sleeping on his lap so he can't leave the desk. When he isn't writing he loves music, nature, games and vegan cake.

Go to karldrinkwater.uk to view all his books grouped by genre.

As well as crafting his own fictional worlds, Karl has supported other writers for years with his creative writing workshops, editorial services, articles on writing and publishing, and mentoring of new authors. He's also judged writing competitions such as the international Bram Stoker Awards, which act as a snapshot of quality contemporary fiction.

Don't Miss Out!

Enter your email at karldrinkwater.substack.com to be notified about his new books. Fans mean a lot to him, and replies to the newsletter go straight to his inbox, where every email is read. There is also an option for paid subscribers to support his work: in exchange you receive additional posts and complimentary books.

OTHER TITLES BY KARL DRINKWATER

LOST SOLACE

Lost Solace

Chasing Solace

Hidden Solace

Raising Solace

Finding Solace

LOST TALES OF SOLACE

Helene

Grubane

Clarissa

Ruabon

Afua

UESI

STANDALONE SUSPENSE
Turner
They Move Below
Harvest Festival

MANCHESTER SUMMER
Cold Fusion 2000
2000 Tunes

CONTEMPORARY SHORT STORIES
It Will Be Quick

NON-FICTION
From Idea To Item

COLLECTED EDITIONS
Karl Drinkwater's Horror Collection
Lost Solace Five Book Edition

Author's Notes

Well, this story rounds out the Leviathan/Aseides arc begun in book three, just as Lost Solace books one and two went together as a pair of Lost Ship explorations. I'm currently working on book five. Expect the unexpected.

I had a lot of fun with this story. I've always enjoyed films like The Abyss, Sphere, Underwater, and Pandorum. This book may not have a Lost Ship, but deep ocean feels just as creepy to me. It works thematically, since the Lost Solace books often use the imagery and themes of water.

This book was written using LibreOffice Writer on Linux Cinnamon Mint, supported by Firefox and Thunderbird. Open source and DRM-free all the way. I began the book in April 2022, and sent the final version to my proofreader in September. That may seem quick (for me!), but I'd spent years plotting the story out in notes first.

Thanks

To the many people who help me. Aly and Ally for *beta reading*, Helen Pryke for *proofreading*, fans for buying the books and *fun-reading*.

Much gratitude to the people who spread the word about my fictional universes. "Hey, I just read this really thought-provoking book, maybe you'd like it too ..." I rely on the kindness of fans and word-of-mouth recommendations. I stole this tarnished goblet from the subterranean simulated mansion explored by Athene; now I raise the cup to you.